FRIENDS WITH BENEFITS

A DIRTY LOVE NOVEL

R.L. KENDERSON

For my handsome husband, Hon.
Thank you for giving me our three beautiful mixed babies and showing me beauty comes in all different looks, shapes, and forms.
And for my beautiful sons, Kaiden and Karter.
Luke was inspired by you two, and I hope you both know that you are handsome and wonderful and that any woman would be lucky to have you someday. Please don't ever let society tell you that you are not attractive or good enough because you are.

STAY TUNED...

Stay tuned at the end of *Friends with Benefit* for exciting bonus content!

CHAPTER ONE

E lise Phillips scanned the bar and grill as the door closed, leaving the June warmth behind her.

An arm toward the back of the room shot up, waving. Next, she saw her college friend's light-brown hair, and then Rachel Garwood's pixie face lit up as she beckoned her to the table.

When Elise approached, Rachel stood and squealed, her hazel eyes shining, as she held out her arms for a hug. Rachel had to step on her tippy-toes while Elise had to bend down. Elise was five-seven, but Rachel was only five-two.

"I'm so happy you're here," Rachel said. "I can't believe you get to come out with us whenever you want now."

About a month ago, Elise had moved back to the Minneapolis-St. Paul area, where she'd gone to high school and college. She'd found out her father was sick, and she wanted to be close to him just in case he didn't have much time left. Even though Rachel had also been born and raised in the Twin Cities, they hadn't met until they became room-mates at the University of Minnesota.

"Me either," she said as she stepped back from her friend.

"So, how's the house-hunt going?" Rachel asked as she took her seat.

Elise sighed as she hung her purse on the edge of the chair next to Rachel and sat next to her. "Okay. I'm so glad my old house sold; that's a relief. I really like the realtor you referred, but so far, I haven't found something I really like and want to buy."

"I'm so glad you like Cara. She's great. And I know what you mean. Sean probably would have been happy with the ten other houses we saw, but I didn't have that I-could-live-here feeling." Rachel had just bought a home with her fiancé, Sean, about six months earlier. "I'm sure you'll find one you like sooner rather than later."

"I hope so. I can only live with my parents for so long before they drive me completely nuts. I'm twenty-nine, but sometimes, I think they forget that I've been living on my own for over a decade."

"Ah, they're sweet."

Elise snorted. "You don't have to live with them."

Her mother had always been protective, but her hovering had gotten worse ever since her father was diagnosed with colon cancer.

"Well, let's agree to disagree. I'm just happy you're home."

So was she. Elise had enjoyed living in Denver since finishing graduate school, but it felt good to be home. And, while she would miss it, she didn't regret coming back once she learned her father was sick.

Elise gestured to the four open seats at the table. "Who else is coming?"

"Do you remember Shelly and Joe Howard?"

"Hmm." Elise couldn't quite remember them off the top of her head. "Oh. Did I meet them one year at your Christmas party? Shelly teaches with you, and her boyfriend is Joe. Both redheads?"

"Yes, that's them. Although they're husband and wife now. Shelly is actually pregnant. They are going to have the cutest little ginger baby."

Elise chuckled. "That's so great for them," she said, meaning it even though she felt slightly let down.

When Rachel had asked her to have dinner and drinks, Elise had assumed it was going to be a girls' thing. While she remembered liking Shelly and Joe, they were a couple, which meant one of the six seats belonged to Sean. So, either it was a couples' get-together and Rachel was setting her up with someone or she was going to be the dreaded fifth wheel. Neither option sounded appealing.

"So, Shelly, Joe, and Sean are coming. Is the sixth seat someone you're trying to hook me up with?" she asked just as Rachel said, "Oh, look. There are Shelly and Joe now."

Her friend stood and waved to catch the newcomers' attention.

Despite the two of them speaking at the same time, Rachel had heard her question. She sat back down and cocked her head. "I wouldn't do that to you. I know how much you hate being set up on blind dates."

Fifth wheel, it was then. Elise didn't know whether to be relieved that she wouldn't have to fake interest in someone—because she really didn't have the energy for that tonight—or disappointed that she was going to be the poor single girl.

Turned out neither because Rachel then said, "No, the last seat is for Luke Long. Do you remember him?"

Elise's answer was a groan of irritation. Oh, she remembered him all right. So did every other member of the student body—at least, those with ovaries. Girls' IQs dropped when Luke was around. It almost made her embarrassed to be a member of the female sex.

Thankfully, Shelly and Joe walked up, so Rachel didn't hear her response because Elise knew Sean and Luke had been good friends in college. Greetings were made, and Elise was reintroduced to the couple considering it had been a few years since she last saw them. They talked about Shelly's ever-expanding belly. She was huge, but she still had seven weeks to go. Shelly was barely over five feet while Joe was a former football player and closer to six feet tall, and they joked about how she was going to have an enormous baby. Thankfully, the group's joking had Elise almost forgetting all about the previous conversation.

When the door opened, she was sure she could feel a breeze all the way at the back of the room as Sean and Luke walked in. The two of them contrasted each other. Sean was blond and blue-eyed and only about five-eight while Luke was over six feet with thick dark brown hair and chocolate-brown eyes. Sean was showing Luke something on his phone, and Luke threw his head back and laughed, catching all the attention in the room. Elise swore she saw drool on a couple of ladies' chins.

Barf.

To be fair, Luke wasn't a horrible person, and she hadn't seen him in years, since college, so he'd probably matured... hopefully. But, back in school, he'd been quite the man-slut. While he hadn't been truly arrogant—she'd known some conceited assholes, and Luke had never been like that—he was gorgeous, and he knew it. Girls had practically thrown themselves at him, and he'd had no shame, sleeping his way through the female student body and leaving a trail of broken hearts.

Elise hadn't been a saint. She'd had a few one-night stands and even a couple of exclusive friends with benefits, but she'd like to think she'd had some discretion. She certainly hadn't slept with every guy who had hit on her.

Luke looked at one of the girls—probably ten years his junior who was staring wide-eyed at him, and he winked at her.

Elise rolled her eyes. She might have given him too much credit on the maturing thing.

Luke and Sean reached their table, and she realized that she had watched them walk through the whole restaurant. God, she was such a hypocrite. Her only defense was that she didn't have her tongue hanging out, and she'd never been dumb enough to hop into bed with Luke.

Sean leaned down and kissed Rachel before taking the seat across from her in the middle chair. Shelly and Joe were already sitting on opposite sides of the table, so all the girls were on one side, which only left the seat directly on the other side of Elise open.

Great. This was supposed to be a relaxing night out with friends. She really didn't feel like being near King Flirt all evening.

It wasn't that she thought she was some irresistible beauty. In fact, he probably didn't even remember her. It was just that the Luke she remembered flirted with everyone who had a vagina.

Case in point, Luke walked over to Shelly and kissed her on the cheek. "Hey, gorgeous. How's my baby doing?"

Everybody laughed, even Joe. Elise snorted.

"You wish, Luke," Joe said.

Then, Luke kissed Rachel on the cheek. "Hey, beautiful. When are you going to leave that loser over there and marry me instead?"

"Never," Rachel told him with a grin on her face. "But I'll keep you in mind for when he kicks the bucket."

"Hey!" Sean exclaimed. But he was laughing, too. "I'm never dying, woman. You're stuck with me forever."

Luke went around to his side of the table and sat down across from Elise.

Sean pointed to her as Elise held out her hand to shake. "Luke, I don't know if you remember—"

"Elise Phillips," Luke said as he met her eyes. Taking her hand, he kissed the back of it, his trademark cocky smile on his face. "Of course I remember her. How could I forget?"

Like she said, flirt.

Luke Long watched as Elise rolled her eyes, cupping the back of her hand where he'd kissed it, and he chuckled. He remembered that, back in college, it had always been easy to get a rise out of her, and it seemed things hadn't changed very much.

He knew she thought he was a dog, but it wasn't his fault that he liked sex and that women liked him. It wasn't as if he forced ladies to sleep with him. In fact, he usually waited for them to proposition him, and Elise probably wouldn't believe it, but he had said no a time or two.

But *she* had never been one of those girls. She'd never hit on him, and out of respect for his friendship with Sean, he'd never hit on her. Even though he knew she found him attractive. He'd seen the way she stared at him when he walked in the door today although she tried to hide it.

He always thought that one of the reasons she looked down on him so much was because there was unmistakable chemistry between them, and she hated it. While most girls had liked him back in college because he was a jock who played hockey, that hadn't seemed to impress Elise. This had only made him want to goad her more. Maybe it was the ten-year-old boy in him.

He could acknowledge that he might go a little overboard on the flirting, but flirting was fun, and he might as well drive Elise nuts since he couldn't sleep with her. Because, unlike her, he could admit he had wanted to—and apparently, still did.

She was pretty but not exceptionally beautiful, yet there was something about her. She was taller than most women, which he always liked since he was tall himself, and she was thin but not skinny. She had curves in all the right places, and she'd even filled out significantly more since college. She wasn't too big or too small. Like in *Goldilocks and the Three Bears*, she was *just* right. She had long dark blonde hair and large green doe-eyes. And big red lips that the guys in college had labeled DSL—dick-sucking lips.

He snickered, just thinking about it, and Elise narrowed her eyes at him.

Ha.

If she knew what he had been reminiscing about, she'd probably deck him. It was a good thing he wasn't going to tell her.

No, he wasn't going to say anything, and he'd do his best not to torture her tonight. He knew from Sean that she'd recently found out about her father's cancer, and she was busy moving and starting a new job. While Luke liked to provoke her, he'd like to think he wasn't a total asshole.

Yep, tonight was going to be nothing more than just a bunch of friends hanging out.

CHAPTER TWO

Despite Elise's initial concerns, dinner had been enjoyable, and Luke hadn't flirted much. Maybe she was right, and he had matured.

Right now, he was in a heated conversation with Sean and Joe about politics. They were all on the same side, but the conversation was still fairly animated. The women were talking about Shelly's upcoming baby shower and birth, but Elise found herself catching bits and pieces of the things Luke had to say. She was impressed with his knowledge on the subjects they were discussing. He'd obviously done his research, and she was surprised. And rather turned on.

She'd always found intelligence sexy. Not that she didn't find muscles and a hard body sexy because she was a living, breathing woman after all. It was just that she'd always been attracted to wit. But, right now, Luke was showing brains, and he already had brawn. And she was horny.

Although she'd had two beers with dinner, so that was probably the alcohol talking. That, and the fact that she hadn't been with anyone for seven months, two weeks, and four days. Not that she was counting or anything, right?

God, she missed sex.

Thankfully, she wasn't drunk, just tipsy, and she planned to keep her skirt and underwear right where they were. On her body.

But it didn't stop her from stealing glances at Luke. His deep brunette hair was short and coarse, his coffee-colored eyes were round and large, and his lips were on the full side and naturally rosy. His eyebrows were dark and thick, as were the eyelashes that she would kill for because it would mean never having to wear mascara again. His skin had a beautiful golden tan that she couldn't help but notice whenever his biceps flexed under his tight T-shirt. He was half-Caucasian and half-Asian—Chinese, if she remembered correctly—and that was where he got his dusky features from. She'd always been a sucker for brown eyes and brown hair. That described almost all of her ex-boyfriends. But none of them had been as good-looking as Luke.

Ugh.

She looked away from him and down at her beer. She should really stop drinking. Otherwise, she was going to go home, feeling sorry for herself, and end up masturbating to images of Luke going down on her while she grabbed on to his short hair.

She looked to her friends to see if they could tell what she was thinking, but they weren't even paying attention to her. She turned to look at Luke, and he was staring at her with a smirk on his face. But there was no way he could know what she had been thinking, could he?

"Okay, enough talk about babies and politics. Joe and I don't have many more kid-free nights," Shelly said, turning Elise's gaze away from Luke.

"What are you thinking, babe?" Joe asked.

"First, everyone needs to get another drink since I can't."

"Works for me," Joe said as he raised his arm to catch their waitress's attention. "I'm going to enjoy having a DD for as long as I can."

"Uh...I'm not sure I should drink anymore," Elise said.

"Why not?" Rachel asked. "Tomorrow is Saturday, and this is the first time you've come out with us since you moved back. We should be celebrating."

Elise didn't answer because she couldn't tell the whole table her lame reason for wanting to cut herself off.

"Yeah, Elise, why not?" Luke joined in.

She couldn't tell if he was mocking her or not, but she didn't want to disappoint Rachel. Elise was certain she could stop thinking about Luke sexually, so she said, "Okay, order me another beer."

"Woohoo!" Rachel said. "That's the girl I remember from college."

Elise laughed as their waitress approached.

"Refills for everyone," Sean said. "And five shots of Jäger-meister," he added, wiggling his eyebrows.

Elise groaned. "Oh God. Jäger was my go-to shot in college. I used to get so drunk off that stuff."

"And that is why I ordered it."

"Your fiancé is evil," Elise told her friend.

Rachel laughed. "Nah, we just want you to have fun with some reminiscing on the side."

Their server brought back their five shots along with one shot of Coke. "I didn't want you to feel left out," she told Shelly.

"Aw, that's so sweet," Shelly said. After their waitress walked away, she added, "Someone's getting a big tip." She picked up her shot, and everyone else followed. "What are we toasting to?"

"Good friends."

"Healthy babies."

"Getting laid."

"*Sean*," Rachel chided.

"What? I've been gone all week on business. You *know* you're going to be giving it to me later."

Rachel set her full shot glass on the table. "Yeah, but you don't have to tell everyone. I work with Shelly. I don't want her thinking you're a pervert."

Joe laughed. "Babe, you wouldn't think that about Sean, would you?"

Shelly shook her head. "Never." She put her free hand on Rachel's arm. "And, if it makes you feel any better, this baby was conceived in the back of Joe's SUV at his brother's wedding."

Everyone laughed, except for Joe, his face serious.

"Baby, we promised to never talk about that. If my mom ever finds out that I had sex in the church parking lot, she's going to make sure this baby is baptized the minute it comes out, and she'll make me attend confession every day for a year. At least."

Shelly stopped laughing. "You're right. She already thinks her Protestant daughter-in-law corrupted her Catholic son." She pointed her finger around the table. "Not a word to anyone. I can't even use the I-was-drunk-when-I-said-that, it's-not-true excuse."

Elise understood where Joe and Shelly were coming from. She hadn't grown up Catholic, but her parents were religious.

"Don't worry; we won't say anything," Rachel promised. She picked up her shot again. "Okay, where were we?"

"To good friends, healthy babies, and getting laid," Elise said.

Everyone repeated the words, and they all clinked their glasses together and downed their shots.

"Who wants to play pool? There's one table open," Sean asked after they all deposited their shot glasses on the table.

"I'm in," Joe answered.

"I'll take winner," Luke said.

The guys got up and headed toward the pool tables. Since their table was in the back of the room, the girls would have a clear view of the game without leaving their seats.

"How did Sean and Luke start hanging out again? I haven't seen him since, like, junior year or something, and I haven't heard you talk about him in forever," Elise asked.

Luke and Sean were two years older in school than Elise and Rachel. The girls had met the guys their freshman year, but Rachel hadn't started dating Sean until she was a sophomore. Sean and Luke had been roommates, and since Elise and Rachel were good friends, the four of them had seen a lot of each other. Both guys had finished their bachelor's degrees and stayed on for graduate school, but by that time, Elise had started dating Tyler. She was ashamed now by how much she'd thrown herself into that relationship. She'd barely even seen Rachel their senior year because she was so caught up with her boyfriend.

After Elise and Rachel had finished their undergraduate degrees, they'd both stayed at U of M for graduate school. Elise had been going to school full-time, working as many hours as possible, and moved in with Tyler, so she still hadn't seen Rachel that much although they both tried.

From what she remembered, the same thing had kind of happened with Luke and Sean. They had both gotten busy, seeing each other less and less, especially since Rachel and Sean lived together, until the two guys no longer hung out and then lost touch. Thankfully, that had never quite happened to Elise and Rachel, and they had remained friends, even when Elise moved to Colorado. It probably helped that Rachel was the shoulder that Elise had needed to cry on when she and Tyler broke up right before her move to Denver.

"I know. It's kind of crazy. Sean ran into Luke at our local Home Depot, of all places. Did you know that Luke works at Southdale? I was kind of surprised when I found out."

Elise knew Sean had gone to school for his MBA and worked for a big-box store. It wasn't hard to believe that Luke had graduated with a master's, too, and gotten a job at somewhere like Southdale Center, the mall in Edina. He was a womanizer, not an idiot.

She was just about to ask what Luke's role was when Rachel continued with her story, "Anyway, that's how we found out we only lived a few blocks away from him. Go figure. We'd practically been neighbors for about two years.

After that, it was almost like the two of them had never been separated."

"Good for them," Elise said. "It doesn't seem like Luke has changed all that much."

Rachel laughed. "You mean, because he's a flirt and a half? Yeah, he's still kind of a man-ho. I swear, he dates a different girl every weekend. That's probably the only thing I don't like about Sean being friends with him. But Luke has never tried to push his singleness on Sean, and Luke seems genuinely happy that the two of us are getting married."

"Joe and I have gone out with him only a few times," Shelly said. "He is totally a flirt, and the women are always eyeing him." She nodded her head toward the guys. "Like now."

Elise looked over and saw a beautiful woman sliding up to Luke and getting as close as possible to him.

"But, to give him credit," Shelly continued, "he doesn't dog on women when he comes out with us. When he spends time with us, he spends time with us. I can't even blame all the girls who hit on him. He's hot. If I were single..."

The woman hitting on him put her hand on his arm. While Luke smiled politely at her, he was standing with his feet spread apart, and his hand on his pool cue, his body facing the pool table. Elise got the distinct impression that he wasn't interested. The woman slipped a piece of paper in his back pocket and walked away. As soon as she turned, Luke took the paper out and chucked it into the trash can in the corner of the room.

Elise was impressed again because the Luke she'd known

in college probably would have ditched them all and walked out the door with the woman without a backward glance.

Luke looked up from the garbage, his eyes colliding with Elise's so swiftly that she turned back to the girls and took a couple of sips of her drink. She hoped he didn't think she'd been staring at him.

"I guess it's true that men can change," she said, almost forgetting what they had been talking about.

"Nah, we don't change that much," a deep voice said in her ear.

She jumped in her seat and turned. "Shit, you scared me." She hadn't heard Luke come up behind her.

He was way too close for her liking. He smelled wonderful, a natural muskiness with a hint of aftershave that was utterly male. She wanted to bury her nose in his neck and breathe him in.

Had she mentioned that she missed sex?

She tried not to lean too far away because she didn't want him to know that he affected her or how confused she felt when she was near him.

He tugged on a piece of her hair. "Another table opened up. Come play pool with me?"

She welcomed the distraction. Now, pool, she could definitely manage.

She raised her brow at him. "Are you sure you want to play against me?" she asked sweetly.

"Sure. You can't be that bad."

Elise just laughed.

♡

"You kicked my ass." Luke sighed, surprise showing on his face. "And here I thought, I was good with *my* stick and balls."

Elise ignored his sexual innuendo and smiled. "I asked you if you wanted to play against me," she said in a singsong voice.

Luke narrowed his eyes. "That was when I thought you were bad at pool."

She shrugged innocently. "That'll teach you to assume things about women."

He snorted. "I didn't assume you were a bad player because you were a woman."

She put one hand on her hip. "Then, why did you think I was bad?"

"Because I remember you being kind of a fuddy-duddy."

"*What?* I was not. Just because I didn't fall into bed with you like every other chick does not mean I was a fuddy-duddy." She swept her hair over her shoulder and stepped closer to him, looking him in the eye. "I'll have you know, I had plenty of sexual conquests in college. You just didn't happen to be one of them."

He grinned down at her. "See, I know you're trying to make me feel inadequate because we didn't have sex, but all you're doing is making me hard."

She rolled her eyes. "You're hopeless."

"Nah. Wanna play again?"

"Sure."

She was actually having fun with Luke. She liked playing pool, and Luke was a good opponent.

"Do you want another beer first?"

She looked into her almost-empty glass. "That'd be great." After all, she was drinking for the pregnant lady, and she'd managed to keep her hormones in check so far.

"You set up, and I'll go get us drinks."

Elise grabbed the triangle and began racking the balls, putting them in their proper place. She grabbed the one ball and put it at the apex when Rachel walked over and leaned against the side of the pool table.

"Are you having a good time?" her friend asked.

"Yeah. I'm glad you asked me to come. I totally kicked Luke's ass."

Rachel smiled, but it was hesitant.

Elise stopped what she was doing. "What's wrong?"

Rachel stood up straight. "I think we're going to take off. I don't feel well. Shelly and Joe are leaving, too. Shelly's tired, and she wants to go home and put her swollen feet up."

"Are you okay?"

"Yeah," Rachel said, putting her hand over her stomach. "I think it was something I ate."

Elise narrowed her eyes and studied her friend. "Liar. You just want to go home and get laid."

Rachel blushed. "Guilty. I haven't seen Sean for a week." She stuck her bottom lip out.

Elise laughed. "I understand. Go have fun with your man."

Rachel looked around the room, as if she was calculating the situation.

"What is it?" Elise asked.

"Nothing."

"Rachel, just spit it out. What's wrong?"

"I don't want to leave you here with Luke."

Elise shook her head. "I'll be fine. We're having fun. I'm not ready to go home yet."

Her friend looked over her shoulder to where Luke stood at the bar, talking to Sean. They seemed to be having a serious conversation. She looked back at Elise. "I just want you to be careful."

Elise tilted her head. "How do you mean?"

"It's been over six months since you and Jason broke up. I don't want to see you get hurt again."

Elise shook her head in confusion. "I still don't get it. Why would I get hurt?"

Rachel sighed. "Just don't sleep with Luke, okay? He's grown up quite a bit, but he's still Luke. I've never seen him get serious with anyone, and I don't want your heart to get broken."

Elise threw her head back and laughed. "We are just playing pool. Nothing's going to happen."

Rachel didn't laugh. "I know you haven't slept with anyone since before you and Jason broke up." She leaned in close and lowered her voice. "And I know how horny you get when you've been drinking. I also know that sex with Jason was mediocre, at best, so you're probably really jonesing for sex now. And let's face it; we both know that Luke probably fucks like a rock star."

Elise laughed again and shook her head. "Trust me, Rach, you have nothing to worry about. I am never going to sleep with Luke Long."

CHAPTER THREE

The next morning, Elise woke, flat on her stomach, disoriented, with a piercing headache that only came from a hangover. While she'd been living with her parents for about a month now, she'd often still wake up in confusion from forgetting where she was at first. It'd sometimes take her a minute to realize she wasn't in her house in Denver anymore. She opened one eye to check the time, but the alarm clock wasn't hers or the one in her parents' guest room.

She sat up, jarring her already-sore head, and let out a moan. Thankfully, dark shades were covering the windows, casting the room in shadows and hiding the evil sun.

What happened last night? Her memory was fuzzy, and it hurt to think.

She realized she was naked and pulled the sheet up to cover herself as she slowly looked around the room, recognizing nothing. Nothing but the sleeping naked male lying on the bed next to her.

Oh God. No! Panic raced through her body, and memories rose to taunt her.

She'd slept with Luke Long. She'd slept with. Luke. Long.

She whimpered and closed her eyes. She had managed to escape college without screwing the guy, only to have dirty, dirty sex with him last night. And that was only the stuff she could remember.

She was never drinking again.

If Rachel ever found out, she was going to give Elise so much shit—after she quizzed Elise on whether the whole fucks-like-a-rock-star thing was true.

Elise couldn't recall everything from last night after the rest of their friends had left the restaurant, and Luke and she had decided it would be fun to take a bunch of shots. But, now, she did know that, yes, Luke Long did indeed fuck like a rock star. Her sore vagina could attest to that.

I hate you, alcohol.

Luke shifted beside her, but the arm he had over his eyes remained where it was, and his breathing regulated and deepened again.

She really should get out of there before he woke up, but instead, she found herself staring at his beautiful body. *Why does he have to be so gorgeous?*

She moved her gaze from his face to his muscular chest and stomach and noticed a blemish of some kind. She leaned closer to look at the red mark directly above his hip.

Are those teeth marks?

A memory surfaced. She'd bitten him so hard that she

bruised him...*after* she went down on him...*again*. She dropped her head in her hand. She was such a slut.

She looked again at the wound, and her gaze moved to the thin white sheet that was covering one leg and only part of his penis. God, even flaccid, it was thick and long. She remembered thinking it was perfect. She might have even told him that she wanted to mold his dick, so she could use it on herself when she was alone. She moaned softly with embarrassment.

"Jesus, would you stop thinking? You're making my hangover ten times worse."

Elise jumped. "Would you stop scaring me?"

Luke chuckled and moved his arm from his face. His brown eyes glittered with amusement. "Sorry," he said, but his tone indicated that he wasn't the least bit remorseful.

And, now, she was regretting not getting the hell out of there right away. She looked at the floor next to the bed and only saw a few items of clothing and nothing that looked like the shirt or skirt she'd been wearing last night. Nothing to cover her up so that she could make her escape. Then, she spotted them by the door on the other side of the room and winced.

She looked at Luke, hoping maybe he'd shut his eyes in an attempt to go back to sleep, but luck was not on her side this morning, and she found him watching her. It was making her self-conscious, knowing all the naughty things she'd done with him and to him last night.

"Can you please close your eyes, so I can get dressed?"

This made Luke laugh, but she didn't find it the least bit

funny. She needed to get up and out of there before Rachel called her or her parents called Rachel. She really didn't need a lecture about sleeping with Luke right now—from her parents or Rachel. Especially after she'd told her friend it was never going to happen.

"I think that ship has sailed, Lise. I already saw everything last night, babe." He looked down at her crotch. "*Everything*."

She fidgeted on the bed. First, she didn't know if she liked him shortening her name like they were close now or something, and second, she suddenly pictured him kneeling between her legs as he parted her and blew on her nether lips right before he—

Luke threw back the covers and sat up on the edge of the bed, giving her a clear view of his back. Even his back was sexy. Except for the red claw marks there.

Holy shit. Had she possessed any restraint last night?

Luke stood and walked to the door to retrieve her clothes. He didn't seem to care that he was naked because he didn't bother dressing. Of course, he had a world-class butt. Elise tried hard, but when he turned around, she couldn't help staring at his morning wood, and she grew wet between her legs.

"Can you put on some clothes, please?" Her tone was bitchier than she had meant it to be, but she really needed him to get dressed before she threw back the bedsheet and spread her legs for him, begging him to fuck her again.

He raised an eyebrow.

"I know, I know. We already had sex, so what's the big

deal? And I'm sorry for being rude, but I'm finding it hard to think with you walking around..." *With your big, beautiful dick saluting me.*

Luke snickered as he tossed her clothes on the bed, as if he knew exactly what was going on in her head. But he didn't object as he went into his walk-in closet.

As soon as he was in there, she quickly yanked on her clothes, except for her underwear. She didn't see them anywhere, and since Luke would walk out at any second, she opted for going commando. It wasn't ideal since she was wearing a skirt, but at least she wasn't nude anymore.

Luke exited his closet, wearing a pair of nylon shorts and holding a T-shirt in his hand. The bite mark she'd left stood out against the light gray of his shorts. She considered just pretending like she didn't know it existed, but she was maturer than that. Or, at least, she wanted to think she was.

"I'm sorry—"

"If you apologize for fucking me..." Luke's lips were in a hard line, and his eyes had lost all humor. He almost looked hurt. "Look, we're both adults, both single, we used protection, and no one got hurt."

She sat on the side of the bed. "Well, see, that's not exactly true..." She waved her hand toward his lower body.

He shook his head, obviously not understanding. "What's not true? Are you trying to tell me you have a boyfriend?"

"No."

He frowned. "Are you saying, we didn't use protection? Because I might have been drunk, and you did almost jump the gun there the first time, but I distinctly remember using condoms."

Her cheeks got warm as she vaguely recalled pushing him down on the sofa, slipping her underwear off, lifting her skirt, and—

"Open your eyes and watch me while I fuck you, Elise. I want you to know whose cock you're riding."

She shook her head before she turned red, clearing the memory. "No, that's not it either."

"Okay, Lise, you're just going to have to spit it out then."

"Hurt. You're hurt." She pointed to his hip and sighed. "I hurt you."

Luke lowered his head and examined her bite mark. "Oh, yeah, I remember that." He looked up at her and grinned. "I never would have taken you for a wildcat in bed, but damn, I liked it." He shrugged and put his shirt on. "Besides, I sort of got you back." He waved his hand over his neckline.

She gasped and jumped up, bolting for the bathroom. "You didn't!" she yelled at him before she flipped on the light switch. She lifted her chin up and to the side, and there it was —a big ole hickey right on her neck. Thankfully, the top she'd worn last night had a low collar, so she should be able to find a more modest shirt to cover it for work, but she sure as shit didn't know how she was going to walk into her parents' house and not let them see it.

He came up behind her. "I'd tell you I was sorry, but then I'd be lying. If it makes you feel better, I don't remember doing it, and I didn't do it on purpose."

She angled her head to look at it again. "Fat lot of good that does me. It's there whether you meant to do it or not."

He leaned in closer to her, meeting her eyes in the mirror. "Well, at least I didn't bite you," he teased.

Embarrassed, she didn't reply. Instead, she worked on straightening her appearance. She finger-combed through her long hair to get the snarls out and used hand soap and water to get rid of the mascara that rimmed her eyes.

She almost forgot he was still there when he said, "I'm going to get coffee. I'll meet you downstairs."

She hurried up, trying to make herself look presentable, and quickly used the facilities before heading downstairs.

If she wasn't hungover and freaking out about sleeping with Luke, she would have taken the time to admire his beautiful home. But, at the moment, she wanted to forget that she had ever been there and get the hell home.

She quickly scanned the living room for her missing article of clothing, but with no luck, she met Luke in the kitchen where he handed her a glass of water and a couple of pills while the smell of coffee brewing filled the kitchen.

"Ibuprofen," he explained when she gave him a questioning look.

"Thank you," she said. Swallowing the medicine, she downed the whole glass in a few gulps. She hadn't realized how thirsty she had been until now.

She handed him the empty cup, and he put it in the sink. After he poured himself some coffee to go, he grabbed his keys off the counter.

"I rode with Sean last night, so my car's here. You need a ride, I'm assuming?"

"Yes, please."

"Do you want any coffee?"

She shook her head.

He reached for something else on the counter and handed it to her. It was her purse.

"Do you have everything?"

Everything but her underwear, but she wasn't going to tell him that. She slung her purse over her shoulder. "Yep, I'm ready."

CHAPTER FOUR

L uke watched Elise slip out of the passenger side of his car.

She turned around. "So, we agree to keep this between us? No telling Rachel or Sean or anyone else, right?"

He nodded. "Agreed." He was more than happy to go along with this deal since Sean and Rachel would kill him if they found out.

He made sure Elise unlocked her car and got in before he took off to head back home.

He had screwed up last night. No pun intended. Sean had specifically told him not to fuck Elise. And what had he done? The one thing his friend had asked him not to.

But, if he was being fair, she had been the one to fuck him. After she'd unzipped his pants in the back of the cab they took to his house, she had taken him all the way to the back of her throat, not caring that the driver only had to look in the rearview mirror to get a show. She'd shocked the hell out of him because he wasn't a small guy. He wasn't trying to brag about his size; he was just stating a fact. He'd had plenty of girls who couldn't take his entire length, but Elise...damn. He was getting hard, just remembering her deep-throating his dick until he'd exploded in her mouth and she swallowed all of him.

Then, when they'd gotten to his house, she'd practically shoved him through the door once he unlocked it. She'd kissed him before he could even say anything, which was fine with him because he hated wasting time on small talk. Plus, he was all about kissing, and that girl could kiss. He could still taste himself on her, and it wasn't long before he'd been ready to go again.

He'd shoved his pelvis between her legs, making her moan, and she'd pushed him down onto the couch, pulled his pants down, slipped her underwear off, and sat on his cock. He'd barely had time to put a condom on before she slid all the way down his length.

He adjusted his erection in his shorts because, now, he was fully aroused.

When he'd asked Elise to play pool with him, it was just because he'd thought they'd have fun playing together. He'd always liked her and figured it was a way for them to get to know each other better. He hadn't known it would lead to a bunch of shots.

He hadn't planned to ask her to come home with him right away. When he had, he'd thought he'd have to do some convincing to get her into bed, but it'd turned out, the female was like a fucking wet dream. She'd been virgin tight, yet at the same time, she'd fucked him like it was some sort of contest, and she was aiming for first prize. She'd been hot and wet, and just thinking about her made him want to fuck her all over again.

He'd really wanted to have sex with her again this morning, especially when he'd caught her eyeing him a couple of times. He knew she'd liked what she saw. It didn't hurt that she'd told him last night in explicit detail how much she loved his body. But, this morning, she'd been skittish, and he'd had no doubt she would turn him down. Even if she had taken him up on his offer, she would have regretted it later, and she'd already seemed to be sorry, concerning their night together.

This was why he preferred sleeping with women he didn't know well—or women who weren't friends with his buddy's fiancée. He shook his head. He should have kept the phone number that had been slipped to him last night and called that woman up instead. So what if he hadn't been interested in her? At least, he wouldn't be in the situation he was in now.

This was what he got for thinking with his dick. He was thirty-two years old. He was supposed to be past this kind of thing. He'd worked hard to show people that he wasn't just some lucky jock who'd breezed through school. He'd come a long way since then, only to make such a freshman move.

The grown-up thing to do would be to tell Sean and take his punishment like a man, but, one, Elise had asked him not to say anything. Two, he didn't kiss and tell anymore. Three, despite Sean and Rachel feeling like Elise's sex life was their business, it really wasn't. And, four, when he thought about it, he really didn't feel that guilty. What he felt was guilt for not feeling guilty. But he just couldn't summon up any true regret when it came to sleeping with Elise because she might be the best lay he'd literally ever had.

Besides, history was not going to repeat itself, so he might as well enjoy what had already happened, guilt-free.

Elise quietly unlocked the front door to her parents' house, hoping she could slip up to her room without being seen. Her religious parents would never understand premarital sex, no matter how old she was. They'd never known she lived with her boyfriend at the time, Tyler, which wasn't always easy to pull off. So, while she'd lied to her parents before, she was still feeling raw from last night, and she didn't know if she could do it right now.

Luckily, her parents were gone. They'd left a note, saying that they'd be back before lunch, so she had about an hour before they got home. She headed to her bedroom and stripped off her clothes, shoving them into her laundry basket.

Elise looked at the beautiful purple-and-black bra she owned and took a second to mourn the loss of the matching panties she'd somehow misplaced at Luke's. They were from a boutique store in Denver from several years ago, so they'd be almost impossible to replace. She loved the matching set, and it hadn't been cheap. This had to be the universe's way of punishing her.

Throwing her bra in the hamper, she walked naked to the bathroom since she was alone. She really needed to work on moving out. Elise loved her parents, but she missed having the freedom to do what she wanted, like walk from the bedroom to the bathroom in the nude.

She turned on the water and got under the hot spray. It felt refreshing to wash the night away. The cleansing was only metaphorical since nothing could erase what she'd done, but it did help her feel better about it.

She hadn't had sex for over seven months and had missed it. She was an adult, like Luke had said, and they'd used protection, so she shouldn't feel ashamed.

She'd always really liked sex, and the sex she'd had with her ex wasn't that great. Her and Jason's love life had been average. He was a nice guy, so he had worked hard to give her an orgasm, but the key words there were *worked hard* because he'd truly had to sometimes. They both had really. After all, she had been the one actually trying to have an orgasm. She had been the one under pressure.

Men didn't know how lucky they were. Pee standing up. Orgasms essential to create life. No bleeding from a part of their body for five days every single month. The feminist in her would like to believe that God was a woman, but let's face it; the orgasm thing alone proved God was a man. Periods were just icing on the cake.

Elise put body wash on her loofah and began soaping her body. Her nipples puckered as the abrasive material scraped over them. They were tender from Luke's mouth after he'd sucked on them over and over. She moaned at the memory. In the privacy of the bathroom, with the hum of the water running, it was easier to let herself think about last night.

She moved the loofah down her belly and in between her legs. There, she was sore and sensitive, and she used her free hand to examine herself. Her lips were puffy and swollen, and when she slipped a finger inside, she could tell how tender she was. A shiver went up her spine at the memory of how she'd gotten that way.

She didn't really know how many times she and Luke had had sex because some of last night still blurred together, but she was pretty sure that she'd climaxed every single time. The kicker of it was that Luke hadn't even had to try. She knew there was no such thing as premature ejaculation in women, but she'd always kind of liked the idea that a guy had to earn her orgasm. She'd climaxed the first time she put Luke inside her. She'd had to try really hard to hold it at bay. Guys weren't the only ones who had to think about things like sports and their grandmothers. It was almost humiliating to think that she'd almost come from just one thrust. Premature ejaculation indeed.

Elise was getting aroused and considered staying in the shower for a little longer to pleasure herself. She couldn't believe that she was even considering that with the amount of sex and number of orgasms she'd had last night, but apparently, just even thinking about Luke turned her on.

And that thought—she didn't like that he had so much power over her—along with the knowledge that her parents would be home soon got her moving, and she finished her shower.

She got dressed, finding a shirt with a high enough neckline to cover her ridiculous hickey, and was just grabbing some coffee and a late breakfast at the kitchen counter when her parents got home. The door to the garage opened, and Elise's dad walked in, carrying several bags of groceries. She hurried to set her bowl down and jumped off the stool to grab the sacks.

"Here, Dad, let me help."

Her dad let her take the food with a big sigh. Elise's mom came in right behind her dad as he exhaled.

"What's wrong, Ward?"

"Your daughter is treating me like I'm an invalid."

Elise's mom regarded her with a questioning look.

"All I did was take the bags from him, Mom. I hardly think that counts as treating him like an invalid."

"Ward," Elise's mother said in her mom tone.

"Suzanne, I've been on this planet for over fifty years. I know when I'm being babied. If this cancer doesn't kill me, then boredom and feeling worthless will."

Elise set down the box of mac and cheese she had taken out of one of the bags and walked over to her father. "Dad, it's just that I love you, and I worry."

Her dad smiled. "I know, peanut."

"Will it make you feel better if I insist you help Mom put the groceries away while I finish my cereal?"

Her father nodded and smiled. "I think it will."

She kissed her dad on the cheek, and she knew moving back to Minnesota was the best decision she could have made for her family.

Elise sat down and finished her breakfast while her parents put the food away.

"Did you have fun last night?" her mom asked.

"Yeah. I'm glad I went."

"We didn't hear you come home. You must have stayed with Rachel."

Elise had just taken a big bite of cereal, thankfully, so all she was able to do was mumble, "Mmhmm."

"I'm glad you didn't drink and drive. And, even though Rachel lives with her boyfriend, I'd rather have you going over there than getting hurt or hurting someone else."

"Mom, Rachel and Sean are engaged. They are getting married. Besides, it's 2017. Living together before marriage is not that big of a deal."

Her parents turned to look at her.

"To some people. It's not that big of a deal to some people," she quickly added.

"Well, it's still a big deal to us," her father said. "And I'm finished with my half of the groceries. I'll be in the den."

After her father left the room, her mom said, "Look, honey, your father and I like Rachel, and we always will. It's just not something we want for you. You shouldn't live with a man until he's your husband."

Elise nodded her head but said nothing. She'd heard this all before, but it still made her feel like her parents lived in the dark ages, which was why she never told her parents a lot of things she'd done in the past.

Her mom grabbed the empty grocery sacks, stuffed them under the sink, and then walked over to Elise. She ran her hand down Elise's hair. "I know you think we're old-fashioned, but that's how your father and I were raised, and that's how we wanted to raise you and your sister."

And that was why, when her sister, Kristen, had gotten pregnant, she had gotten married so young and was now having marital problems. But Elise wasn't going to point that out to her mom. Her parents still wouldn't understand—or wouldn't want to understand. They would spin the situation to suit how they viewed the world. Her parents weren't bad people, just super conservative in their thinking.

"Sex is meant to be between a husband and wife. It's how God planned it. I hope you understand." Her mother kissed her on the forehead. "You're going to be home tomorrow to go to church with us, right? Maybe now that you're home, you'll find a nice man there to marry."

Elise only nodded because her last bite of cereal was stuck in her throat. Her mom turned and left the room, and Elise forced her food down.

If her mother and father knew where she had really stayed last night and what she'd been doing, her mother would be disappointed, and her father wouldn't even need to worry about cancer killing him because he'd die from shock.

And forget marrying someone from church. Elise might not be a wild child, but she wasn't uptight and stuffy either.

Moving back might have been right for her family, but she needed to find her own place ASAP.

CHAPTER FIVE

Elise sat in her office on Monday morning, going over her schedule. As a speech therapist, she saw all different kinds of patients—from young children to adults, from those who had had traumatic brain injuries to those who had had strokes. But one of the nice things was that she saw her patients routinely. She really got to know them and could find out the best way to help because everyone was different, and what might work with one patient might not work with the next.

She was just finishing up some notes and had about fifteen minutes before her first patient arrived when her phone buzzed.

Unknown number: How was the rest of your weekend?

Elise frowned.

Elise: Who is this?

Unknown number: Sex God, giver of
orgasms.

Elise rolled her eyes, laughed, and added the number to her Contacts.

Elise: Charlie Hunnam, you know who I am?

Luke: Ha-ha. You know this is Luke.

Elise: Oh, I do, huh?

Luke: Who else made you come multiple
times this weekend?

She considered pretending like he wasn't the only one she'd slept with just to tease him but went a different route instead.

Elise: Maybe I was faking it.

Luke: Bwahahahaha!

Elise frowned again.

Elise: What's so funny about that?

Luke: Baby, there is *no way* you were
faking it.

Elise: Maybe I'm that good of an actress.

> Luke: Nobody's that good. You might have pretended with other guys, but I know you didn't with me. You can moan and throw your head back like a good actress would, but there is no faking the way your face flushed as you climaxed or the way you scrunched up your nose right before you came or how you were so wet that it coated your thighs. And there is definitely no faking the way your pussy milked my fucking cock like it was holding on for dear life. Nobody is that good.

Elise looked around her empty office, as if someone might see his text message. It was absurd because there was no one in the room, much less someone looking over her shoulder. Even though she was alone, her face flushed from his words, and she was squirming in her chair because, now, she was thoroughly aroused. At work, of all places.

> Elise: I'm not sleeping with you again.

> Luke: Ha-ha-ha. I don't recall asking you.

Well, damn.

She'd just been put in her place. Just because he'd turned her on didn't mean that he had meant to do it on purpose. And it didn't mean he wanted to do anything about it.

> Elise: You're right. How did you get my number BTW?

> Luke: I asked Sean. I told him I needed to get ahold of you because you left something behind on Friday.

He added a bikini emoji, which she took to stand for the underwear she'd lost at his house. Her face got warm again, but she ignored the missing panties situation.

If he didn't want to sleep with her again, why had he texted her?

Elise: What did you need then?

Luke: Nothing.

Luke: I just wanted to see how you were doing after Friday night/Saturday morning.

Aw, that's kind of sweet of him.

Elise: I'm fine.

Luke: You don't hate me?

Elise: No. I was just as much responsible as you were. I don't blame you.

Elise: Plus, I went to church on Sunday and cleansed my soul.

Luke: Ha-ha. Good to know.

"Elise?"

She looked up to see her coworker Lora standing in her doorway. She quickly set her phone facedown on her desk. Lora wasn't her boss—she was another speech therapist—but Elise was still new, and she didn't want anyone to think she was slacking off when she should be working.

"Yes?"

"Your eight a.m. is here," Lora said with a smile.

"Okay, thank you."

Lora turned and walked away, and Elise picked up her phone. Luke had texted her while she wasn't looking.

Luke: I'll be sure to dirty it again.

She forgot what they'd been talking about. And, while she should be telling him she had to go, she was too curious not to ask. Thankfully, she still had seven minutes before it was actually eight o'clock.

Elise: Dirty what?

Luke: Your soul.

Luke: Oh, I have to run. Duty calls.

Wait! Elise thought.

Elise: Wait. I thought you didn't want to sleep with me again?

Luke: When did I ever say that?

Luke: Now, I really gotta go, babe. We'll finish this later.

Elise waited, but there were no more texts. Yes, he'd said he had to go, but that was before he'd asked that last question. How could he leave her hanging like that?

She shouldn't care because, when she'd said she wasn't sleeping with him again, she'd meant it. Yet she wanted him to text her again.

She sent a quick reply, threw her phone in her purse, and

grabbed her first patient's folder before heading for the waiting room. She loved her career and usually lost herself in her work.

But, today, she couldn't help wondering if she wasn't in just a fair bit of trouble where Luke was concerned.

Luke finished up his last report before signing off the computer. It had been a long day at work. He was tired, and he couldn't wait to go home. He knew he wasn't original in his pain, but he hated Mondays. Sundays were worse, but thankfully, he hadn't worked the day before.

He packed up his things and got ready to leave for the rest of the afternoon. He shut his locker door and headed for the parking lot. As he walked, he pulled out his phone.

After texting back and forth that morning with Elise, he'd been so busy that he didn't have time to check it all day. Not even at lunch, which had consisted of standing in the break room, shoveling as much food into his mouth as he could in less than ten minutes.

He was beat and hungry, but as soon as he pulled out his phone and saw what Elise had texted him after he had to go this morning, it made him smile.

> Elise: Just like a man to start something and not finish it.

He hadn't meant to start anything this a.m. when he sent her the first message. In fact, he hadn't even meant to flirt. It'd just happened. When he was young, his mother repeatedly told him that he was a natural-born flirt, and he often thought she was onto something there. Besides, flirting was just flirting. It didn't mean anything was going to go beyond that.

> Luke: Ouch. My poor manly pride is ruined.

He didn't think she'd reply right away, but she must be near her phone because, a minute later, his phone beeped.

> Elise: "Ladies, if a man says he will fix it, he will. There's no need to remind him every six months about it."
>
> If the meme fits...

He threw his head back and laughed.

> Luke: Now, I'm offended for the whole male population.
>
> Elise: Hey, there are a ton of those out there, so it must be true.

Luke got in his SUV but had to reply before he drove off.

> Luke: You might think we're lazy, but we're actually smart. It's called strategy, baby. If we pretend not to be able to do something, we know you women will get frustrated and do it for us.

> Elise: I knew it! My college boyfriend was the worst when it came to doing the laundry. He even shrank my favorite sweater. I finally told him to stop and let me do it. I always suspected it was a ploy.

Luke remembered the guy Elise had dated in college. *What a tool.*

Luke: What a dick.

Elise: What can you do? Men suck.

Luke: We don't suck; we lick. You're the one who sucks.

As far as replies went, he knew it was pretty cheesy and immature, but he couldn't resist. He'd been thinking about how Elise had sucked all weekend, and he couldn't get it off his mind.

Elise: Real smooth, Lucas.

Luke: Had to be done.

Luke: Off work now. Have to drive home. Talk later?

Luke sat and stared at his phone, actually worried she'd say no.

Elise: Sure. Later.

Luke threw his phone on the passenger seat and shifted

into drive, all the while grinning from ear to ear. He couldn't wait to see what she would have to say next.

CHAPTER SIX

Elise looked around the house, trying to decide if she liked it. But the fact that she was trying to decide already gave her the answer she'd been looking for.

No, she didn't.

At this rate, she was never going to find a place to live.

Elise's sister, Kristen, walked into the kitchen. "I don't think it's you."

Kristen had dark hair like their father while Elise was blonde like their mother, but they had the same green eyes.

Elise sighed. "Me either."

"How many have we looked at today?"

Elise had to think. "This is number seven."

"Dang, you're picky."

Elise stuck her tongue out at her sister. "I can't help it. None of them feel right."

"Then, we'd better go tell your realtor. This is the last one, right?" her sister asked as they headed toward the front of the house where Cara was waiting.

"Yes."

"That's good because I'm tired, and if we look at one more and you say no, I think Cara might fire you."

"I will not," Cara said with a laugh after hearing the end of their conversation. "After all this work I've put into your sister, I'm getting the commission."

"You two are so funny," Elise said dryly.

They all stepped outside, and Cara locked up the house. "Don't worry, Elise. The right house is out there somewhere. We'll find it."

"I hope you're right."

"We'll be in touch," Cara told Elise before heading to her car and driving off.

Elise and Kristen got in Elise's car.

"Where to?" It was dinnertime, and Elise was starving.

They looked at each other and said, "Granite City," at the same time. It was their favorite restaurant.

They laughed, and Elise said, "I don't know why I bothered asking."

They made it to the restaurant in less than fifteen minutes. It was a shame that she hadn't liked the last house because she'd have been close to her favorite place to eat.

After they were seated and their server took their drink orders, Elise finally asked her sister the question she hadn't wanted to ask in front of Cara, "So...how's everything going with James?"

Kristen fiddled with the silverware and napkin in front of her. "Okay."

"Oh, hon, things still haven't gotten any better?"

Her sister sighed. "No, and I really don't think they will."

She looked up at Elise. "Honestly...I think we're headed for divorce."

"What?" Elise had known things weren't great, but she hadn't thought her sister and brother-in-law were this bad.

"Yeah. We've been trying to keep things going smoothly for Jennifer's sake."

Jennifer was their six-year-old daughter, and the major reason they had gotten married in the first place.

"But even Jennifer doesn't seem to be a strong enough reason to make it work. Can you believe it? I'll be a divorcee at twenty-five. I can't imagine what our parents are going to say. I dread telling Mom and Dad."

James's parents were just as religious and conservative as her and Kristen's parents. That was how they'd met. They were from the same church.

"But that's only if you get a divorce. I wouldn't worry about what Mom and Dad might say until it actually happens. I know they can seem scary, but it's not like they'll disown you or anything."

Kristen tilted her chin down and arched her brow, her look clearly saying, *Oh, really?* "So, now, you're all tough, huh?" She reached into her purse and slowly pulled out her cell. "How about I just call Mom right now and tell her how you lived with Tyler in college and how you almost moved in with Jason before you two broke up?" She wiggled her phone, moving it closer and closer to Elise. "Huh? Huh?"

Elise slapped her hand away. "Okay, okay, I get it. You don't want the wrath of our parents coming down on you."

Kristen set her phone down. "Oh no, there would not be wrath. They'd be like, 'We're not mad...'"

"We're disappointed," the sisters finished together.

"Ugh. Even worse," Elise said.

"Right? No, thank you. Plus, I can't put the extra strain on Dad right now. I want him focusing on his health."

"Yeah, I see your point, but if you're having problems, their disappointment is worth not staying in a loveless marriage."

"Yeah, well, it's more complicated than that."

"What do you mean?"

Kristen opened her mouth, and it looked like she might tell Elise, but that was when their server chose to come over and ask them what they wanted to order. They hadn't taken the time to look at the menus, but they'd been there countless times, so they didn't need to look. They put their food order in, and the server walked away.

Elise hoped her sister would finish her earlier thought, but she completely changed the subject, and Elise let it go. It made her sad to think of her sister's marriage failing though. She and James had been together since high school and always seemed perfect for each other. If they couldn't make it work, who could?

Elise and Kristen finished dinner and went back to their parents' house where Kristen's car was. Elise asked her sister to come inside for a while, but she begged off, saying she had to get home to Jennifer. Elise wasn't sure if it was the truth or if she didn't want Elise asking any more questions about her marriage. Elise didn't press the issue, instead giving her sister a hug to let her know she cared.

Elise walked into the empty house and put her leftovers in the fridge. After, she went to the den and turned on the TV. For some reason, Elise was lonely, sitting there on a Saturday night, all by herself. The weird thing was, if she were in her own house, it would be okay. But there was something about living with your parents, and while they were out, you were stuck at home, doing nothing, on a weekend night. It was embarrassing to think her parents had more of a social life than she did.

Elise knew that Rachel and Sean already had plans. Elise considered calling Shelly, but she still didn't know her that well. Also, it seemed awkward when Shelly was at a totally different place in her life, being married and ready to have a baby while Elise wasn't even in a relationship.

Elise didn't really know anyone else to call. She'd lost touch with pretty much all of her high school friends, and a lot of her college friends had gone back home after graduating.

Not knowing what else to do, she picked up her phone and called one of her best friends in Denver. That turned out to be a big mistake because Kit was out with all their friends. Everyone told her how much they missed her and asked her when she was moving back. It made her feel loved yet, at the same time, very sad and a tad lonesome.

She knew that moving back to Minnesota was the right choice. So far, her father's prognosis was pretty good, but if that changed and he didn't have a lot of time, she would hate herself for not being with him as much as she possibly could.

Resigned to sitting at home, Elise decided she might as well go all out and put on sweats and wash her makeup off. As she rose from the couch, her phone buzzed.

She unlocked it to see it was Luke.

Luke: How did the house-hunting go today?

It had been two weeks since they slept together, and they'd been texting back and forth almost every day. Usually, it was just little things, but she couldn't stop the smile from forming across her face. It was nice that he remembered and thought to ask.

Elise: Not well. It looks like I might be living with the 'rents forever. Kill me now.

Luke: LOL. That bad, huh?

Elise: Yes. I'm just starting to feel like it's a pointless task.

Luke: You could always come live with me. I've been looking for a housekeeper/sex slave.

Elise snorted. *Because those two things go so well together.*

Elise: You couldn't afford me.

Luke: You're probably right.

Elise: What are you doing right now?

Luke: Trying to decide what Die Hard movie
I should watch.

Elise didn't reply right away. She bit her lip as she hemmed and hawed before finally pulling up her phone app and dialing.

"Hey," Luke answered, his voice smooth and deep.

How had she never noticed how nice it sounded before?

"I think you should go with the first one."

"And why is that?"

"Because we all know it's the best."

Luke chuckled, the rich sound vibrating in her ear and making her grin. "I'm not so sure about that. I think you might be hanging out with the wrong people. Everybody knows *Die Hard* 2 is the greatest."

"We should take a poll or something."

"I don't have time to find out the results. But I'll tell you what. If you come over and hang out, we'll watch the first *Die Hard*."

"Okay," she heard herself say. It was definitely better than staying there, feeling sorry for herself. "Just a couple of things."

"What?"

She could hear the smile in his voice.

"There must be popcorn."

"I can do that."

"No drinking. I promised my mom I'd go to church early in the morning."

"That's no fun but done."

"And no sex."

Luke laughed. "And here I was, looking forward to dirtying your soul before you went to church tomorrow."

"Luke."

"I'm just kidding. No sex. I promise. And, if it makes you feel any better, I rubbed one off before I texted you, so I'm good for at least an hour."

"Oh my God, Luke. Have you ever heard of TMI?"

"Nope. Now, get your hot ass over here, so I can start this movie."

She turned off the TV and picked up her keys. "I'm leaving right now."

"Wait."

She stopped in her tracks. "What?"

"Wear something sexy."

Elise laughed and rolled her eyes. "Good-bye, Luke. I'll see you soon."

CHAPTER SEVEN

"Alan Rickman was such a good actor. I wonder if he was a nice guy in real life, and that's why he played such an excellent bad guy. It's sad he passed away," Elise said from Luke's couch.

She was sprawled out on it like she owned the place, her blonde hair fanned out around her head, but he didn't mind. After she'd gotten to his house, he'd made sure to sit in his recliner, so she would know that he had been serious when he assured her there would be no sex.

Or rather, he was serious about it for tonight. Because he'd already decided that he was going to fuck her again.

Yeah, yeah, so he'd promised not to sleep with her in the first place, and when he had, he'd promised himself it wouldn't happen a second time. Except he'd been thinking about it almost nonstop during the last two weeks. He'd been dreaming about fucking her, only to wake up hard, aching, and disappointingly alone. And that was when he had known he had to get inside her again. That was the only way he was going to stop thinking about it.

He was an adult, Elise was an adult, and what the two of them did in the privacy of the bedroom, living room, or back of a taxi wasn't anyone's business but their own. Their friends could just kiss off because Sean wasn't the one walking around with a permanent boner.

"He was a good actor, but he hasn't played that many bad guys, has he?"

"Yes. Hans Gruber in *Die Hard*, Sheriff of Nottingham in *Robin Hood*, Judge Turpin in *Sweeney Todd*, Professor Snape in the Harry Potter movies, and Harry in *Love Actually*."

"*Love Actually?*"

"Yeah. You know what I'm talking about."

"Sorry, babe, no clue."

Her mouth dropped open. "Are you telling me, you've never seen *Love Actually*? That's only, like, one of my favorite movies."

"Nope."

"But...why?" she asked, clearly dumbfounded.

"Two words—*chick flick*."

She shook her head. "I can see why one would think that, but it's more than just a chick flick. It's a holiday movie with a great message. You're really missing out."

Luke cocked an eyebrow.

"I'm serious."

"*Yeeaaah*...I think I'll just take your word on it."

"I can't believe no woman has gotten you to watch it."

"Many have tried; none have succeeded," he joked.

"Hmm..." she said with a glint in her eye.

"What?"

She shook her head and smiled. "Nothing. Just that I'm going to make it my mission in life to make you watch that movie."

"Ha."

"So, what would it take, huh?"

Luke grinned at her.

She pointed a finger. "And don't say sex."

"Aw, shucks." He feigned disappointment.

"Come on."

Because he had no plans to watch that chick flick, he told her, "Fine, I'll watch it with my future wife."

This way, they both won. He got her to leave him alone, and she got him to agree to watch the movie.

"Mission complete."

She huffed, "Hardly. But I'll concede for now."

He laughed. "What makes Alan Rickman the bad guy in that movie anyway?"

Elise snickered. "Wouldn't you like to know?"

He didn't want to admit it, but he would. But he wasn't going to tell her that. He shrugged. "Whatever. I'll find out someday." *Someday far, far from now...maybe.* Because Luke had no plans to get married in the near future.

They continued to watch the movie, subject dropped.

After the movie was over, Elise made no move to leave, so he asked, "*Die Hard 2?*"

It almost looked like there was some relief in her eyes.

But she shrugged her shoulders, like it was no big deal, and said, "Sure."

"Do you want to change the movie while I go and make you the popcorn I promised you?"

"Oh, yeah. I almost forgot about the popcorn. You've got yourself a deal."

Luke walked to the kitchen and pulled out the popcorn, oil, pan, bowl, and butter. The only way to make popcorn was on the stove. He didn't like any of that microwave shit.

While he waited for the oil to heat up, his phone rang, and since Elise was in the other room and they weren't in the middle of a movie, he answered, "Sydney, what's up?"

"How's my favorite brother?"

Between him and their other two siblings, Luke was not her favorite. "What do you want?"

"Lucas, what makes you think I want anything?"

"You're calling me."

Luke loved his sister, but she really never called unless she needed something. He would like to think it was because she was young and the baby of the family, but sometimes, he wondered if that was the kind of person she was always going to be.

"Maybe I'm calling you because I love you."

"What do you want, Syd?" he asked again.

Elise walked into the kitchen. There seemed to be some uncertainty in her eyes and maybe, possibly, some jealousy. Luke could only hope because, if she was jealous, she was interested, and if she was interested, he had a shot of getting in her pants again. But he didn't want her feeling envious. He wanted her to be relaxed and enjoying herself.

So, he mouthed, *Sister*, to her and turned back to the heating oil.

He checked to see if the popcorn kernel he had thrown in there popped. *Not yet.*

Luke realized he had missed everything Sydney had said because he wasn't paying attention. "Hold up. Can you repeat that?"

Luke looked over to see Elise coming up beside him before his sister said, "Ugh, Luke. Will you pay for my acting classes or not?"

Easy question. "Not."

"Luke," his sister whined.

"Sydney, I am not giving you money for acting classes."

Luke looked at Elise and shook his head as he grimaced. Elise giggled.

"Come on. You're rich; you can afford it."

"First, I am not rich. There are these things called student loans, which I will be paying back until I'm dead, not that you would know anything about it. Second, what did Mom and Dad say?"

"You suck."

Translation: Mom and Dad had said no.

"Syd, you know I love you, but at some point, you have to stop wasting money and figure out what you really want to do."

Getting down and serious was a sure way to get his sister off the phone.

"I gotta go," she mumbled.

"Okay. Remember, we love you."

"Whatever."

And, with that, she was gone.

Luke tossed his phone on the counter and went back to making popcorn, pouring the rest of the kernels in the pot.

"So, that was your sister, huh?"

Luke snorted. "Yeah. She lives in LA with her yuppie boyfriend while she tries to *find herself*. Why she can't do that while going to college like everyone else is beyond my parents' comprehension. But I kind of don't blame them. It'd be one thing if she supported herself, but she's always asking for money. Today, she wanted money for acting classes. Two months ago, she was going to be an artist. Six months ago, she wanted to design jewelry."

"Wow."

"Yeah."

"How old is she?"

"Twenty."

"Wow," Elise said again. "I can't imagine moving to LA at such a young age with no job or anything. That takes guts."

Luke paused as he shifted the popcorn pan back and forth. "I suppose you have a point. But it's pretty easy to do that when you know your parents are never going to let you starve. Mom and Dad might not pay for her acting classes, but they do pay for her rent and car insurance."

Elise didn't reply and seemed lost in thought.

"You don't want to move to LA with some loser guy, do you?"

Elise laughed. "No, not even close. I was just thinking, it'd be nice to be able to do what you wanted without worrying about your parents judging you."

Luke gave her a questioning look.

"This is between us, but today, I found out my sister

might be getting a divorce, and if she does, my parents are going to be devastated. They're annoyingly conservative. What's ironic is that the reason my sister got married was because she'd gotten pregnant. Can't have a baby out of wedlock, you know. And the only reason she got pregnant was because my parents had refused to discuss birth control. Because, of course, nobody has sex before marriage."

Luke chuckled. "Of course not."

Elise looked at him and turned pink.

"That sucks for your sister."

She sighed. "Yeah, I feel really bad for her."

Luke poured the popcorn in the big bowl he had gotten out. "What about you? What would you do differently if you didn't have to worry about your parents?"

Elise tilted her head to the side. "I don't think anyone's ever asked me that before."

Luke threw the butter in the pan to melt it. "So?" he prompted.

"Well, I still probably wouldn't do anything like your sister, but there is something I've always wanted to do. I'm embarrassed to admit I haven't because I don't want to disappoint my parents."

This, he had to hear. "What's that?"

"Promise you won't laugh?"

He drew a cross over his heart. "Promise."

"I've wanted to get my nose pierced for years. Nothing crazy, just a cute little something. One of my good friends in Denver had one, and I always loved it."

Luke put the pan in the sink and turned on the faucet to fill it with water. "That's cool."

"You don't think it's silly?"

"No, in fact, I think, if it's something you want to do, you should do it. I think it'd be sexy."

Elise laughed and rolled her green eyes. "I'm pretty sure you think everything is sexy." She grabbed the popcorn bowl. "Come on. Let's go watch the movie."

CHAPTER EIGHT

Elise was running late for Rachel's Fourth of July party. She jerked her blue shorts up her legs, yanked her red halter top over her head—careful not to wreck her makeup—and slipped on her white sandals. She brushed her hair, deciding to leave it down, and hurried out of the bathroom.

She'd told Rachel that she would be there early to help set up before everyone else arrived, so running behind didn't leave her much time to help before the guests were scheduled to get there. But, before she could leave, she had to get one thing just in case the opportunity arose to bring it out. Unfortunately, it was in the basement among all her moving boxes. At the moment, she had taken over the lower level of her parents' home with all the things she had moved out of her house in Colorado.

She started in the corner where her living room stuff was, and it took a couple of tries, but she found the item she'd been searching for. She ran upstairs, slipped it in her purse, and grabbed the food she'd made for the party.

Rachel lived about twenty to thirty minutes from her parents', depending on traffic, and since it was a holiday, the drive was considerably better than on a normal weekday.

Halfway there, Elise's cell rang.

"Hello?"

"Hey, are you on your way?" Rachel asked.

"Almost there."

"Can you stop and pick up some ice? I underestimated how much we'd need."

"I told her to get ten bags!" Sean yelled from the background.

"Yeah, yeah," Rachel said. "So, I thought you were exaggerating. I was wrong."

"Elise, did you hear that?" Sean yelled. "She said she was wrong. You're my witness."

Elise laughed.

"Get out of here, jerkface," Rachel told her fiancé, her voice laced with humor.

"So, how many bags do you need me to get?" Elise asked.

"Six," Rachel whispered into the phone.

Elise laughed harder. "You only got four bags? Ha-ha-ha-ha!"

"I know, okay? Don't tell Sean. He's already gloating because I didn't believe him."

"I won't say anything."

"Let me know when you get here. I'll help you bring the ice in."

"You mean, sneak it in."

"Whatever. Just text me when you're here."

"Will do."

"And stop laughing at me."

"I love you!" Elise shouted into the phone before her friend hung up, smiling. She was really looking forward to sitting around, eating, drinking, and watching fireworks with her friends today.

About twenty minutes later, Elise texted Rachel to let her know she was there. She parked on the street to leave the driveway free. The garage was open with tables set up for food to keep it out of the hot sun with the back door of the garage open to the backyard, so people could walk back and forth.

Elise got out of her car and started unloading the ice and food on the lawn when Luke strolled out of the garage. She hadn't seen him since she hung out at his house a week and a half ago when they watched the first two Die Hard movies. She hadn't realized how much she'd been looking forward to seeing him until now.

The front door opened, and Rachel came flying out, shouting, "Sean's in the shower! Hurry, hurry, hurry."

Elise laughed. "Rach, it's not that big of a deal."

Rachel grabbed the first two bags. "Oh, he has been giving me so much crap this morning, especially after I admitted I was wrong. I might just strangle him, and I really don't want to go to jail tonight."

"Whatcha ladies doing?" Luke said from behind Rachel.

Rachel jumped a foot in the air. She turned around and actually attempted to step in front of the ice, which proved to be pointless because there was so much. "Luke, you're supposed to be in the backyard."

Elise laughed at her friend's panic, grabbing the last few things out of her car and locking it.

Luke looked at all the items strewed on the lawn. "That's a lot of ice."

"I know," Rachel said in a biting tone. "Now, shoo." She waved her arms, as if Luke were a dog or something.

Luke ignored her. "Are you sure you don't need help?"

"Fine." Rachel pointed a finger at Luke. "As long as you don't say anything to Sean."

"I can keep a secret." He looked from Rachel to Elise. "Right, Elise?"

Elise made a strangled sound in the back of her throat and almost dropped the ice she'd just picked up.

Rachel swung around to look at her. "Huh?"

Elise ignored Luke's question. "Let's just get this done before Sean comes out. Where do you want this?"

Rachel had them split up the ice between the coolers and then store the rest in the deep freezer in their basement.

They had just finished up when Sean walked into the kitchen. "Hey, Elise. Thanks for running that errand for us."

"Hey, Sean. Not a problem. I was already in the car."

"Well, ya know, if someone—"

Rachel held up the knife she'd just reached for to cut up fruit. "Babe, are you sure you want to finish that sentence?"

Sean shook his head. "No, ma'am."

"That's what I thought."

Rachel went back to cutting fruit, and Sean came up behind her, slipping his arms around her waist.

"You know I was just giving you crap. It's not every day you mess up, so I had to give you a hard time. But, if I hurt your feelings, I'm sorry."

Aw, so sweet.

Rachel's face softened. She put down the carving utensil, turned, and kissed Sean, rubbing her watermelon-soaked fingers over his T-shirt. Sean didn't seem to mind because he moaned and tugged Rachel closer.

*Aaannnd...*that was Elise's cue to leave the room.

"Just a reminder, you have guests coming soon," she called over her shoulder as she opened the sliding glass door to go outside.

Rachel and Sean's home was older and didn't have the walk-out basement that was so popular nowadays. So, their deck was only a couple of feet off the ground. That made it convenient for parties because people didn't have to crowd the deck where the grill was.

Elise grabbed the folded chairs that had been set on the side of the house and started setting them out. She set some up on the lawn and some on the deck. Then, she went into the garage to grab herself something to drink. She couldn't decide between a mixed drink or a beer or if she should just stick with pop for now.

"Are you trying to kill me with that outfit?" a voice from behind her spoke against her ear.

She barely managed not to flinch. Once again, Luke had scared her. She didn't know how he kept doing that.

She looked over her shoulder to meet his eyes. "After your comment to Rachel, you deserve it."

Luke grinned, his beautiful brown eyes lighting up, and she couldn't help smiling back.

"You're a butthead, you know that?"

He shrugged one shoulder. "Guilty."

She turned toward him and asked, "What if Rachel had questioned what you meant by asking me if you could keep a secret?"

"Nah, she was too busy freaking out. I heard her yelling something about Sean being in the shower and for you to hurry. She was too worried about her own thing."

"Yeah, but it could have happened. I mean, what if she had figured out about...you know?"

He raised his brow. "That I fucked you?"

She quickly scanned the garage, despite knowing they were the only ones there. "*Luke.*"

He snickered. "Oops, I meant, that you fucked me."

Her cheeks heated. "Uh...I don't think so."

"Hmm." He pretended to look confused. "What do *you* call it when you pull down a guy's pants, whip off your panties, and sit on his cock?"

She covered his mouth with her hand, her embarrassment now spread across her whole face and down her neck. "Oh my God, be quiet."

He pulled her hand away from his mouth but only far enough so that he could speak, "I can't." Then, he kissed her palm.

Her skin tingled where his lips touched, and she stood there in a trance, unable to move. He pulled her arm down and used it to tug her close, lacing their fingers together. With his free hand, he stroked his fingers over her cheek and down her chin.

Unsure of what he was going to do, she held her breath—afraid he'd do more and, at the same time, afraid he'd stop.

He threaded his fingers through her hair and pulled her mouth to his. "I can't stop thinking about the two of us together," he whispered.

Then, he kissed her.

Elise sighed and opened her mouth to let him in, grabbing on to his hip to anchor herself to him.

Luke wasted no time in taking possession of her mouth, and she could do nothing to stop him. She didn't want to do anything to stop him. Although they were just kissing, Luke had complete control, and it made her hot. He swept his tongue into her mouth and then sucked hers into his. She grew wet between her legs and had flashbacks to the night they'd spent together.

She admitted it; she wanted to feel him inside her again.

But Luke made no move to go any further. Unlike the night they'd slept together, this kissed lacked urgency. What it lacked in urgency was replaced with intensity. Luke took his time as he just kissed her and kissed her and kissed her. Soon, it was only him, her, and their mouths.

She wanted to kiss him forever and forget about the rest of the world.

Unfortunately, reality intruded with the sound of a car door slamming, and Elise stepped away.

She put her fingertips to her lips. Even without a mirror, she knew they were red and swollen. She quickly reached into a cooler, grabbing the first thing she touched. She put the cold glass to her lips for a few seconds and then opened the bottle before taking a big gulp.

"Yuck." She made a sour face and looked at the beverage for the first time. "I hate this kind of beer."

Luke laughed at her expression, and then they both turned to see who was coming up the driveway. She pushed him toward the guests because somebody had to greet them, and she was too stunned at the moment.

She took another sip of the god-awful beer she clutched in her hand. The couple entered the garage, and Luke welcomed them both. The woman set some sort of dish on the table, and then Luke introduced Elise to them.

She forgot their names two seconds after they stepped into the backyard.

"I'll go tell Rachel and Sean they're here," she told Luke, heading for the house.

She needed to process the kiss they'd just shared anyway.

CHAPTER NINE

Luke frowned as Elise escaped into the house. While he had hoped to kiss her sometime today, he hadn't planned to do it before the party even started. But she'd stood there, smelling like heaven, in her sexy outfit with her skintight top and shorts that showed off her legs, looking at him with her big eyes, and he'd wanted her something fierce.

He hadn't been able to resist teasing her about their night together, and he'd enjoyed the blush that spread from her face down to her chest. She'd flushed like that when she came, too. Luke adjusted himself in his shorts, grateful that he was alone in the garage at the moment.

The sound of more car doors shutting told him that more guests had arrived. He directed everyone to the backyard, where the previous guests were, after showing them where the food and drinks were located. He was starting to wonder who the host and hostess of this party were when he saw a figure coming up the driveway that caused him to run scared into the house.

Elise was alone in the kitchen, cutting up the fruit that Rachel had previously been working on.

"Where are they?" He didn't wait for her to answer. "Sean! Rachel!" he called down the hall.

A second later, their bedroom door opened, and they stepped out. Rachel was finger-combing her hair, and Sean was tugging down his shirt.

Oh, nice.

So, while they had been getting it on, Luke was preparing himself to fight off unwanted attention all day. This was supposed to be a fun, relaxing holiday.

"Why the hell did you let Molly bring her little sister?" he asked his friends.

Rachel covered her mouth with her hand as she tried not to laugh.

Luke pointed a finger at her. "This is not funny."

"It kind of is," she countered.

Sean sighed. "For the record, I told Rachel no, but Molly begged Rachel to let her come. Something about how her sister was sad because she'd just broken up with her boyfriend, and Molly couldn't leave her home alone."

Luke threw his hands up in exasperation. "Great. Now, she's going to be even clingier than usual. Doesn't that girl have any friends of her own?"

"Apparently, they all went away for the week or something," Rachel said.

"Wait a second," Elise spoke up. "What am I missing here?"

"My friend Molly has a younger sister who"—Rachel paused, as if searching for the right words—"has a bit of an interest in Luke."

Luke snorted. "A bit of an interest? The girl—and, when I say girl, I mean, *girl* because she's only, like, nineteen—will not leave me alone whenever I see her. I practically have to peel her off me."

Elise laughed.

"Oh, Barbie's not that bad," Rachel said.

Elise laughed harder, clutching her stomach. "Her name is Barbie? This keeps getting better."

"Ha-ha," Luke said sarcastically. "It's hilarious."

"Sorry, man," Sean told him.

Inspiration struck, and Luke snapped his fingers. "I know. Elise, pretend to be my girlfriend. She'll leave me alone then."

Elise shook her head, still giggling. "No way. I wouldn't miss this for the world."

"You suck. I hate you all," Luke told the room.

He stomped out of the house, Elise's and Rachel's laughter trailing behind him.

He went over to the stereo on the deck, plugged in his iPod, and cranked up the music to a loud but tolerable level. Then, he grabbed a beer and threw himself into a chair to pout. He grabbed his phone out of his pocket and pretended to be busy on it while sipping his beer.

It didn't work.

Ten seconds later, Barbie sat beside him, and he groaned into his drink. She had her platinum-blonde hair in big, fluffy curls, and she wore what looked like a truckload of makeup. Her outfit was way too revealing for an afternoon barbeque. She looked like she was ready to go out to the club.

"Hi, Luke," she said, full of excitement.

Luke leaned his head back against his chair. "Hey."

He had to tread cautiously with Barbie. He didn't want to lead her on or give any indication that she had a chance with him. Yet he had to be very careful that he didn't hurt her feelings. She was at an age where she was finding herself, and he didn't want to be the jerk older guy who crushed her spirit and made her hate men forever.

God, he was glad he wasn't in college anymore.

"How are you, Luke?"

He looked around for Molly, who knew that her sister had a thing for him, but she was off in the corner, talking to someone. So, Luke sipped his beer and tried not to fidget.

"Good," he answered Barbie. He didn't want to be rude, but he also didn't offer any more information than that.

He spied Elise walking out of the back of the house.

Although I could be better, he thought when he saw her.

She stood close enough to listen to him and Barbie but didn't approach them.

"And you?" he asked Barbie, whose back was to Elise.

Barbie shrugged. "I'm doing okay."

Clearly, she only said she was okay, so Luke would ask why. But he wasn't about to mention that he'd heard about her breakup because he didn't want her thinking he'd been talking about her. She would surely take it as a sign that he was interested.

His phone buzzed in his hand.

He nodded. "That's good," he said as he unlocked his phone and pulled up his messages.

> Elise: She's cute.

> Luke: Ugh. She reminds me of my little sister.

Luke looked over at the deck. Elise stood there with a smirk on her face, looking at her phone.

"Yeah, I just broke up with my boyfriend," Barbie said, her head down as she gazed up at him through her lashes.

Luke quickly looked away as his phone buzzed again.

> Elise: Can she be any more obvious that she wants to do you?

> Luke: God, I hope not.

"Oh, that sucks. Breakups are no fun," Luke told Barbie. *Buzz.*

> Elise: What is it with women wanting to sleep with you?

> Luke: I'm irresistible. Although not irresistible enough. You don't want to sleep with me again.

> Elise: Who said I didn't want to sleep with you again?

He read Elise's text just as Barbie said, "Yeah, I'm hoping to have a little rebound sex."

Holy hell.

He'd been in the middle of taking another sip of his beer and practically choked on it after reading Elise's message and listening to Barbie blatantly hit on him.

It was a good thing he was coughing from his drink going down the wrong tube, so he didn't have to respond to Barbie right away. Meanwhile, Elise was trying not to die from laughter.

Luke quickly picked up his phone when it buzzed again.

> Elise: Bwahahahaha.

> Luke: If that's not true, then how about you come over here and sit on my dick again? That'll let Barbie know I'm interested in only you.

> Elise: And give everyone in the backyard a show? I don't think so.

> Luke: Okay then, how about you please get your sexy ass over here and rescue me?

> Elise: I don't know. I like watching you squirm. It's not every day that Luke Long is uncomfortable. I'm kind of enjoying this.

> Luke: Please. I'm begging you.

> Elise: Okay, but you owe me.

"Luke," Barbie said, "are you going to be okay?"

Luke was still coughing, so he hit his fist against his chest a couple of times, trying to clear his lungs. "Yeah, I think I'll live."

"About what I said…" Barbie started but didn't get to finish because Elise approached them.

"Hey, Luke?"

"Oh, hi, Elise. Elise, this is Barbie. Barbie, this is my good friend Elise."

"Hello," Elise said cheerfully.

"Hi," Barbie said, clearly unhappy.

Luke smiled at Elise. "What's up?" he asked Elise, pretending like they hadn't been texting back and forth.

"Could you come into the house for a minute? Sean needs you."

Luke jumped up from his seat. "Oh, sure." Feeling slightly bad for Barbie, he turned back to her. "Sorry. Gotta go."

"Bye, Luke," she said, obviously disappointed that he was leaving.

Luke threw his arm around Elise's neck, pulling her close as they walked toward the house. "Thank you, thank you, thank you," he whispered in her ear.

Elise wrapped her arm around his waist. "You're welcome."

"I owe you."

"How about you just watch my back? Because, with the daggers Barbie is sending my way, I'm afraid she might go a little *Fatal Attraction* on me. Make sure you inform the police about your admirer-slash-stalker when I turn up dead."

"She's not my stalker. I rarely even see her. It's just that, when I do…"

"She wants to have rebound sex with you," Elise said with a laugh.

Luke shuddered. "Please do not say that again. I wasn't lying when I said she reminded me of my sister. It creeps me out."

They reached the sliding glass door and dropped their arms to turn toward each other. Elise had an odd look on her face.

"What?" he asked.

She shook her head and smiled at him. "Nothing. You'd better get in there and *help Sean* before Barbie sics herself on you again."

"You joke, but it's true."

She laughed. "Go on. Find something else to do for a few minutes. I'll keep an eye on Barbie and make sure she doesn't follow you inside."

Luke kissed her on the cheek. "Thanks, babe."

CHAPTER TEN

Several hours later, Elise was in the front yard, talking to a couple of Rachel's friends, Heidi and Tera, about one of her favorite subjects—books. All of them were romance novel fanatics and had started comparing favorites and then offering suggestions of what the others should read, forming a fast friendship.

They'd ended up in the front yard because Tera wanted to show Elise and Heidi the book she was currently reading, which she had left in her car, because neither of them had heard of it. Tera still enjoyed the look and feel of holding a real book in her hand. After that, they hadn't moved very far, staying in the front of the house rather than going to the back again since it was quieter and easier to talk there without the loud music.

"We should really exchange info, so we can get together or something. Maybe we can form our own book club," Elise suggested.

"Good idea. I would love to have an all-romance book club," Heidi suggested.

Heidi was a curly redhead with blue eyes and a kind smile.

"I'm open to trying a book club. I've tried them before, but someone always wants to include something just because it looks good. I'm a smut reader and proud of it," Tera said.

Tera was a blonde with short hair and brown eyes. She seemed like she had a feisty streak in her.

Elise had liked them both immediately.

Tera and Heidi hadn't met each other until that day either, and they all had just finished exchanging phone numbers and finding each other on Facebook and Instagram when they heard a loud, "Whoop, whoop," and a high-pitched whistle from the backyard.

"Ooh, I think we need to go and see what we're missing," Tera said.

They all stowed their phones in their pockets and trekked to the back of the house. They walked through the garage, snagging a few snacks to take with them as they went.

When Elise stepped through the back door, all she saw at first was lots and lots of skin.

Sexy, sweaty male skin.

And her eyes zeroed in on one male in particular. *Damn, that boy is fine as hell.*

It made her wish their night together was clearer. She remembered it, but since she'd been drunk, parts were still fuzzy and didn't have the clarity of a recent memory. Instead, it seemed like it had happened a long time ago, almost like a dream, which was a damn shame. Next time, she was going to be stone-cold sober.

Next time? Ha.

"Wow," Heidi said beside her. "Break me off a piece of that." She pointed to a guy. "Or that." She pointed to another one. "Or that." She pointed to a third guy. "You know what? Just give me a taste of everything."

Tera added, "Oh, me, too. I'm willing to share." She held out her arms. "Come to me, gorgeous men. I am yours for the taking."

The three women fell into a fit of laughter, and a few people around them looked at them and smiled while some looked at them like they were a bunch of weirdos. It only made them laugh harder.

"I'd even take one of the...less fit guys," Heidi said tactfully. "It's been a long time for me—if you know what I mean."

"I know exactly what you mean," Elise said. "I've thought about buying stock in Energizer and Duracell. BOB sure goes through them fast."

"It's only been over two months for me," Tera said. "And, before that, I had a long dry spell. I think the hardest thing about being a woman is that I can live without sex, but I just don't want to."

"Amen," said Elise.

"Word," said Heidi.

And the three of them clinked their cups together.

Heidi turned her head to the side. "Of all those fine men out there, who do you think would be the best in bed?"

"Sean. Hands down, Sean," Rachel said, coming up behind them.

Tera rolled her eyes. "You can't say that. You've actually had sex with the man. This is supposed to be a hypothetical. We're guessing. You actually know what it's like to have sex with Sean."

"Okay, okay, I see where you're coming from." She put her finger to her lips. "Hmm..."

Since Elise had had a few drinks and the conversation was going the way it was, she asked her friend, "Is Sean *really* that good in bed?"

Elise admitted to herself that she'd always wanted to know. Sean was built with nice muscles and a six-pack, but he wasn't as tall as some men, and he was on the thin side. In fact, Elise had never known the guy was so muscular until the first time she saw him without his shirt. He reminded her of Adam Levine. Another guy whom she'd had no idea what he was packing underneath his clothes until he did that photo shoot a few years ago.

Elise's eyes moved from Sean to Luke. If Sean was Adam Levine, then Luke was Jason Momoa. Big, broad, and alpha-like. Sean was good-looking, but Luke was sex on a stick.

A stick she wanted to lick.

"Hell yeah," Rachel said, answering Elise's question. "Do you really think I would have dated someone this long or promised to marry him if he were a dud?" She shook her head. "No way, no how. If I'm going to have sex with one guy for the rest of my life, he'd better know what he's doing in the sack. Plus, Sean might be short, but he's not *short*." She smirked. "If you know what I'm sayin'."

"Hey, why did it take the two of you so long to get engaged?" Tera asked, changing the subject.

Rachel told them about how she and Sean were in college at first and nowhere near thoughts of marriage, and then they'd broken up for a few years before getting back together. Elise had already known all this and had heard it all before, and she found herself contemplating what Rachel had said about enjoying sex with Sean.

In Denver, Elise and her ex Jason had actually talked about marriage a few times, and she had often thought that was where they would eventually be headed until they broke up. Yet she and Jason had had a very mundane sex life. Then, she thought about some of her other exes. Tyler, the college boyfriend whom she'd lived with, again, was just okay in the bedroom department. Also, there were Zach and Mike. She hadn't thought about marriage with either of them, but she had dated each of them for about a year. Both could have used some pointers on pleasing women. Yet she'd had some one-night stands and friends with benefits who were great in bed.

Was it a coincidence, or did it mean something else?

Elise was jarred out of her thoughts when the girls started jumping up and down, shouting and yelling at the game. Elise hated to admit it, but she didn't know all that much about football. She didn't know exactly what had gotten her friends excited, but she clapped along with them.

Then, Luke threw a pass to some guy—Elise couldn't remember his name—and the guy made it into the end zone and scored. She didn't know much, but she did know how a goal was scored. Sean high-fived Luke and then smacked him on the butt, the two of them grinning and drawing the eyes of the female partygoers.

"Now, there is one fine specimen of man meat," Tera said.

"Who?" Elise asked.

Probably ten to fifteen guys were playing out there, and part of her—a jealous part—hoped that she wasn't talking about Luke.

"Luke," Tera said with a sigh. "He is *so* hot."

"Oh my God, *so* hot," Heidi added.

Elise mentally winced, prepared to hear about how these females had slept with Luke. She didn't want to be envious, picturing him with other women, but she was afraid that was exactly what was going to happen. She could already feel herself getting resentful, and it made her uncomfortable. She didn't want to be jealous, nor did she have a right to be.

"I agree, and I'm engaged," Rachel just had to chime in.

Now, if Elise didn't say something, they'd think something was up.

"He's hot," Elise agreed. "But he's kind of a player. At least, he was in college."

"Man, I wish," Tera said. "I've been trying to get with him since Rachel introduced me."

"Same here. He never takes me up on my offers. And I don't think I'm being subtle."

"What? Are you sure we're talking about the same person?" Elise asked, shocked.

"Yes," Tera and Heidi said at the same time.

"To be fair, Elise is right. He was a total player back in college, and he still gets around some," Rachel said. "Now, he doesn't sleep with just anyone though. He totally would have taken you both up on your offers back then. Now, he stays away from anyone who is friends with Sean and me. Thank God, too. I lost a few friends back in college because Sean's friends had slept with them and never called them back."

"Man, I'm about ten years too late," Tera said. "Does that mean you slept with him?" she asked Elise.

"Huh? What?" She hadn't expected that question. "Oh, you mean, back in college? No, we never had sex back then." No, instead, she'd had sex with him last month.

"Damn, I was going to live vicariously through you."

"Sorry," she said with a shrug.

"So, do you think Luke is more of a McDreamy or a McSteamy?" Tera asked.

"Ooh...that's tough because he's dark like McDreamy, but he's built more like McSteamy," Heidi said.

Elise didn't understand why they were comparing Luke to the *Grey's Anatomy* doctors whom all the females on the show thought were hot. She guessed it was because he was good-looking, like the actors on the show had been.

"I say McSteamy," Rachel concluded.

"Yeah, you're probably right. Elise?" Tera agreed.

Elise shrugged. "McSteamy." She'd always found McSteamy more attractive than McDreamy.

"Hey, I have to go inside and do a couple of things. I'll talk to you guys later," Rachel said. She stepped around them to head for the house.

Nobody else said anything, and the ladies concentrated on the game while Elise's thoughts turned inward again.

She didn't know what to think about Luke. She was

slightly amazed that he hadn't slept with either Heidi or Tera. And, earlier, when he had turned down Barbie, she'd been surprised. Barbie might have been young and brash, but she was a cute young thing. There is no way Luke would have said no to her back in the day. But he had told her he wouldn't go there and that the whole situation creeped him out. Maybe Luke had matured more than she gave him credit for.

Of course, that was when the guys decided to take a break from football. Luke picked up his bottle of water and took several long drags. She stared at his throat as he swallowed. It was tan and sweaty, and she wanted to kiss him there and taste the sweat on his skin.

As if he knew that she was watching, he put the water down with one last big drink and looked at her. At the same moment, the stereo began to pump out "Inside of You" by Hoobastank, and Luke knowingly smiled at her. As the lyrics continued, he practically mouthed the words as her eyes caressed him. She knew she should look away before someone noticed, but she couldn't. The words were making her hot. Her breathing became labored as Luke licked his bottom lip and stared at her like he had that night he fucked her. Of course, that part, she remembered perfectly.

Somebody laughed and broke her trance. She quickly glanced around to see if Tera and Heidi were paying attention, but they were looking at something on someone's phone next to them. Elise had to use all her willpower to not look at Luke again. She turned and went into the garage to compose herself because she was only so strong. She took a position by the food table in case someone else walked in. Thankfully, although people were in the front yard and right outside the back door, she was alone, so no one asked why she stood there, breathing hard and staring into space.

Because the music was loud, she didn't hear Luke approach, but she sensed him through her whole being. She didn't turn to look at him, but she felt the length of his body almost touch hers, only millimeters separating them. He moved her hair off one shoulder and put his mouth right on her ear where he sang the chorus of the song as it came to a crescendo. She moaned softly because she wanted the same thing as the lead singer of Hoobastank did. As Luke did.

The words were over, and all that was left was music. Luke pulled his mouth away and pushed her hair back around her shoulder. When the song was done, she turned around, and he was gone.

Heidi and Tera came through the door.

"Hey, there you are," Heidi said. "Are you getting something to eat?"

"Oh, uh...no, I thought about it, but nothing looks good."

"Come back out here then," Tera said.

"Oh, sure." Elise put the plate down she hadn't even realized she'd picked up. Her fingers ached from where she'd been clutching it.

"I love the song they just played," Heidi said when Elise joined them.

"Oh, me, too. It always gets me in the mood," Tera said.

"Same here. Whenever I hear it, I fantasize about a guy singing it to me from the other side of a room as he looks at me like he wants to do me."

"Shit, yeah. To know a guy wants you that bad...H-O-T hot," Tera said.

"Don't you agree, Elise?" Heidi asked.

Elise squeaked out a sound and gave a small nod, unsure if she was actually able to form any words at the moment. Part of her wanted to brag that it had just happened to her from the guy they'd been fawning over earlier, but the other part of her wanted to keep it to herself. For some reason, it made the whole thing hotter that way.

It was her dirty little secret.

Suddenly, Elise looked at her new friends and smiled. "I definitely agree."

If these ladies only knew what had just happened...

As if on cue, "Dirty Little Secret" by The All-American Rejects filled the backyard, and Elise laughed.

CHAPTER ELEVEN

After the guys were done playing football, they got out the fireworks and were setting them off in the driveway and on the street. There were certain laws in Minnesota about what kind of fireworks you could have and set off, especially in town. Not that the guys cared about the rules too much. Elise was pretty sure there were a few that would get them in trouble if someone turned them in or if the police drove by. But the neighbors who were outside around Rachel and Sean's house were pretty much doing the same thing.

Up until now, Barbie had been leaving Luke alone. It had helped that he was playing football and then helping Sean grill the burgers and hot dogs they had for dinner.

But, now, she was marching up to him and holding out her hand for him to look at. A second ago, Barbie had been near a firework that went off. She had squealed and jumped away, startled, but in no way had she looked hurt. Until her eyes had focused on Luke with determination.

Elise wanted to pull Barbie aside and tell her to lay off the man. Not because Elise was jealous or anything like that, but because it was so obvious that Barbie wanted Luke, and it made her look desperate. Elise had heard a couple of people snicker behind Barbie's back, and her heart went out to the girl. She remembered what it was like to be young and unsure of herself, and then to add liking a boy on top of that was the worst.

Molly, Barbie's older sister, was a few feet away, and her attention was drawn to the situation. Molly's face fell when she heard one guy's comment about how, if Luke didn't want Barbie, then he would screw her, like her little sister was some kind of thing. Molly hurried over to where Luke was inspecting Barbie's hand and shaking his head, like he didn't see anything wrong. Molly pulled Barbie away and spoke into her ear. Barbie looked around before hurrying off to run along the side of the house. Molly sighed as her shoulders slumped, obviously frustrated, and ran after her sister.

Luke walked over to Elise.

"So, did your admirer have a boo-boo she needed you to look at?" Elise felt bad for Barbie, but she still had to tease Luke a little.

"She was just fine."

"If you say so."

Luke ignored her joking. "Are you ready to set off a firecracker?"

Elise laughed, shaking her head. "No way. I'd probably shoot myself in the face and have to go to the hospital."

"No, you won't. Besides, I'll help you. I won't let you get hurt."

Elise squinted at him. "What about the fact that it's illegal?"

Luke stuck his fingers in his ears. "La-la-la-la-la. I can't hear you." He put his hands down. "I'm sorry. I don't know what you're talking about. Now, are you going to do this or not?"

"Not."

"Wrong answer," he said, grabbing her hand and pulling her over to the corner of the driveway. He bent over and sifted through the assortment of fireworks there. He grabbed one, stood up with a huge grin on his face, and handed it to her.

"What am I supposed to do with this?" she asked.

It was cylinder-shaped, about two inches in diameter, and six inches tall. It did not look small, and she was already worried.

"Go and set it in the middle of the road, and light it."

When she just stood there, he pulled her out to the street, took it out of her hand, and set it down.

"Now, you have to light it."

"Are you sure I won't get hurt?"

Luke held up three fingers. "Scout's honor."

She snorted. She doubted he'd ever been a Boy Scout.

She bent, pulled the tape off of the fuse, and drew it away from the firecracker.

Luke handed her something. "It's called a punk."

She snatched it from him. "I know what a punk is."

He chuckled and raised his eyebrows. "Well, excuse me."

Elise lit the firecracker, and then she quickly stood and backed up.

She made it almost to the sidewalk when Luke pulled her onto the lawn. "Watch out!"

"Shit!" she screamed as she ducked.

What kind of firecracker had he given her? That'd teach her to always read the label.

She heard a pop and turned around. Luke pointed up in the sky to what looked like a parachute.

Yep, that's a parachute. Why all the excitement then?

She turned to Luke, who was stifling a laugh.

"You are such an ass," she said as she pushed him, which only made him laugh harder. "You scared me. I thought it had exploded all over."

Luke kept on laughing, as did everyone else around him.

"I hate you. It's not funny," she said as she walked away.

"It's kind of funny!" he shouted after her.

She reached Rachel, Tera, and Heidi, who were all giggling but at least looked like they were trying not to.

Rachel said, "That was hilarious. You should have seen your face. You looked so afraid."

"Hardy-har-har. I was terrified. He had me thinking I was going to blow up or something." She added, "The big jerk," loud enough for Luke to hear.

He turned, smiled at her, and winked.

Elise rolled her eyes.

Heidi looked at her. "Gurl, did he just wink at you?"

"Yes, but only because he thinks the stunt he pulled is hilarious."

"Uh-huh," Tera said.

But it didn't look like she believed Elise, and Rachel just stared at her but didn't say anything.

Elise was done talking about the whole thing, so she changed the subject. "Hey, Rachel, how come Shelly and Joe didn't come today?"

"Oh, I forgot to tell you. Shelly is on bed rest these last few weeks of her pregnancy. She was pretty disappointed she couldn't come. And Joe decided to stay home with her."

"Aw, that's sweet. Tell her hi for me the next time you talk to her."

"Will do."

Apparently, her changing the subject hadn't worked too well because all three of her friends were studying her. She didn't understand what the big deal was. So, Luke had played a joke on her. It wasn't like it'd meant anything.

Tired of being scrutinized, she told them, "I'm going to get something to drink."

Before heading over to the beverages, Elise went into the house and used the bathroom. She dawdled in there for a bit, needing some time away from people. Everyone was outside, so she was alone—thankfully. Next, she cleaned up some plates and cups that were sitting around the kitchen and living room before heading back to the garage.

She mixed herself a drink when she realized she could hear voices coming from the backyard. There was so much commotion up front that she hadn't heard other voices drifting from the opposite direction until that moment.

Curious, Elise stepped outside, into the back. At first, she didn't see anyone, but then, off to the right, almost hiding behind the deck rails, were two people sitting down. She stepped closer, suddenly realizing it was Luke and Tera.

Tera looked up at Elise, and a look flashed across her face that almost appeared to be guilt, but it was gone so soon that Elise thought she might have imagined it. Tera threw her arm in the air and waved Elise over. When she reached them, she stood behind Luke's chair, so Tera was facing her. She saw that Tera had her leg on Luke's lap, and he was running his hand down her calf, pausing to squeeze it as he moved his fingers lower.

"Hey, Elise. Luke here was kind enough to look at my leg. Some dummy shot a bottle rocket, and it slammed into my calf."

"How nice of him," Elise tried to say in a perfectly normal voice.

But watching him touch Tera like that made her uncomfortable. And, worse, it made her jealous.

So much for not feeling possessive.

Luke seemed to be inspecting Tera almost clinically, and he didn't even look up at Elise. That hurt. Like he didn't even care that she was watching him touch her.

She told herself to let it go. But hadn't he just kissed her several hours ago? And hadn't he asked her to be his pretend girlfriend? And to rescue him from Barbie? And, after she had, he'd put his arm around her and kissed her cheek, like she was special. And then he'd had the gall to come behind her and sing the naughty lyrics of a song in her ear, as if he really had wanted to get inside her again. And then the joke and the wink? They weren't boyfriend and girlfriend, but she had thought they were friends. Or was he just using her for his own amusement?

Normally, Elise prided herself on being pretty level-headed and calm. She got angry and upset like everyone else, but in her line of work, she had really mastered having patience and not showing others when she was mad or distressed.

But, today, almost as if someone else had taken over her body, Elise took a swig from her big red Solo cup and then proceeded to dump the remains down Luke's back.

Luke cursed and jumped up from his chair, knocking Tera's leg off his lap, and Elise immediately regretted her childish act.

"Oh my God, I am so sorry," Elise told him.

She couldn't believe she'd done that. She had no claim on Luke. They weren't in a relationship. She didn't even think she wanted one.

What the hell is wrong with me?

Luke stood, hunched over, back still to her, with his arms out, just standing there and letting the liquid drip off him.

She wanted him to turn around and look at her, so she could read his face.

She didn't get a chance because Sean and Rachel came out from the garage.

"Tera, Rachel just told me—" He stopped when he saw Luke. "Oh, man, Luke, what in the hell happened to you?" Sean started laughing at his friend.

"I think Elise got revenge on him for the fireworks thing," Tera said, giggling.

"What? No. I didn't—I mean—it was an accident, okay?"

Rachel held her hand over her mouth to try to stifle her laugh as Elise shot past her and into the house.

Elise ran to the bathroom where she quickly grabbed a towel and took it outside to Luke.

When she got back out there, he was stripping off his shirt, and he still had his head down, so she couldn't see if he was mad. He took the cloth from her and began drying himself off.

"Give me your shirt, Luke, so I can throw it in the wash," Rachel said.

"It's okay. I can take it home."

"Don't be silly. Give it to me."

Luke handed it over while he dried his head and back. "I'm going to head to my house to change real quick," he said.

Because he was broader and larger than Sean, there was no way Luke could wear a shirt that belonged to Sean.

Luke handed Rachel the towel and took off through the neighbor's yard, in the direction of his home.

After he left, the backyard was silent.

"That was awesome," Tera finally said. "You should have seen his face. Classic."

Elise didn't even try to tell her again that she hadn't done it as a joke. What was she supposed to say instead? That the green-eyed monster had taken over her body, and she had acted immaturely? No, she definitely wasn't going to say that.

"Remind me never to cross you," Sean told Elise.

Rachel took Luke's shirt and the towel into the house. Sean turned and followed.

Tera stood up from the chair and approached Elise. She patted her on the arm. "Don't worry; he'll get over it." Then, she continued on into the garage and disappeared.

Alone, Elise admitted to herself that she'd acted juvenile,

and she felt guilty. She was maturer than that, and the grown-up thing to do was go and apologize.

Not bothering to say good-bye to anyone, Elise took off after Luke.

CHAPTER TWELVE

Luke cut through a few yards to make it home as fast as he could. He didn't know what Elise had had in her drink, but it must have been sugary because he was sticky, and he smelled fruity. He needed to get to his house and get in the shower ASAP.

Luke made it there in record time. He used his garage code to open the automatic door and head inside. Since he was leaving again soon, he didn't bother shutting it.

He went up to his bedroom and stripped, throwing his soaked shorts and boxers in his laundry basket in his closet. He walked into his master bath, hopped in his shower, and quickly went about cleaning Elise's drink out of his hair and off his skin.

He felt a little bad for just leaving like that because he sensed Elise's guilt for what had happened. She hadn't laughed like everyone else and had seemed shaken up. But Luke had just wanted to get home and get clean. The sooner he was back to normal, the sooner he would talk to Elise and tell her he wasn't mad that she had spilled her drink on him. He would survive getting wet.

Luke was almost finished with his shower when he heard a noise.

Is that my garage door?

He wasn't sure, but that was definitely someone calling his name. Luke hastily rinsed off the last of the soap, shut off the shower, and stepped out. He grabbed a towel to throw around his waist and stepped into his bedroom as the door to the hallway opened, and Elise walked in.

She quickly turned around. "Oh my God, I'm sorry. I didn't know you'd be naked."

Luke laughed. "It's okay, Lise. You've already seen everything anyway. Besides, I have a towel on." He tucked one side of his towel into the waist to keep it from falling down.

She slowly turned back around, but if he wasn't mistaken, her cheeks were slightly flushed, making her green eyes pop.

He stepped toward her. "What's up?" he asked.

She took in a deep breath and squared her shoulders. "I came to tell you, I'm sorry."

He waved it off. "It's okay. It's not a big deal. So, you spilled your drink on me. It's not like I melted or anything."

She squared her jaw. "I appreciate that, but I really need you to accept my apology."

He started moving closer to her. *Hmm...*

"Why is this so important to you?"

She rolled her eyes. "It just is, okay?"

When Luke reached her, he studied her face. She looked determined yet embarrassed, and he didn't think it was because he only wore a towel.

Realization dawned.

"Holy shit, you were jealous."

That certainly hadn't been his intention. There had been absolutely nothing sexual going on with Tera. She'd been hurt, and he had been making sure she was okay. But, since he had made Elise envious, he couldn't deny that he was a little pleased with her reaction to him.

Elise scoffed. "No, I wasn't."

He wasn't convinced. "Yes, you were," he insisted.

She put her hands on her hips. "Okay, so what if I was? I made a rash decision. It was immature and childish, and I'm sorry. So, just accept my apology."

Luke shook his head and licked his lip. "Lise, that is hot as hell."

She furrowed her brows. "That I was immature and childish?"

"No, that you were jealous. You want me."

She shook her head and stuck up her nose. "No, it was a fluke."

"Fluke, my ass," he said before kissing her.

Luke gave Elise no warning before he pulled her close and took her mouth. He smelled like soap and man. Elise groaned against his lips as he swept his tongue between them. God, he tasted good. And smelled good and felt even better.

Is there anything about this man that isn't good?

At this moment, the answer was an obvious no.

Maybe she should be playing hard to get. After all, she

was in the bedroom with a known player. But she didn't really want to be *gotten* in the first place. She just wanted to have some good old-fashioned dirty sex. Sleeping together did not equal a relationship, and she was totally okay with that. Some women might think Luke was using her, but she wanted him for the exact same reason. It was mutually beneficial to the two of them, and if they were both happy, then that was just fine.

Elise clutched his shoulders and then ran her hands down his smooth chest and over his washboard stomach. Then, she moved her fingers up the muscular expanse of his back and down again to circle his towel with her fingertips.

Then, she ripped it off him, tossing it aside.

Luke, who had his arms around her, pulled her closer to him and growled. But Elise didn't want to be closer to him. She wanted...she shoved her hand down. She just needed a tad more room...and she pulled her body away until...*ahh*... she circled him with her fingers and squeezed.

"Jesus," Luke said, breaking their kiss.

God, she loved his dick. It was long and thick and freaking perfect in every way.

She wanted to taste him again.

She backed away to get on her knees.

Luke grabbed her upper arms and made her stand. "No fucking way. Me first this time."

Elise didn't get to protest because Luke yanked off her shirt, flicked off her bra, and pulled her shorts and underwear down within seconds. He kissed her again and guided her toward his bed. When the backs of her knees hit it, he pushed her over. She scooted her body up, so she wasn't hanging off the bed as Luke quickly removed her sandals.

He then dragged her right back to the edge as he dropped to his knees. He put his mouth directly on her clit and sucked.

Elise's hips shot off the bed, and she moaned.

Luke released her clit and kissed each side of her labia before giving her one long lick. He then proceeded to fuck her with his mouth. She squirmed and tried to rub herself against his face. He kept giving her clit the attention it needed, but when she got close, he'd pull away. This happened several times.

"Oh, please, Luke. Please, please, please, let me come. I need it so bad."

He stood and rose over her, licking the taste of her off his lips. "Why didn't you say so?"

Luke opened his nightstand drawer and pulled out a condom. He quickly made work of the wrapper and covered himself. He spread her thighs with his hands, pushing her legs wide, and entered her in a single thrust.

Elise moaned long and loud. He felt fantastic. Like he was made to be there.

Luke leaned over her, and she enveloped his body with her arms. He wrapped his around her, too, and maneuvered them to the middle of the bed.

When they got there, Elise began to pump her hips. She was tired of letting him play around with her. She wanted to come, damn it.

But he had other plans. Luke raised his body up and away as he moved inside her. She rolled her hips, trying to reach her orgasm by bringing the two of them closer. Luke kept trying to keep her still, as if he knew her body better than she did.

He leaned down and spoke in her ear, "You are one feisty girl. Do you not trust me?"

Her answer was to tug his head down for a kiss and arch up on his cock. He tasted like her, and she loved it.

Luke groaned but pulled his mouth away. He shook his head as he smiled. "I guess we're going to have to do this the hard way."

He took both her arms and drew them up over her head. He brought her wrists together and held them with one of his hands. With his other hand, he held down her hip, pinning her to the bed. She tried to fight him at first, but then he began fucking her. Like *really* fucking her. He pounded in and out of her, as if that were his mission in life.

She tried to fight him at first because she wanted him to rub up against her clit, but she should have known he'd know what she was doing. As he powered inside her over and over, he hit a spot deep inside her pussy that made her see stars. She forgot all about her clit as she begged him to fuck her harder. Longer. To never stop.

Then, she came, and it was all over. It wasn't one of those cute little orgasms that fluttered through a woman's body, making her look sweet and feminine. No, this was a convulsing, screaming full-body orgasm. She knew she probably looked like she was having a seizure or something, but she didn't care because she came and she came and she came. It was the best orgasm of her life.

After her body calmed and she was able to pay attention

to other things around her again, Elise realized Luke did know her body better than she'd thought he did. She'd never had a vaginal orgasm before, except for maybe their first night together. If only she could remember that.

Luke let go of her wrists and leaned back on his legs, pulling hers over his hips. He slowly brushed his hand all the way down her arm and over her shoulder. He swept it over her chest, pausing to caress her breasts and giving each nipple a tweak, before stopping close to where their bodies joined. He looked up into her eyes. His brown eyes were full of intensity as he dropped down onto his forearms and began to move inside her again.

She moaned and wrapped her legs around him. Now, it was his turn, and she wanted to feel him come inside her. For the first time that she could remember, she cursed STDs and unwanted pregnancies because she wanted to feel him with nothing in between them.

As Luke thrust in and out of her, she tugged him close to let him know that she was okay, and he could go faster. Luke picked up his pace as he panted near her ear, his breath catching every few seconds. She loved that she was making him breathe like that.

With this new position, Luke's pelvic bone rubbed against her clit. Here was what she'd been seeking before, and now, she didn't need it. But it didn't matter because, as Luke continued to move inside her over and over, it wasn't long before she came again. And, this time, Luke was right there with her.

For the second time that night, Elise saw fireworks.

CHAPTER THIRTEEN

L uke closed his eyes for a moment and waited for his breathing to even out and his heart rate to slow. He grabbed a tissue from his nightstand to remove the condom and threw it in the wastebasket he kept next to his bed. Then, he flopped back and stared up at the ceiling.

"Holy shit," Elise said beside him, sounding as winded as he felt.

He turned his head to look at her. "You okay?"

She rolled up onto her side, toward him. "Hell yes." She cleared her throat and shifted her eyes away from his, like she was nervous. "How did you learn how to do that?"

He shook his head, not understanding. "Do what?"

She met his eyes for a brief instant. "Sex."

Luke laughed. "I'm pretty sure every guy learns about sex while in middle school. Who I actually learned it from, I don't know. That was a long time ago."

She sighed. "No, not sex in general."

She rolled onto her back, further away from him, so he

reached over and pulled her toward him, resting her head on his shoulder.

"Where did you learn how to have sex like that?" she asked.

He shrugged. "I don't know. Practice, I guess."

She traced lines across his chest. "No, it's more than that." She paused and raised her head to look at him. "I can't believe you're going to make me say it."

Now, he was really confused. "Lise, I have no idea what you mean, so I'm sorry, but, yes, you're going to have to say it."

She placed her head back on his shoulder. "Where did you learn to fuck like that? To make me come like that?"

Luke chuckled. "Oh. Well...the answer's still the same for the most part. Practice. And paying attention to a woman's body." He cupped the back of her neck and drew her head away from him, so he could look into her eyes. "Why? Was it good for you?" He already knew it by the huge climax she'd had, but he didn't want to sound cocky and say it out loud.

She smiled. "Very." She looked at her hand. "Can you believe I've never had an orgasm like that before?"

He wrinkled his brow.

She looked at him, noting his expression, and explained, "A vaginal orgasm. It's always been a clitoral orgasm for me." She rolled her eyes. "And, sometimes, not even that."

"What?"

"What do you mean by, what?"

"How could you not come? You're so...responsive."

Luke was mystified how anyone could not get this female off. She was like dynamite in his arms.

"Yeah, well, it's definitely happened."

He snorted. "Losers."

"Hey," she protested.

"Them, not you."

"But I dated them."

"Well then, maybe you were a loser, too."

She reached over and pinched him on the side.

"Ouch. That hurt."

"You deserved it." She laughed.

He held up the hand that wasn't around her, giving her an exaggerated shrug. "If the shoe fits."

She extended her arm again, and Luke rolled off the bed. "No pinching."

She sat up on her knees, her beautiful breasts swaying and her blonde hair falling around her shoulders. She looked at him with a knowing smile. "Fine. No blow jobs for you. Not from me anyway."

Luke laughed and headed to the bathroom. He turned when he reached the door. Elise didn't look happy that he was mocking her threat.

"Babe, you can't stay away from this dick. You said so yourself." He pivoted and entered the bathroom.

"I did not!" Elise shouted. Two seconds later, she said, "Oh, crap, I did." She growled, "Damn alcohol."

Luke chuckled to himself at her revelation while he used the facilities.

"We'd probably better go." Elise raised her voice, so he could hear her. "It's going to be dark soon, and we want to be back before the fireworks show starts."

He exited the bathroom to find Elise pulling on her

shorts. He moved toward her, still naked, and pulled her close. "I don't want you to put your clothes on."

She placed her hands on his bare chest and rubbed. "Me either. But we have to get back."

Rather than argue, he kissed her.

She only hesitated for a second before she kissed him back. He had her right where he wanted her. He kissed his way down her neck and tilted her back over his arm, so he could kiss her breasts. How had he missed these before? He sucked a nipple in his mouth, and a moan escaped out of the back of Elise's throat.

He released her and said, "I'm sorry I didn't give these the attention they deserved earlier." He then moved on to the other breast and gave it the same consideration as the first.

"Oh, Luke, that feels so good," she told him, panting out the words.

"Does this mean, you'll take your shorts off?"

She made a cry of distress. "No, we can't."

He released her nipple with a pop and set her on her feet. "What—why'd you stop?"

"If Luke can't have fun, then Elise can't have fun."

Elise's expression changed from confusion to conniving. "In that case..." She wrapped her whole hand around his cock and pumped him in her fist as she leaned in and gently sucked on his neck.

She pulled away and smiled at him.

He put his forehead on hers. "Baby, you play dirty."

She laughed but released him down below. Then, she stood up on her tiptoes and brushed her lips across his. "Now, go get dressed before people start asking questions."

He reluctantly did what she'd asked. Even though he wanted to stay there, naked, with her all night, he knew their friends would start to wonder why they were both gone.

Luke grabbed some clothes from his closet and dresser and put them on while Elise looked over her appearance in the mirror. Then, they headed out.

As they got closer to Sean and Rachel's, he asked, "Do you want us to separate, or do you not care if we show up together?"

"I'm going to tell them I went to apologize to you, so there's no need to hide that we're together. But how about we walk around the front of the house? That seems less conspicuous for some reason."

He shrugged. "Sure. Whatever you want."

They had a few blocks to go, and they were taking their time.

He was surprised when Elise asked him about sports, "So, I saw you playing football earlier, of course. I thought hockey was your thing?"

He shrugged again. "I like all sports actually. Hockey is just the one I was the best at."

"I remember. You got a scholarship to U of M, right?"

He nodded. "I did. Do you like hockey?"

"Well...I have a confession to make."

He stopped in his tracks. "You don't like hockey?" he asked incredulously. "I'm sorry, but I can no longer have sex with you."

Elise laughed. "No, it's not like that. I guess you could say, I don't like it"—he gasped mockingly—"but I don't dislike it either. The thing is, I really don't get it."

They began to walk again.

"You don't get it?"

"Until high school, I did most of my growing up in South Dakota. I don't think I knew one person who played hockey. We moved to Minnesota, and here, everybody and their fricking dog plays hockey. My coworker has a hockey rink in her backyard for her kids. My other coworker has a son and daughter who are each captains of their college teams. And the thing I really don't get is that it's ridiculously expensive, yet everybody plays. I know hockey is big in New England, but I still think Minnesota is up there right after Canada."

"Hmm, I guess I never knew there was such a difference from one state to the next."

"Me either. Hockey, snowmobiles, and boats—that's my description of Minnesota."

Luke laughed. "That's about accurate." He hip-checked her. "So, does that mean you never saw me play?"

She smiled coyly at him. "Well, now, I never said that."

Luke wanted to throw his arm around her and pull her close, but they were almost to Sean and Rachel's, so he settled for a smack on her butt. "Tease," he told her.

Only a few people were hanging out in the front yard. Most of them didn't pay any attention to Elise and him as they walked toward the back of the house. They made it to the garage when Elise muttered something about being starving and thirsty. He discovered he could use some water himself. He hadn't realized how parched sex had made him.

"There you are," Luke heard a male voice say behind them.

He and Elise turned around.

"Where have you two been?" Rachel asked with Sean standing beside her.

Sean looked at Luke. "Barbie wanted to tell you good-bye, but nobody could find you anywhere."

Luke ignored the Barbie jab. "I told you, I went home to change. I also had to take a shower because I was all sticky."

Rachel looked at Elise, raising her eyebrows. "And what happened to you?"

"I felt bad about what had happened, so I followed Luke home to apologize."

Sean and Rachel suspiciously looked at them.

"Did you now?" Rachel said.

"It's true, Rachel. She came and apologized," Luke defended Elise.

"See? Thank you," Elise said before taking a big drink out of her water bottle.

"But then we had crazy monkey sex before I finally had to make her leave to come back here."

Elise spit her water all over the ground. "Oh my God, Luke," she said, wiping her chin.

Man, I love giving her shit.

Sean and Rachel laughed, thinking he was joking, but the best part was that he was pretty much telling the truth.

"Well, come out back when you're done rummaging for food," Rachel said.

After Rachel and Sean left, Elise whacked him in the stomach.

"Oomph."

She tried to shoot him a stern look, but she was laughing.

"I cannot believe you just said that. You're so immature at times."

"Sometimes, the best thing to do is tell the truth. I knew they wouldn't believe me and that they'd think it was funny."

"Well, it wasn't."

"Then, why are you laughing?"

She stuck her tongue out at him.

"Now, who's being immature?"

She shook her head and laughed. "You are so lucky that you're cute."

He wiggled his eyebrows. "So, you think I'm cute?"

She leaned toward him and dragged his earlobe between her teeth before whispering in his ear, "I think you're fucking hot, and I can't wait to fuck your brains out later."

He risked putting an arm around her and pulling her closer. "Do you promise?" he whispered back.

She bit her bottom lip and nodded, promising him everything with her fuck-me eyes.

He pulled her close again and put his cheek against hers. "I'm going to hold you to it."

He let her go. Then, he grabbed a beer out of the cooler and headed outside.

It was going to be a long night.

CHAPTER FOURTEEN

E lise leaned back in her chair as fireworks lit the sky. They didn't have a front row view, but the show was still pretty impressive from Rachel and Sean's backyard. Rachel was curled up on Sean's lap while Elise was sitting with her new friends, Tera and Heidi. Luke was sitting a couple of feet away with a few of his buddies.

Elise wanted to be snuggled up on his lap.

She had no idea what that meant.

The two of them did not have a relationship. She would go as far as to say they were friends, but that was it. Friends who'd had sex twice now and who had plans to have it again later. But they never talked about having anything exclusive. She didn't even know if that was what she wanted.

When she asked herself the question, right now, the answer was no. Luke was handsome and fun, but she could never see him being husband or father material. She didn't even know if he was boyfriend material. And that was if he even wanted to be someone's husband or father someday.

For all she knew, he might have plans to be single for the rest of his life. The only thing she'd ever heard him mention about being serious with someone was when he'd said he'd watch *Love Actually* with his future wife. And Elise had been around long enough to know that he'd told her that, so she'd quit bugging him to watch the movie.

She didn't know what to do. She thought she'd grown out of the one-night-stand and friends-with-benefits stages of her life. She was going to be thirty next month, and she wanted to get married and have kids before it was too late. It didn't matter how much people said that thirty was the new twenty because her biological clock was still working on ancient time. And, if she factored in meeting someone, dating them for at least a year, getting engaged, planning a wedding, getting married, and enjoying some time with her new husband before having kids, that didn't leave her with much time to have children.

She slumped down in her chair, suddenly depressed.

Elise's gaze wandered over to Luke again. She didn't want to stop this thing they had though. She liked being with him, and it wasn't like there were any prospects for future boyfriends hanging around, so she might as well enjoy Luke for now.

Suddenly, there was a chorus of, "Ooh," and, "Aah," around her, and Elise looked to the sky to see what had to be the big finale of the show.

After the fireworks were done and there were a few disappointed sounds, Rachel stood up. "Okay, everybody, I know most have to work tomorrow—"

"Boo!" someone yelled.

Everyone laughed.

"Stupid weekday holiday," somebody else chimed in.

This year, Fourth of July was on a Tuesday. Something Elise had not been thrilled about before, but now, it gave her a chance to leave and go to Luke's house because the party wasn't going to last forever.

"Since most of you have to work tomorrow," Rachel continued, "but not all of you are ready to drive home, we thought we'd put a movie on, so you could relax and sober up. It's actually a tradition that Elise and I used to do in college, and since she's back, I think it's the perfect solution for anyone who's drunk. It'll be like old times," she said right to Elise.

Damn it.

Elise smiled, but she was secretly somewhat disappointed. She loved the fact that Rachel was bringing back their tradition, but now, she didn't know if she would get to go to Luke's. She was one of those people who had to work the next day, and she didn't know if she would have time for movie and sex.

"If you feel like you need to stay over, we have two guest beds," Rachel added.

Everyone else got up from their chairs, and most people started helping Rachel and Sean clean up by folding their chairs and picking up their glasses and plates. They had put most of the food away before the fireworks, so that was one less thing to worry about.

They were just finishing up with the stuff that couldn't wait until the next day when Elise caught Luke's eye from across the garage, and he smiled his handsome, cocky smile.

"Say, Rach?" Elise said to her friend.

Rachel looked up from wiping the table down. "Yeah?"

"How much would you hate me if I didn't stay for the movie? I love that you thought of us and our tradition, but I'm not drunk, and I do have to work tomorrow."

Rachel's face fell, and guilt flooded Elise for even asking. What kind of friend was she to put sex before her friend of over ten years?

"You know what?" she said, not giving Rachel a chance to even say anything because she would never tell Elise how upset she was. "Why don't I stay for at least the first half? If I'm not feeling tired, I'll stay for the whole thing."

The relief across Rachel's face was immediate. "Yay! I'm so glad you're not leaving. It wouldn't be the same without you. I've been doing it off and on with Sean, but he's not you. I always miss you on the Fourth."

"Aw," Elise said, touched. "I always miss you, too."

Now, she was almost wondering how she'd ever thought about leaving with Luke.

"I'll take the plates and cups into the house," Elise told Rachel.

"Okay. I'll see you in there. I'm just going to put all the drinks in one cooler before I come in."

Elise headed inside and didn't notice that Luke had followed her until he was right behind her. They were the only two in the room, and he slipped up behind her as she opened the cupboard to put the stuff away. He reached around and caressed her breasts before sliding one arm down and cupping her between the legs. He used his middle finger to put pressure against her clit, and Elise fought the urge to moan.

Life wasn't fair. And neither was Luke.

Elise turned around and clutched the counter behind her.

Before she could even say anything, Luke spoke, "Uh-oh, you've changed your mind."

"No. Yes." She sighed. "Both. I still want to come over, but I have to stay and watch the movie for a little while at least. It's my and Rachel's tradition. She would be seriously disappointed if I didn't stay."

"Then, you leave me no choice."

Elise questionably eyed him. "No choice?"

"I have to stay, too."

She raised her brow. "You made it sound like you were going to do something bad."

Luke snickered. "Oh, I am. Three words. *You, me,* and a *blanket.*" He wiggled his first three fingers.

"It's July," she pointed out.

"Damn," he said. "I guess I'll have to think of another way to torture you."

Elise laughed at him. "I'd like to see you try."

Nothing else was said as they heard the door open, and he stepped away from her. But Luke's use of the word *torture* reminded her of the item she had searched for before she left the house.

"Hey, Rachel?" Elise asked right as her friend stepped into the room.

"What?"

"Do you care if I pick the movie?"

"Of course not." She held up a finger. "As long as it's one you know I'll like."

"No problem. No action movies, it is."

"Sounds good to me." Rachel grinned.

Elise couldn't keep from smiling at Luke before she headed to Rachel's room where she'd stuffed her purse when she first arrived to keep it safe.

Luke's expression was clearly a what-are-you-up-to kind of look as she walked out of the kitchen.

After Elise grabbed the movie, she quickly put it in and started it. She didn't want the menu to be on the screen when Luke walked into the room.

Not many people stayed. Most everyone had stopped drinking early enough, but a couple that Elise had just been introduced to were still there.

"Oh, I love this movie," the wife, Mandy, said. "Even Nick likes it."

The husband, Nick, said, "Yeah, it was way better than I'd thought it would be."

"*Thank you,*" Elise said. "That's what I've been trying to say. It's great." Once the previews were over, she paused the DVD on a black display to wait for Luke to enter the room.

Everyone else came into the room and sat down. It was just a couple of more friends of Rachel's from work. Elise waited for the sound of Sean's and Luke's voices as they walked toward the family room, and then she hit play. She always loved the beginning of this movie.

When Luke reached the doorway, he paused and studied the screen. "What movie is this?" he asked suspiciously.

Before Elise could say, *Don't tell him,* the title came on

the screen, and Sean said, "*Love Actually?* Ah, man, this is a Christmas movie."

Rachel said, "It's like Christmas in July, Sean."

At the same time, Luke clapped a hand over his eyes and shouted, "My eyes, my eyes," as he backed out of the room. "My manhood has been tainted. I'll never be the same."

"Oh, come on, Luke! It's a good movie!" Elise yelled out to the hall, hitting pause again on the movie.

"You can't fool me with your evil tricks, woman."

"Yeah," Sean said, "Luke and I will go downstairs and watch something else."

"You're no fun," Rachel said.

"Sorry, babe." He kissed his fiancée. "Hey, Nick, you comin'?"

Nick shrugged. "Sure. Why not?"

"I guess it's just us ladies," Mandy said after they all left the room.

"Hit play, Elise," Rachel said.

She sat back in her seat with a huff. Here she'd thought that she found the perfect way to trick Luke into watching the movie, and the turd had escaped.

But, if he thought she'd give up, he was dead wrong. She was going to get him to watch *Love Actually* if it killed her.

The movie went fast because it was one of Elise's favorites. She always got swept up into the story. And the fifteen-minute nap she'd taken in the middle didn't hurt.

Elise stood up and stretched. "I'd better get home."

"Thanks for staying," Rachel said.

Elise smiled at her friend. "I'm glad I did."

A couple of soft snores came from the other side of the room.

"Looks like everyone else liked the movie, too," Elise joked.

"I think they all fell asleep before we were even ten minutes in," Rachel said.

"Their loss. I'm going to grab my purse."

When Elise came back to the living room, she gave Rachel a hug good-bye and took off for her car. When she got home, it was late, and her parents were already asleep.

She quickly washed her face, brushed her teeth, and put on her pajamas. She crawled into bed and was out like a light.

♡

When Elise's alarm went off the next morning, there was a text on her phone from the night before.

Luke: I see that you snuck out.

Hardly.

It wasn't like she had been super quiet and secretive when she left. And she certainly hadn't been about to go looking for him before leaving. That would have drawn too many questions.

She continued reading.

> Just know, this isn't over. I'm going to see you again. You promised me a fuck, and I'm not going to let you forget it. The next time I see you, you'll be on your back, begging for it.

She loved his filthy mouth sometimes.
She texted him back.

> Elise: Correction. The next time I see you, you'll be on *your* back, begging for it.

The second she set her phone down, it chimed, so she picked it up again, not wanting to wait to see what he had written.

> Luke: I already am.

The next text was a picture he'd taken of himself. She could see his powerful chest and muscular abs along with that special V at his hips that only some guys had. And she could see the very beginning of his penis where it came away from his body. Only the very beginning. Of course Luke wouldn't have sent her a full-on dick pic. No, instead of sending something over the top, he'd sent something teasing. Something tempting and provocative. And the look on his face told her that he had known exactly what he was doing when he sent the picture.

Elise set the phone down and went to the bathroom to take a long, cold shower.

CHAPTER FIFTEEN

F our days later, on Saturday, Elise was just getting home from a stressful day of looking at homes and coming up empty. It didn't help that she hadn't been in the mood to look at homes at all today, and she'd had to go all alone.

Friday at work had started out bad and ended worse.

Her first patient of the day had been an elderly patient who was learning to talk again after having a stroke. Her patient was used to being independent and was mad and bitter at the world for her current circumstances. She had taken her resentment out on Elise. Her patient hadn't wanted to do the exercises Elise had given her to do in between sessions, and when she'd shown up, she'd fought Elise on every little thing. Elise had been exhausted with the beginning of a headache after that patient left, and it had only been nine a.m.

Then, her last patient of the day had been a spoiled brat who needed to be punished but never was. She had actually heard the father tell the little boy that, if he cooperated with his session with Elise, he would let the boy punch him in the stomach. Sometimes, you couldn't make that stuff up. Of course, her patient hadn't done anything she'd asked of him. He'd run circles around the room, knocked the binder to the floor...more than once, and kicked his chair over...repeatedly. When he'd gone home, she'd never been happier for the weekend to come in her life because her headache had been in full force by that time. She'd gone home and gone to bed at eight that night. She didn't care if that made her some sort of loser or not.

Thankfully, she'd woken up, refreshed, but all she'd wanted to do today was relax. No patients. Nothing stressful. She'd actually forgotten all about looking at homes until Cara had texted her the night before to remind her. Elise had wanted so badly to cancel, but she had known Cara had put in a lot of work to set up the showings. Maybe, if Elise had found something to buy, it would have been worth it, but, alas...no.

Maybe she was too picky. She needed to reevaluate what she wanted, but tonight was not that night. Tonight, she was going to run the bath, grab a good book, and relax.

Unfortunately, life had other plans.

She entered through the garage door and into the kitchen. "Mom? Dad?"

"In here," her father called out.

Elise walked to the den. "Hey, Dad. You here alone?"

Her father winced as he adjusted himself in his seat. "Yes. Your mom had her Bible study group."

"Dad, are you okay?"

He waved her off. "Yes, I'm fine."

She inspected her dad better. He was pale and looked to be in pain even though he was trying to hide it.

She stepped closer. "Dad, please. I know something is wrong."

"It's no big deal, peanut. Just some leg pain, and now, I feel some pressure in my chest."

"Dad! We are going to the hospital right now."

"Calm down. I looked up *heart attack*, and I don't have any other symptoms."

Elise fought the urge to roll her eyes in exasperation. "Dad, other things can cause chest pain. Like a PE, which sounds like what you might have because you have pain in your leg. We are going to the hospital."

"What's a PE?" her father asked, all the while still sitting in his chair, not moving.

"It's a pulmonary embolism. Get. Up."

"Huh?"

"It's a blood clot in your lungs. It can kill you. Now, will you *please* get your butt off the chair, so we can go to the hospital?"

Her dad finally, blessedly, scooted to the end of his chair. "Jeez Louise, you don't have to yell. Just ask nicely."

She gritted her teeth. She'd already asked nicely, and that hadn't worked.

Her father stood and shook his head, as if she were the annoying one in this conversation. If her father wasn't already dying, she might just kill him.

After what seemed like a year later, her dad had his shoes on and was ready to go.

"Oh, I forgot my car keys," he said as he patted his pockets.

Elise squeezed the bridge of her nose. Her headache from the day before was coming back.

"Dad, you are not driving to the hospital. I am driving you."

He frowned.

"You wouldn't want something to happen and for us to get into a car accident, would you?"

"No," he answered reluctantly.

"Okay then, let's go."

She got her dad in the car, but he grumbled the whole time.

"We're going to Southdale, right? Your doctor still practices out of there?"

"Yeah, fine. Let's get this over with."

When they got to the hospital, Elise checked her father in and then set out to make phone calls. Her mother didn't answer, but that wasn't a surprise. She was forever putting her phone on silent and forgetting to turn the ringer back on. Next, she called her sister, who also didn't answer, so Elise left a message for her. Then, she called her mom one more time before leaving a message on her phone also.

Elise texted Rachel just to let her know what was going on. They were supposed to have brunch the next day, and she didn't know if she'd make it now.

After texting her friends, she scrolled through her messages until she landed on Luke. She hadn't seen him since the Fourth of July, despite their promises to get naked again. She'd thought that maybe they'd see each other this weekend, but Luke had begged off, saying he had to work. She didn't know what kind of work he had to do on the weekend. She'd never asked him what he did, but she assumed he had some office job at the mall. But what if there was somebody else, or he just didn't want to see her again?

Elise looked up at her father.

Why was she ruminating about Luke? She should be worrying about her dad. She knew part of it was because she was trying to take her mind off her father. But another part of it was because she wanted to see Luke. They had been texting back and forth, so she didn't really think he didn't want to see her again. She was just trying to find another problem to focus on even if it was a made-up one. The truth was that she wanted to talk to Luke. It seemed silly. After all, he wasn't her boyfriend, which was why she fought the urge to text him about her father. She didn't want to scare the guy off by being too serious.

After what seemed like forever but was probably only forty-five minutes to an hour, they were called back. The triage nurse asked her father a list of questions. When they got to the medication question, her father shrugged.

"Oh, Dad. You seriously don't know?"

"Peanut, they put me on this and that every time I go to the doctor. I can't keep that stuff straight. That's your mom's job."

Elise explained to the nurse how her father had colon cancer and was going through chemo at the Mayo Clinic down in Rochester and that she would call her mom and ask her to bring her father's meds.

Of course, her mother didn't answer again, so Elise left

another message and an update to tell her that they were getting a room.

Just as they were being led back to a room, her sister called.

Elise stayed a few steps back to answer. "Kristen?"

"Elise, what's going on?"

"We don't know yet. We're just going into a room. I think Dad might have a blood clot in his lungs though. If he does, they'll have to admit him."

"Oh God."

"I know."

"We'll be there as soon as possible. I'm about an hour away, but I'm coming."

"Okay. If we're not in the ER when you get here, I'll let you know. Otherwise, just go to the front desk and ask for Dad."

"Will do."

"Oh, and try to get ahold of Mom. I've called her several times, and she hasn't answered."

"Phone on silent?"

"Probably. But I'd really like to hear what the doctor has to say and stuff, so if you could work on finding Mom, that would be great."

"I'm on it."

"Thanks, sis. And make sure she brings Dad's meds or a list when she comes."

"Got it. See you soon."

Elise hung up just as a new nurse walked in.

"Hello, Mr. Phillips. I'm Amy, and I'll be your nurse this

evening." She was young with dark hair and blue eyes and a bright smile.

Elise liked her immediately.

"Hi, Amy. You can call me Ward."

Amy smiled. "Sounds good, Ward." She looked at Elise. "And is this your daughter?"

"Yes, she made me come tonight. I think she's over-reacting."

"Dad, I am not overreacting. I'm Elise," she told the nurse.

"Well, Ward, we're going to run some tests to see if we find anything. If this is a false alarm, I give you permission to tell your daughter, *I told you so*," Amy said with a wink.

"Ha," her father said.

Elise snorted.

After her father removed his shirt and shorts and put on a gown, Amy took his vitals. "Your heart rate and respirations are a little fast, and your blood pressure is a little low," she told him. "I'm going to put this information in your chart, and then I'm going to let Dr. L know that you're ready for him. Sound good?"

Her father nodded.

Amy did her stuff and exited the room. As they waited for the doctor, Elise's phone rang. It was her mom.

"Finally!" she exclaimed.

"What's finally?" her dad asked.

"Nothing." She hadn't told her dad that she hadn't been able to get ahold of her mom. She hadn't wanted to worry him. "I'm just going to step out into the hallway."

She left the room and stepped far enough away so that

her father wouldn't overhear before answering, "Mom, where are you?"

"I'm on my way. And I have your father's meds. Have you found out anything?"

"Nothing much. His vitals are off, but we're still waiting for the doctor to come in."

"Well, what's taking them so long?"

"Mom, the nurse just left a few minutes ago, and Dad is not the only patient in the ER."

Her mom huffed. "I suppose."

"Just concentrate on driving. We don't need you getting in a car accident, okay? I'm watching out for Dad until you get here."

"Thank you. I'll be there as soon as I can."

Elise hung up and turned around to go back into her father's room. She saw a glimpse of a tall male with broad shoulders in light-blue scrubs. This must be the doctor. Thank heavens he got there before her mother arrived. She didn't need her mom yelling at the ER staff.

She could hear the doctor and her father speaking to one another, and Elise thought the voice sounded familiar.

But...she thought...

Suddenly, she realized that she had made the wrong assumption and was immediately embarrassed. When Rachel had said Southdale, Elise had assumed Southdale Center, but Rachel had actually meant Southdale Hospital.

Elise stepped into the room, and the doctor turned around.

"Hi, Luke."

CHAPTER SIXTEEN

"Elise?" Luke said, surprised.

His patient, Mr. Phillips, said, "You two know each other?"

If he only knew.

"Yes, Dad, this is my friend Luke—or Dr. L, I'm guessing. We went to college together."

Friend?

He was more than her friend. After all, he'd been inside her. Although not as recently as he'd have liked to have been.

Luke shook his head. He really needed to concentrate on his patient. He usually didn't let anything interfere with his work. And he couldn't let this female start now, no matter how badly he wanted her.

For some reason, Elise's face had flushed a bright shade of pink when she came into the room. She seemed embarrassed or ashamed.

Was she feeling guilty that they'd slept together now that

they were in the same room as her father? It didn't seem like her.

And it appeared her father had taken note of her blushing, too. "Friends?" Mr. Phillips asked doubtfully. He had dark hair sprinkled with gray and green eyes, like his daughter.

"Yes, Dad."

"Mr. Phillips, I'm friends with Sean, Rachel's fiancé. We were roommates in college."

"Oh," his patient said. "And you can call me Ward."

Luke took that as a good sign.

He pulled up the stool from near the computer. He preferred getting down on eye-level with patients. They always seemed more comfortable and more likely to talk to him that way.

Amy walked back into the room and pulled up Mr. Phillips's chart on the computer as Luke began asking questions about his patient's condition.

"So, I've read your chart, and Amy gave me a rundown of your history. But I'd like to hear the information from you. Can you tell me what brought you in here tonight?"

"My daughter."

Luke chuckled as Elise rolled her eyes. "Okay. Can you tell me what symptoms brought you here tonight?"

"I have some pain in my chest. And my leg was bothering me earlier, but it doesn't really hurt anymore."

"I'm going to take a look," Luke said as he pulled back the blanket. "Which leg?" he asked as he examined Mr. Phillips's lower limb. He already knew which one his patient was going to say.

"My left."

"I can see that it's red and swollen." Luke pulled the covers back up. "Can you describe your pain? Is it a pinching pain? Does your chest feel tight?"

"Yeah, tight. But that's it. I'm starting to feel like someone is hugging me securely."

Luke turned to Amy. "I'm going to have you put in an order for a chest CT, and let's get Ward ready to go right away."

"Do you want the usual labs?" the nurse asked.

"Yes." Luke moved back to his patient. "Amy is going to take some blood and start an IV while we continue to talk, okay?"

Mr. Phillips nodded. "Sure."

"When did this pain start?"

"I don't know. Probably two to three hours ago."

"Oh my God, Dad."

Elise's father waved her off. "She worries about me too much."

Luke smiled at Mr. Phillips, but he silently agreed with Elise. "Has the pain and tightness been constant, or has it gradually gotten worse?"

"Gotten worse."

Out of the corner of his eyes, Luke saw Elise bite her lip, like she wanted to say something but was restraining herself.

Luke asked a few more questions and asked about Mr. Phillips's cancer history and treatments.

"All right, Ward, we're going to start with this blood work. Then, we'll get a urine sample, and we're going to order a chest CT. You've had a CT before, correct?"

"The CAT scan thing? Yes. That's how they found the cancer."

Luke stood. "Okay, I'm going to go and make sure all your orders are in the computer while Amy finishes up with your lab work."

Luke nodded at Elise and exited the room.

He went to his own computer and put in his notes and orders for Mr. Phillips. While he did that, he kept an eye out for radiology to come and pick up Elise's dad to take him to CT.

As soon as they wheeled Mr. Phillips out of his room, Luke went back in and closed the door.

Elise, who had been facing the corner with her phone in her hand, spun around upon hearing the door latch.

"Luke," she said with tears in her eyes.

Luke stepped toward her with open arms, and she slid into his embrace.

He held her for a few minutes, letting her lean on him and absorb his strength.

"Are you going to be okay?" he asked her.

She pulled away, far enough for him to see her face. "I'm scared."

He reached up and wiped her tears from under her eyes.

"It's a PE, isn't it?" she asked quietly.

He was kind of surprised she knew what that was. "Most likely."

"Oh God."

"Hey. I know it's scary, but we can treat it."

"I know. And I know it's not the same thing, but I keep

thinking about my patient on Friday who had a stroke. I don't want my dad to be like that lady."

"Patient?" he asked, recognizing that he didn't know exactly what Elise did for a living.

Of all the things they'd talked about in their time together, that had never been one of them. They'd texted back and forth from work, but they hadn't really discussed their jobs when doing so. It was kind of pathetic that he didn't know, but at the same time, it meant they'd seemed to have plenty of other things to talk about.

"Yes, I'm a speech therapist. I've been dealing with a difficult stroke patient."

"Ah," he said, understanding. "I guess I never really knew what you did. I didn't pay attention to what you majored in back in college."

Not that he'd really paid attention to what anyone majored in back in college. They had all been too busy having fun when they weren't in class or studying.

She shrugged and stepped away from him. "That's okay. It's not like we're dating or anything."

She was right, but it still made him flinch.

"Besides, I had no idea you were a doctor."

With those words, he felt a wave of relief that was unexpected. In college, most girls had wanted him because he was a hockey player. Now, most of the women he met wanted to date him as soon as they'd found out he was a doctor. He hadn't even realized he'd been worried that Elise's interest in him now due to his profession, as she had stayed away from him in college.

"You didn't?"

"No, Rachel said something about you working at South-dale, and I assumed you worked at Southdale Center. I don't know if it's because you and Sean were friends and room-mates, but I always thought you both had the same major."

Elise was turned slightly away from him, her eyes cast down, and he studied her face. She was red again.

"Why are you blushing?"

She looked at him. "Because it's embarrassing. You know what they say about assuming. I don't know why I didn't ask more about what you did for work. I guess I assumed, again, that it was some fancy title that wouldn't mean anything to me, so I didn't even question it. Now, I understand why Tera and Heidi were asking whether you were McSteamy or McDreamy. And why you were looking at Tera's leg after she got hurt. I feel so stupid."

Luke pulled her into his arms again. "You're not stupid. You're cute."

She shook her head. "I doubt that. I probably look frazzled."

"Sexy frazzled."

Her blonde hair looked like she'd run her fingers through it quite a bit, and she looked tired, but he still found her attractive.

She laughed. "I don't think those two words go together in a sentence."

"Well, I think you're sexy, frazzled or not." He kissed her.

He had meant it to be a sweet kiss to let her know she was beautiful to him and to take her mind off her father for even just a short amount of time. But she turned the kiss into some-thing hungry and urgent. She tried to slip her hands under his scrubs, and, man, did he want to let her. He wanted to strip them both down and slide into her tight heat.

But he was at work. And her father could come back from his test at any moment. They couldn't be caught doing anything unprofessional.

Luke was saved from having to rein them both in by a shrill, "Elise," from the hallway.

Elise stepped back and broke their kiss. Her green eyes were round and panicked. "It's my mother. If she finds me kissing Dad's doctor, I'll never hear the end of it."

He wiped the moisture of her bottom lip and asked, "Why? Because she'll think you're distracting me?" He pulled her close for a second and rubbed his hard dick across her stomach. "Because you are."

She looked down at his obvious erection that his scrubs did nothing to hide. "Oh my God, put that thing away."

Luke laughed. "It's not that easy, babe. I can't just make it go away like that." He snapped his fingers. "Especially with you still looking at it."

Her eyes flew up to his, and she looked guilty. "I'm sorry."

He brushed a finger down her cheek. "I'm not," he said, grabbing something off the desk in the corner. "That's what clipboards are for," he said, waving it.

He walked over and quietly opened the door. A blonde lady was marching down the hallway toward Mr. Phillips's room. Now, this lady looked frazzled. Her blue eyes were bright with worry.

"Where's my husband?"

"Are you Mrs. Phillips?"

"Yes," she said, walking past him and into the room. She

looked around, and upon seeing it empty, except for her daughter, she said, "Oh no. Oh no, Elise."

"Oh, Mom, no, no." She rushed over and put a reassuring hand on her mom's arm. "Dad is just getting a test done."

Mrs. Phillips put her palm on her chest and sighed with relief. "Thank you, Lord." She whipped around to look at Luke. "And who are you, young man?"

Luke had to stifle a laugh at her authoritative tone. "I'm Dr. L, Mrs. Phillips."

"Dr. L? Did your parents not give you a full last name?"

"It's Dr. Long, ma'am. I go by Dr. L though. It's easier that way."

Mrs. Phillips frowned. "How does it make it easier?"

"Then, I don't get any jokes about my last name."

Elise giggled and covered her mouth.

Her mom looked at Elise and then back at Luke. "I don't understand," she said, seriously confused.

Luke cleared his throat. "Um...well...you know...my last name is *Long*."

"And?"

Oh, jeez, how was he supposed to explain that, just because he worked with medical professionals, it didn't mean they didn't make inappropriate jokes? Most of his coworkers seemed to have their minds in the gutter seventy-five percent of the time. And don't even get him started on the smart-ass teenagers and young adults he had to deal with. Dr. L was easier for everyone involved.

Elise came to the rescue. "Mom, Luke is a doctor in the ER, where it can take a *long* time to be seen. People like to complain and make jokes about his last name, like, *Oh, your name is Dr. Long. That's why I had to wait forever.*"

Luke mouthed a, *Thank you,* to Elise behind her mom's back.

"Oh," Mrs. Phillips said. She turned back to Luke. "Why didn't you just say so?"

"Uh..."

She didn't even give him a chance to finish, her mind already on the next thing.

"Elise, did you just call this young man by his first name?"

"Your daughter and I went to college together," Luke offered.

"Are you single, Luke?"

Luke backed up a step without even realizing it. "Uh... yes, ma'am."

"You know, my Elise is single, too."

"Mom. Leave him alone."

Elise mouthed, *I'm sorry,* to him.

"I'm just asking him some questions," her mom defended herself.

"Mom, did you bring Dad's meds?"

Thank God Elise had changed the subject, and her mom let her.

"Oh, yes," she said, pulling out a list from her purse.

"Good. We need to get that to the nurse."

Luke saw his escape and was about to tell them he would get it to Amy when Mrs. Phillips said, "I'll go find her," and charged out of the room.

"Ma'am," he called after her.

"Too late. She's already gone," Elise said, coming over to him. She put her hand on his chest. "I'm so sorry. She doesn't normally come across this...strong. I think she's worried about my dad."

"Does she always try to set you up with guys?"

"Not always. Only when she sees someone who she thinks would make a good prospect. Now, you know why I didn't want her to know that we were kissing. She'd have been writing out our wedding invitations by midnight."

Luke laughed, and surprisingly, he wasn't completely frightened by the idea.

CHAPTER SEVENTEEN

Kristen showed up a few minutes before Elise's dad came back to his ER room. Her sister walked in with her good friend Ashley. Elise and Kristen were sisters, but they weren't best friends. Elise was closer to Rachel and some of her friends back in Denver than she was to Kristen, and Kristen was really close to Ashley. Those two had been friends since high school and now lived only two doors down from each other.

Kristen gave their mom a hug.

"Hi, sweetie," their mother said to Kristen.

She gave Ashley a brief nod. She had never completely warmed up to Kristen's best friend.

"Have you heard anything yet?" Kristen asked.

Elise shook her head. "No, but the doctor thinks it's a blood clot in Dad's lungs."

"Oh my God, that sounds horrible," Kristen said as Ashley put her hand on her arm.

Her mother frowned at Ashley's act of comfort. "Kristen, do not take the Lord's name in vain."

"Sorry, Mom," Kristen apologized. But then she rolled her eyes and stuck out her tongue when their mom turned her back.

Elise stifled a laugh as the door opened, and their dad was wheeled back into the room.

After the radiology technologist left the room with a thank you, their mom immediately went over to their dad and clutched his hand.

"Ward, how are you?"

His father used his hand to pat her hand. "I'm sure I'll be fine, dear."

"Did they tell you anything?" Kristen asked.

"No, they said the radiologist had to read the exam."

"I hate all this waiting," Elise's mom said.

"I'm sorry to have ruined everyone's night."

"Dad, you didn't ruin anyone's night. I was going to hang out at home tonight anyway," Elise told him.

"Yeah, Dad, Ashley and I were only going to go to a movie. We can always go another time. You're more important."

There was a knock on the door, and Luke walked in.

"Hello, everyone. I see we have a few additions."

"I'm Kristen, the other daughter, and this is my friend Ashley."

Ashley raised a hand. "Hi."

Elise inspected both women, and neither seemed to be blinded by Luke's handsomeness. That was a first.

"I'm Dr. L," Luke told them.

"Elise knows Luke," Elise's mom told Kristen and Ashley with a satisfied smile on her face.

"Mom, he's Dr. L here. And will you please leave him alone and let him do his job?"

Jeez.

Luke chuckled. "It's fine." He turned to her father, and his face grew serious. "Ward, the radiologist has taken a look at your CT scan, and it looks like you do have a couple of blood clots in your lungs."

"Oh no," Elise's mother said, tears forming in her eyes.

"We're going to admit you for at least tonight. We need to get you started on blood thinners, so your clots can be broken up by your body. Then, we're going to have to speak to your oncologist about what he wants us to do after that."

Luke turned and looked at the rest of them and addressed their mom, "Mrs. Phillips, this is a very serious condition, but it is treatable. I don't want to tell you not to worry, but I don't want you to stress yourself out either. Your husband needs you to be strong right now."

"Listen to the doctor, Suzanne. Don't stress yourself out. We'll get this taken care of." Her father tried to reassure her mom.

Luke nodded once. "I'm going to go get the paperwork started to get you admitted." He left the room.

"Excuse me," Elise said before running out after him. "Luke?"

He turned around upon hearing his name.

"Is my dad really going to be okay?"

He walked back to her and put his hand on her upper

arm but kept his distance. She wanted him to pull her close and comfort her again.

"As far as the blood clots goes, he should be fine."

"Thank you."

He dropped his arm and said, "You're welcome." He looked like he wanted to say more, but he looked around the semi-crowded hallway and stayed quiet. "I'd better get your dad's paperwork started."

"Luke?"

"Yes?"

They still hadn't talked about where the two of them stood, and her father's condition was kind of serious territory.

But she bit the bullet and asked him the question she'd wanted to since she first saw him, even knowing he might say no, "Will you call me when you're off work?"

He smiled, his beautiful brown eyes full of kindness. "Of course. I'm off at ten."

She returned his smile, and then she turned and walked back into her father's room.

"Dad, is there anything you want from home? Kristen and I can go and get your things. You, too, Mom. Are you staying here tonight with Dad?"

"Yes. I'll give you a list," her mother said, already pulling out paper and a pen from her purse.

After she was finished writing out everything she wanted for herself and Elise's dad, Elise, Kristen, and Ashley took off for their parents' home.

"Do you think Mom will be okay here tonight, alone with Dad?" Kristen asked.

Elise thought about it. "Yes. She'll have the hospital staff if she has questions or needs help. And I think Dad will be more comfortable without us here all night. What if they make him pee in a urinal or something? He doesn't need his daughters seeing that."

"True story."

"I'm parked over there," Elise told her sister. "I'll meet you at Mom and Dad's, okay?"

"Okay," Kristen said as she and Ashley headed to their vehicle on the opposite side of the parking lot.

Elise turned to look back at them once. Ashley put her arm around Kristen, and Kristen lay her head on Ashley's shoulder. It seemed quite intimate, but Elise wasn't going to judge anyone for seeking comfort when it was offered from someone they cared about.

Hours later, after getting her father settled in and dropping off his and her mother's stuff, Elise was just getting home when her phone rang.

"Hello?"

"Elise, I just got your text message. How's your dad?"

"Hey, Rach. He's doing okay. He has blood clots in his lungs, so they admitted him."

"Oh no! How are you doing?"

"I'm okay. Tired. I just got home."

"I bet."

"Hey, guess who my dad's doctor was?"

"Who?"

"Luke."

"Really? What's he like as a doctor?"

"Good. He took very good care of Dad. And he's quite professional." Except for when he'd kissed her in her father's ER room. "Very different from the player we knew."

"I've never seen him in action at work."

Elise then had to tell Rachel about her mom not understanding why Luke went by Dr. L and how her mother could not get that *Long* was used to make sexual jokes.

"Oh, man, your mother. I do not know how you grew up to be so unrepressed, but I'm so glad you are not like them. Your parents are sweet but very reserved."

"I think I owe it all to public school. If it wasn't for my friends, I wouldn't know what a period was or how to use a tampon. My mom about died when I told her I got it for the first time. I thought I was going to have to use my babysitting money to buy my own stuff. And sweet, my butt. My mom was practically planning my wedding to Luke right there in the hospital. She had the balls to ask him if he was single, and when he said yes, she told him that I was single, too. She's so embarrassing."

Rachel was on the other side of the phone, busting a gut.

"It's not that funny."

"Oh, yes, it is. Did Luke look like a deer in the headlights?"

"No, he was really patient with my mom. If I were him, I would have lied and said I was married with a mistress on the side. Definitely not marriage material then."

"Why is your mom pushing for you to find someone so badly all of a sudden?"

"Because I'm going to be thirty, I think. She was already

married with two kids by that age. Plus, she won't say it, but I think she thinks that, if I find someone here and get married, then I won't move away again. Especially if something happens to my dad."

"Oh, that's kind of sad," Rachel said.

"Yeah, it is."

"Say, did Luke happen to mention if he had plans tonight?"

"Uh..." Elise said.

He'd only talked about having plans to call her, but it was still plans, and Elise didn't want to lie.

"Of course not," Rachel answered her own question, saving Elise from answering. "He was probably too busy playing doctor."

"Why do you ask?"

"Sean asked him if he wanted to have drinks after work. Luke said he was busy, but he didn't say why. Sean and I were thinking that maybe it was some girl."

Elise had no idea how to respond. "Oh. Wow."

"Right? Anyway, I'd better let you go, so you can get some rest. We'll talk tomorrow, okay?"

"Okay."

Elise and Rachel hung up, and Elise thought about what Rachel had said.

Some girl indeed. If Rachel only knew...

CHAPTER EIGHTEEN

E lise was dragged from sleep by the ringing of her phone. Disoriented, it took her a few seconds to realize that she had fallen asleep on her parents' couch. She had only meant to sit down and rest for a few minutes, but she'd fallen asleep—and in an awkward position no less. She'd somehow managed to drift down onto the armrest but with her feet still on the ground, and now, her neck hurt.

Her phone was still ringing, and she rotated her head to try to get out the kinks and shake off the mental cobwebs before answering, "Hello?"

"Hey," Luke's deep voice said.

"Hey," she answered as a smile crossed her face.

"Did I wake you?"

"Yeah."

"I'm sorry."

"No, don't be. I fell asleep on the couch. I'm not in bed or anything."

"Darn it," he joked.

She chuckled. "What time is it?"

"Almost ten thirty. I got out of work a little late. It was crazy tonight. It's a full moon, ya know. How's your dad doing?"

"You don't know?"

"Once he leaves my ER, he's not my patient anymore. It's a HIPAA thing."

"Of course. He was doing good when I left. My mom is staying with him tonight, so he's not alone."

"So, does that mean you're alone?"

"Yeah," she said, letting her voice drop a touch. "Do you want to come over?" She could use a little bit of Luke right now.

"Yes. Text me your address. I have to go home and shower first though."

"No. You can shower here."

He laughed. "Are you sure?"

"Yes."

"Okay then, I'm on my way."

They hung up, and Elise sent him her parents' address. Then, she quickly went up to her room to make sure it wasn't a mess because she was sure that the two of them would end up there tonight.

Next, she went to inspect herself in the mirror since she had no idea what her hair and makeup had done while she was sleeping. She was able to run a brush through the blonde strands, making it mostly presentable. She performed a quick touch-up to her makeup, removing the mascara that had built up underneath her eyes.

Last, she called her mom to see how her dad was doing and to make sure her mom wasn't coming back that night. If her mother came home to she and Luke having sex, then Elise would have two parents in the hospital.

She was just about to hang up with her mom when Luke knocked softly on the front door. She opened it, put a finger to her lips, and motioned for him to come inside.

"Yes, Mom. I'll call you right away when I get up in the morning. I love you. Now, try to get some rest. Bye." She closed the door behind Luke and locked it as she hung up the phone.

"Everything okay?" he asked.

"Yes."

Everything was so much better now that he was there. What that meant, she didn't know, and she wasn't about to psychoanalyze it either. At least, not tonight.

Luke had brought a backpack with him, and he set it down against the wall. He was wearing street clothes, having changed out of his scrubs. His jeans fit him amazingly. The back pulled tight across his butt as he bent over. And his T-shirt was fitted well across his chest, a stupid barrier between her and his delicious skin.

When he stood up to face her, he had his mouth open to say something, but she didn't let him get a word in as she practically attacked him.

He caught her as she hurled herself at him. She pulled his mouth down and kissed him. He tasted good, like mint and Luke. She slipped her hands underneath his shirt, so she could feel him against her fingertips. She loved how smooth his skin was, and she wanted him naked.

Luke must have needed the same thing because he picked her up and urged her to wrap her legs across his back. He broke the kiss to ask, "Where to?"

"Upstairs." She pointed behind him even though he couldn't see. "First door on the right."

He kissed her again as he turned and headed for the stairs. It made their progress slow because it was hard for Luke to see, but she didn't care because she loved kissing him. She shouldn't have been surprised that Luke was a great kisser, but she was. So many guys thought they just had to focus on the actual sex part, but Elise always thought that kissing was just as important. She loved kissing, and if a guy was a bad kisser, she didn't have much hope for him in other areas of the bedroom.

When they reached her room, Luke dropped her legs, so she could slide down his body. His dick was hard and big, and she wanted it—like, now.

Elise ripped Luke's shirt off over his head and then her own along with her bra. She reached up to kiss him again as she pushed her jeans and panties down with one shove, so she could kick them off. She grabbed for Luke's button and fly, but she only managed to brush her fingers against his jeans when he picked her up and flung her on the bed.

She squealed with laughter, and hastily and somewhat clumsily, she got to her knees. Luke stood next to the bed, and she went for his pants again. She pulled at the tab and unzipped his jeans. He wasn't wearing underwear, and his beautiful cock sprang out into her waiting hand.

She immediately bent and took him in her mouth. She grabbed on to his powerful thighs with her hands as she worked him all the way down her throat. She loved the taste of him here as well as his mouth. He tasted salty and smelled like the musky fragrance of pure man. Elise didn't always like giving blow jobs, but she already knew that she loved giving head to Luke.

He moaned above her and caught her hair in his hands. He slightly tugged on it when he didn't like something she had done, like run her teeth against him, but it only made her do it more. She loved the bite on her scalp when he pulled her hair. It made the swollen, achy spot inside her throb with want.

When he seemed to have had enough of her teasing, he drew her head back, so it fell against her shoulders. She smirked up at him and reached for his cock with her hand. He nudged her arm away, let go of her hair, and pushed her back against the bed with a grin on his face.

"You're going to get it now."

She licked her lips. "Promise?"

He jerked his jeans down and off. His only answer was to climb on top of her. He kissed her again and rubbed his hardness over her tender and empty pussy, but he didn't enter her.

She kissed him back and worked to get enough leverage so that she could roll them, ending with her on top. She sat up and arched her back, and this time, she rubbed her wetness on him.

"Oh, fuck," he said, panting out the words. "You're killing me."

She leaned over him again. "We can't have that, can we?" she said. She reached down to grasp him and place him at her center.

"Elise," he gasped right as she sat down on him, taking him all the way inside her.

She moaned high and loud. God, he felt so good inside her.

She made a move to rise up on him and lower herself back down again, but he grasped her hips, holding her pelvis to his. Since he was buried inside her to the hilt, she rotated her hips instead, rocking back and forth until his dick hit that amazing spot inside her that only he'd been able to find.

"Elise," Luke said again through clenched teeth.

He was trying to keep her still as she moved back and forth. She didn't understand why because she could tell she was making him feel as good as she felt.

She bent over and kissed him. "Why aren't you letting me move?" she asked between kisses, which he was having no trouble returning.

"Condom," he gasped. "Oh God, I don't think I can hold out much longer. Your pussy feels incredible."

Elise chuckled. *Oops.*

So, that was why he wouldn't let her move. In her haste to get him inside her, she'd completely forgotten.

She pulled his hands off her waist and brought them over his head. Normally, there was no way she'd be strong enough to overpower Luke, but since he was close to orgasm, he didn't fight her much.

She began to sway, slowly at first. "It's okay. I'm on the pill."

"What about—" he started before letting out a deep groan as he gave a halfhearted attempt to get her to release his upper limbs.

"We're both clean," she answered for both of them.

If you had asked her that night in June if she'd have unprotected sex with Luke Long, she would have answered, *Hell no.*

But, now, over a month later, she knew that she could trust him. A lot could happen in such a short amount of time.

"And we're only fucking each other, right?" When he nodded, she said, "Then, it's all good."

He stopped fighting her completely, and she knew she had him right where she wanted him. She began to fuck him just the way she'd wanted to since he walked through the front door. She used his big, beautiful dick to rub that sensitive spot deep inside her over and over and over again.

It wasn't long before she was right on the cusp of having a glorious orgasm when she opened her eyes to see Luke watching her. The tendons on his neck stood out as he held off his own climax until she reached hers, and that was all it took to push her over the edge.

She fought to hold on to his arms, but she came so hard that she almost lost her balance. Her nails dug into his forearms, and they scraped him from wrist to elbow. But Luke didn't seem to mind.

Then, he gently moved her arms aside as he grasped her hips again, thrusting once, twice, and a final time inside her. The hot release of his seed burned as she collapsed on top of him.

She buried her nose in his neck, and he lazily rubbed her back.

This was exactly what she had needed tonight.

CHAPTER NINETEEN

Luke caressed Elise's bare back, brushing his fingers up and back down again. They were lying on their sides, still naked, on Elise's bed.

They'd just finished some of the best sex he'd ever had. He couldn't remember the last time he'd had sex without a condom. With the exception of Ava, it had probably been back in high school. It had felt incredible. Elise had felt incredible.

He was trying not to let it bother him, but he was uncomfortable with Elise assuming he was STD-free. Not because he wasn't; he got himself tested regularly. He'd seen too many patients who didn't practice safe sex or get themselves tested between partners. No, his issue was whether Elise would have said that last night before finding out what he did for a living. Did she trust Luke the doctor or Luke the man? He knew he shouldn't let it get to him, and he tried to ignore the thought, but it lingered in the back of his mind.

Elise rolled onto her back and winced.

"Hey, are you okay?" he asked. "I didn't hurt you or anything, did I?"

She smiled at him. "No. My neck is sore from falling asleep in an odd position on the couch. It's a good thing that you called and woke me up. I can only imagine what I'd have felt like if I'd stayed there until morning." She grimaced.

"Show me where it hurts, and I'll rub it for you."

She grinned. "You don't have to give me a neck massage. I already slept with you, and I'm probably going to do it again."

He laughed. "Just show me."

She rubbed her neck and shoulder on the side closest to him.

"Roll away from me again."

She did as he'd asked, and he started kneading her neck.

"Oh," she moaned. "That feels great."

He massaged her for about five minutes when he realized that Elise had fallen asleep. He was tired, too, but his mind was still running, so he slipped quietly from the bed.

She rolled onto her back. "Luke?" she said, still half-asleep.

"I'm going to go shower."

"M'kay," she said as she turned onto her side again.

Luke went across the hall and into the bathroom where he found a towel and got in the shower.

He'd just finished washing his hair when the curtain was pulled back behind him, and Elise stepped into the tub.

"Hey, I thought you were gonna sleep," he said, drawing her toward him.

She put her hands on his chest. "I was, but then I realized

that I probably needed a shower, too," she said as she looked down at herself.

Ah, yes. One of the drawbacks of no protection. Messier sex.

He grabbed the body wash on the shelf next to his head and began lathering her body. "Sorry about that."

She closed her eyes and dropped her head back against her shoulders as she let him wash her. "I'm not. You felt awesome inside me."

He stood from where he was washing her legs. "Keep talking like that, and it'll happen again."

She slid her arms around his neck and rubbed her soap-covered body against his. "God, I hope so."

He maneuvered them under the spray to rinse away the suds. Then, he pushed her against the wall. He stared into her eyes as he lifted her up and draped her legs around his waist. He placed himself at her entrance, searching her face for any indication that she didn't want this.

"Put yourself inside me, Luke," she whispered.

And he did as the lady had requested.

They both groaned as he thrust inside her. She was hot, tight, and wet.

Will I ever get enough of this woman?

Right now, he was a little terrified that the answer was no.

After they showered, they were drying themselves off when Elise's stomach rumbled.

"I guess I'm hungry," she told Luke with an awkward laugh.

"Maybe we should order pizza."

"I think we might have a few frozen ones. Then, we don't have to wait."

"Sounds good to me."

She scanned his towel-clad body. "Do you have anything to wear? I feel bad for insisting that you come over, not letting you go home."

"Don't sweat it. I have a clean pair of scrub pants and boxers in my backpack."

She wrapped her own towel around her body. "Hold on. I'll go get it for you."

Normally, he had no problem with walking around naked, but it didn't feel right, doing that in Elise's parents' home. "Thanks."

When she returned to the bathroom with his bag, she was wearing yoga pants and an oversize U of M T-shirt. Her wet hair hung down her back, and she was sans makeup. He thought she looked beautiful.

She handed him his pack. "I'll go put the pizza in the oven. Wanna watch a movie while we eat?"

"Works for me," he said. Unzipping his bag, he began rummaging through his stuff.

He didn't register the smile on her face until she slipped out of the bathroom.

He rushed to the door and swung it wide. "Elise?"

She turned, her face a touch too innocent. "Yes?"

"No *Love Actually*."

She wrinkled her nose at him. "You suck."

He laughed and went back into the bathroom. After he dressed, he met her downstairs in the den. "What did you end up picking?" he asked her.

"Since you ruined my plan, I went with *Lethal Weapon 4*."

"*Lethal Weapon 4*? What the heck for?"

"It's the only one I own."

"Then, what's that?" He pointed to a pile of all four Lethal Weapon movies on the shelf behind her.

"Fine." She raised her chin. "I admit it. It's my favorite, okay?"

He stared at her in disbelief. "You're crazy. Everyone knows the first two are the best."

Something beeped from the kitchen.

"Oven's ready. I'll go put the pizza in." She walked backward toward the kitchen and smiled. "No switching the movie while I'm gone."

"You suck," he said, returning her words to her.

She spun and laughed all the way to the kitchen.

She came back a minute later. "Hey, do you want something to drink? I don't have any beer or anything though. My parents don't drink alcohol."

"Really?"

"Yeah, my parents are on the conservative side."

He pointed to the TV. "Yet they watch R-rated movies?"

"Ha. No, those are mine. They would never watch such filth, don't you know?" she joked. "Way too much swearing and forget about the fornicating outside of marriage." She rolled her eyes.

"Wow." He looked at her, remembering the night she had

come to his house. "Is this why you won't get the nose piercing?"

"Pretty much. I know I'm almost thirty, but I can just hear my parents' voices in my head. *Elise, God would frown on you for doing something so shameful to your body.*" She shook her head, as if she were disappointed in herself. "Anyway, what can I get you to drink? I have water, milk, or juice."

"I'll have water."

"Okay. I'll be back in a sec."

She went back into the kitchen as Luke took a seat on the couch.

He sympathized with Elise. He understood conservative. His father had grown up in a traditional Chinese family, and while his father wasn't super orthodox, his grandparents were. One of Luke's uncles had once told him that his grandparents had really pushed their children to marry a Chinese guy or girl, but his father had mostly dated Caucasian women. Whether it was out of some sort of revolt against his parents or because most of the Chinese girls he had known were related to him or reminded him of family members, Luke never knew. But, in the end, it hadn't mattered too much because half of his grandparents' kids had married white people. One had married another Asian, but she wasn't Chinese, and the remaining two had Chinese spouses.

And, despite how his father had grown up, he had married his mother because he'd knocked her up, and he still drank beer, watched R-rated movies, and swore. That, and he supported his wild-child daughter in LA. Something he couldn't see Elise's parents doing if they couldn't even accept a common body piercing.

Elise came back to the den with bottled water and snuggled up beside him. He thought about all the dirty things they'd done in bed together, and he had to wonder if that was how Elise rebelled against her parents. Happy to be part of her resistance, he pushed her hair off her shoulder as she hit play.

They watched the movie and ate their pizza. Even if Luke wasn't a big fan of *Lethal Weapon 4*, it was still a Lethal Weapon movie, and it kept his interest.

When the movie was over, Luke discovered that Elise had fallen asleep on him. He slowly untangled their limbs and carried her upstairs. He laid her on her bed and pulled the covers out from underneath her as best he could without waking her, but he didn't quite succeed.

"Luke?" she said with her eyes still closed.

"Yeah, Lise?"

"Don't go."

"I wouldn't dream of it, baby," he told her.

"Mmm," was her only response. A content smile swept across her face.

He shucked off his pants, so he could sleep in his boxers, and he climbed into bed beside Elise.

He put an arm around her, and she curled up next to him.

"I'm glad you're staying," she whispered.

He kissed her on the forehead. "Me, too, babe."

"I don't want to be alone."

He squeezed her close. "You're not alone. I'm right here."

Elise sighed, hugged him tighter, and fell into a deep sleep.

Luke thought he'd lie awake for a while, but he closed his eyes, and the warmth of Elise's body helped him fall into a peaceful, dreamless sleep.

CHAPTER TWENTY

A week later, Elise was at home with her parents. Her dad had been home from the hospital for a few days, but she couldn't stop worrying about him.

"Will you two stop hovering, please?" her father asked. "I am perfectly capable of getting up and getting my own food and water."

"Ward, you don't mean that," her mom said as she tried to fluff the pillow behind her husband's head.

"Yes, I do. I feel like I can't breathe with the two of you here. And I can certainly adjust my own pillows," he said, yanking it away from his wife.

"Dad, we just care about you, is all."

"Well, if you cared about me, you wouldn't have canceled your plans, and you'd leave the house."

"I didn't—" Elise started.

"I know you were supposed to go on a shopping trip with your friends this weekend."

"I didn't want to go anyway," she lied.

It was supposed to be a trip with her new friends, Tera and Heidi, along with Rachel. She'd been disappointed about not joining them, but she couldn't leave her dad and mom.

Her father gave her a pointed look, but Elise was saved from lying further when her phone rang.

She picked it up and looked at the display. It was her realtor. Elise frowned. She had called and canceled with Cara a few days earlier. She'd had to leave a message, and since she hadn't heard anything, Elise had assumed that Cara had received her message.

"Hello?"

"Elise, please tell me you have an hour free."

She didn't answer directly, instead asking, "Why? What is going on?"

"Remember that house you told me you liked? The one that, if you could buy it, you would?"

Of course she did. It was her dream home. It had everything she wanted, and it was in a great location. It was the example she'd used when Cara asked her what she wanted in a home. It belonged to a couple she used to babysit for, which was the only reason she knew what it looked like on the inside. They'd lived there for as long as Elise could remember, and there was no way they'd ever move.

"Yes."

"A house just came on the market today that is almost identical. I did some research, and they were built by the same builder. It might need a few updates inside, and it's a little farther away than your dream home, but I think you'd still be happy with the location. Do you have time to come look at it? There is already at least one offer on it, but I don't want you to miss out."

Elise looked to her father. He must have known what she was thinking because he motioned for her to leave.

"Text me the address. I'm on my way."

Her father looked relieved.

"Excellent," Cara said.

Elise pulled up the address on Maps on her phone and laughed. It was probably ten minutes from Rachel and Luke.

"What's so funny?" her mom asked.

Elise looked up. "Nothing. I have to go. I'll be back as soon as I can."

As she left the room, her father yelled, "Take your time!"

Elise grabbed her purse and rushed out the door.

When Elise pulled up, Cara was already waiting for her. The house was beautiful on the outside. She dared to say she liked it even more than her dream home.

She climbed out of her car and shut the door. She strolled up the walkway, taking her time in looking around.

"Hi, Elise."

"Hi, Cara."

"As you can see, it is very well-maintained. The roof was replaced less than two years ago, and they painted the outside last summer."

"That's wonderful."

"I agree. Let's go inside."

Cara let Elise inside. The front opened to an entryway with a dining room to their right, a living room to the left, and stairs straight ahead of them.

"Let's go this way first," Cara said, heading toward the dining room.

She led Elise from the dining room to the kitchen, which was nice and large with plenty of cupboard space. The cabinets and countertops were a little old, but they could easily be replaced in a few years. There was a sliding glass door that led to a beautiful fenced-in backyard and a door to the garage. The kitchen also opened to a family room. The family room came through to the living room at the front of the house, where they made a full circle.

Upstairs, there was a master bedroom with an en suite and three smaller bedrooms with one additional bathroom. Both bathrooms were a little outdated, but it was, again, something she could fix.

When they finished looking at the garage and basement, Cara asked, "What do you think?"

"I love it. It's perfect."

Cara sighed with relief. "I was hoping you'd say that. Now, it's a little more than what you originally wanted to pay, but because the inside needs some work, it's significantly less than what you could be paying for it. And, since there is another offer on it, I suggest you offer full price."

"What are they asking?"

When Cara told Elise the price, some of her excitement dimmed. It was more than she had originally planned to spend. But she already knew she was in love with it. She hadn't come close to feeling this happy about any of the previous houses she looked at.

Cara sensed her hesitation. "Is there someone you can

call to come and look at it with you? A second opinion with someone who is a little more objective?"

That was an excellent idea. But who to call? Rachel, Tera, and Heidi were out of town, and Kristen was busy with her own family. Her parents would come, but she wasn't going to make her dad leave the house. Plus, she didn't know if she really wanted her mom's opinion. She was kind of picky. That left one option, and surprisingly, it was exactly the person she wanted to call.

Luke sat up on the bench and used the bottom of his shirt to wipe the sweat off his face. "Your turn," he told his friend Nate.

Nate took Luke's spot on the workout bench, lay down, and picked up the barbell while Luke spotted him. Neither of them said much as Nate benched his set with Luke throwing in a few encouraging words now and then.

Nate and Luke had been friends since elementary school, having first bonded over their mixed races in a school where there weren't many minorities, and years later, they didn't feel the need to fill the silence.

Nate had just finished his set when Luke's phone rang. Nate picked it up before Luke could get to it.

"Elise?" he said, reading the screen. "Is this the girl you've been fucking?"

Luke had used that very word to describe what he'd been doing with Elise, but for some reason, hearing it come out of Nate's mouth rubbed him the wrong way.

He gave his friend a come-here motion. "Hand it over."

Nate smirked at Luke and swiped the green button. "Luke's Palace of Sexual Favors," he said into the mouthpiece.

Luke sighed. "Dude."

"This is Nate. Luke's busy with a client, but I'm available. I'm not as good in the sack as Luke, but I've got a bigger dick, so I think that makes up for it."

Luke could hear Elise laughing through the phone, but he couldn't make out her response.

Nate laughed and pulled the bottom of the phone away from his mouth, grinning. "She told me to prove it. Where'd you find this chick?" He didn't wait for Luke to answer and moved the phone back to his lips. "I think we can arrange that."

Over Luke's dead body.

If people thought Luke was a player, it was only because they'd never met Nate. Nate was one hundred percent womanizer and a dog. He was one-quarter black, one-quarter Mexican, and half-white with a shaved head that he Bic'd every day because he didn't even have stubble. He had light-brown skin with tattoos covering his whole left arm and crystal-blue eyes that stood out against his tan skin. He was about the same height as Luke with a slightly slimmer build but still muscular. He was forever making jokes about Asian dicks being small and black dicks being big, saying that was why women should date him over Luke. Ladies loved him. A lot.

And Luke wasn't entirely comfortable with him and Elise bonding.

"Can I have my phone now?"

Nate held up a finger. "Uh-huh," he said into the phone. He was nodding, and his face was serious. He suddenly grinned. "Babe, you came to the right guy. We'll be there in five minutes. I just have to tell Luke to get dressed," he joked.

Luke rolled his eyes.

Nate hit End on Luke's phone and handed it to him. "We've gotta go. Your fuck buddy needs us. She said she'd text you the address."

Luke picked up his bag. "Please don't call her my fuck buddy. Especially to her face."

Nate grabbed his backpack off the floor and looked at Luke. "Dude, you must really like this girl. Either that or she has a magical pussy."

Luke didn't answer. "Let's just go."

Nate raised his brow but didn't say anything.

They hopped in Luke's SUV and made it to the address Elise had given him in seven minutes. When they pulled up, she ran out of the house.

"Hurry." She motioned them inside. "We don't have much time."

Luke rushed toward the house. "What's going on?"

"I think I've finally found a house I want to buy," she said, full of excitement.

Luke looked around the front yard for a For Sale sign.

"It just went on the market," she explained as Nate reached them. "You must be Luke's friend." She held her hand out for Nate to shake.

He took her hand and kissed the back of it. "Now, I get it," he said.

"Get what?" she asked, confused.

"What Long sees in you. You look sweet with your big, innocent eyes, but I bet you're a wildcat in bed."

Elise laughed in disbelief and stuck her thumb out at Nate. "Is this guy for real?" she asked Luke.

Luke smacked his friend on the back of the head. "Unfortunately, yes. I shouldn't bring him out in public, but he insisted on coming along."

"Hey, I'm right here," Nate said.

Elise laughed. "Come on in, guys."

They entered through the front door where they were greeted by an attractive woman who was about five years older than Luke.

"Cara, this is my friend Luke who I called, and this is his friend Nate." Elise turned to Luke and Nate. "Luke, this is my realtor, Cara. Nate, this is Cara. She's married, so no hitting on her."

Luke laughed and elbowed his friend. "Boy, does she have you pegged."

Nate pouted but didn't object.

Cara extended her arms with a smile. "Go ahead and look around. I'll let Elise show you everything. I'll be out front, making a few phone calls." She looked at her watch. "You have about forty-five minutes to make an offer," she told Elise before stepping outside.

Nate flung his arm around Elise. "Show us the way, FB."

"FB?"

"It's nothing, Elise," Luke told her. "Shut up, Nate."

Nate dramatically rolled his eyes. "Whatever."

Elise shook her head and laughed. "You two are weird. Come on, let's go look around."

CHAPTER TWENTY-ONE

Elise stood back, trying to wait patiently for Luke and Nate to tell her what they thought of the house.

The two of them had shown up wearing tank tops and nylon shorts, their muscles on display for everyone to admire. They were both a little sweaty from working out. She'd seen the look Cara gave her when the guys weren't looking, and Elise didn't blame her. They looked incredibly gorgeous, especially next to each other, but Elise thought Luke was the sexier of the two.

"This home has a nice, solid foundation," Nate said.

Normally, she wouldn't care about what some guy she'd just met thought, but Nate explained that he'd fixed up more than one house and remodeled his own home. Luke admitted that Nate was very good at it and had an eye for these kinds of things.

"Do you fix up houses for a living?" Elise asked Nate.

Nate shook his bald head as he ran his hand over the

woodwork on the doorway. "No, I'm an engineer. But my dad was a contractor, so I've worked on houses since before I can remember."

While Nate was deep in thought, Elise pulled Luke aside. "Is Nate going to tell Rachel and Sean about us?"

"Nah. He and Sean aren't really friends." Luke paused and looked like he wanted to say more.

"What?" When he didn't answer her, she nudged him. "You can tell me."

"Does it bother you that Nate knows we slept together?"

"No." She studied Luke.

Did he think she was embarrassed or something that they were sleeping together? Because she wasn't. In fact, she was kind of sick of keeping it a secret. A part of her was relieved that she hadn't gone on the girls' trip, so she wouldn't have to keep quiet about it all weekend. Especially since she'd seen Luke almost every night this past week.

With her dad in the hospital and her mom staying with him, Elise had been spending a lot of time with Luke. At this point, it didn't seem right to keep their relationship—or whatever it was—a secret.

She stepped closer to Luke. "I'm actually kind of tired of keeping it from everyone. But, then again, I don't want a lecture," she told him.

He smiled down at her. "I totally understand. I mean, we're adults, but, ugh, Rachel will probably bitch about it for a week."

Elise playfully smacked him and laughed. "Hey, that's my friend you're talking about." She tugged him closer. "But it is kind of fun, keeping this secret to ourselves."

"Yeah, it is," he agreed. "It makes it naughtier."

He leaned over, like he was going to kiss her, when Nate interrupted, "Hey, Long, if I work on this house for Elise, are you going to help me?"

"Of course," Luke answered.

"Oh. No, no. I didn't ask you guys to look at the place to put you to work. I just wanted your opinions on whether or not it was a good deal." She didn't want either of them to think she was looking for free or cheap labor.

"Oh, it's a great deal," Nate said.

"I agree."

"Awesome. I can't wait." Elise clapped her hands. "I've finally found a home, and I'll get to move out of my parents' house."

Nate grimaced. "That kind of puts a bummer on getting laid, doesn't it?"

"Do you think about sex all the time?" Elise asked.

Nate said, "No," while at the same time, Luke said, "Yes."

Elise laughed while Nate scowled at Luke.

"Like you're one to talk, Long. You're already pussy-whipped over FB here."

"Shut up, asshole."

"Why do you call Luke *Long*?"

Nate looked confused. "Because it's his name."

"Well, I know that. But you're the only one I know who calls him that."

Nate shrugged. "We've been friends forever, and we've always called each other by our last names."

Elise realized she'd never heard Luke address Nate by his first or last name. "What's your last name?"

171

"Thicke. Like Robin Thicke." Nate threw his arm around Luke's neck. "Everywhere we go, people say, *There goes...*" He trailed off, obviously wanting Elise to finish his sentence.

"Long and Thicke." She snorted with a laugh. "Nice," she said sarcastically.

Luke was shaking his head as he pushed Nate's arm off him.

Elise shot Nate a doubtful look. "Is that really your last name?"

"Nah. It's Hall. It would be kind of cool if it were Thicke though, huh?"

Elise laughed. "You are so full of shit."

"I should never have brought you along," Luke told his friend.

"Well, I answered the phone, so technically, I brought you." Nate turned away from Luke and grabbed Elise's hand, tugging her toward the stairs. "Come on, FB, let's go get you a house."

"Why do you keep calling me FB?" she finally asked as she let Nate drag her down the stairs.

"Oh, because you're Long's fuck buddy or friend with benefits. Either way, FB fits."

Elise laughed out loud, yet a tingle of discomfort traveled down her spine at the title. "Is that what Luke calls me?" she asked as casually as she possibly could, looking behind her to make sure that Luke had hung back enough not to hear her question.

"No. He actually told me not to call you that, but if I were fucking you, I'd want everyone to know. You're hot."

"Thank you?" *I guess.*

"He's probably just afraid of getting hurt after Ava."

"Ava?" Elise had never heard that name.

"Yeah, you know, his ex."

No, she hadn't known. She didn't get a chance to ask Nate any more questions because they reached the front door, and he yanked it open.

"Hey, sexy realtor lady, someone here wants to buy a house."

Cara grinned. "I was hoping you'd say that. I'm already trying to get ahold of the seller's realtor. Why don't you come down to my office, and we can get the paperwork started?"

Luke came up behind them and cupped the back of Elise's neck, pulling her toward him and away from Nate, forcing Nate to drop her hand. She'd forgotten that he was holding it.

It seemed like it was a possessive move on Luke's part, which she admitted that she kind of liked, but when Elise looked at his face, he was smiling and appeared relaxed.

"I hope you get it," he told her.

She smiled, but she was starting to feel butterflies take over her stomach. "Me, too."

Luke pulled her closer and kissed her on the forehead. "Good luck, babe. Call me when you hear something."

Elise looked at Luke. She wanted to ask him about Ava and the other things Nate had said, but now was not the time. "Will do," was all she said instead.

Several hours later, Luke's phone rang. When he answered it, the first thing he heard was a high-pitched squeal.

"I got the house! I got the house! I offered as much as another buyer, but the sellers were in a sudden time crunch. They wanted to close in less than two weeks, and I was the only one who could do that. The house is mine!"

Luke grinned into the phone. "That's great, Lise. I'm so happy for you."

"Let's go out and celebrate."

Shit. "I can't."

"Of course. I'm sorry. You probably have other plans. I already interrupted your morning." She tried to sound nonchalant, but he could hear the disappointment in her voice.

"Hey, you didn't interrupt anything. I was more than happy to come over this morning."

Luke was also secretly pleased that, out of all the people in her life, she'd called him. He knew Rachel was out of town, but he also knew there were other people she could have called besides him.

"It's just that I promised Hall—I mean, Nate that we'd go out tonight and do something." Luke lowered his voice because Nate was in the kitchen, rummaging through his pantry. "Believe me, I'd much rather hang with you tonight."

"Well, that makes me feel better," Elise said.

At that exact time, Nate came up behind Luke when he hadn't been looking. "Hey, I take offense to that. Just because I can't make you orgasm doesn't mean I'm no fun." Nate flopped down on Luke's couch next to him with a bag of Luke's chips in his hand. He rubbed his chin. "Actually, I think I could give you an orgasm. But I doubt either of us would like it."

Elise started laughing on the other side of the phone.

"I guess you heard all that, huh?"

"Yes," she said, still giggling. "Does he ever quit?"

Luke thought about it. "No."

"Does it get old?"

"Hardly ever. He knows when to be serious. Don't you, Hall?"

Nate pretended to be wounded. "Of course I do. I was a perfect gentleman at your grandmother's funeral, was I not?"

"You were," he told Nate. "Did you hear that, Elise?"

"Yes, but still..."

Luke laughed.

Nate might be over the top sometimes, but he was like a brother to Luke. And he always found Nate to be honest. He said what other people were thinking anyway. It was refreshing that Luke never had to wonder what his childhood friend was thinking.

"Meh, he grows on ya."

"Like a fungus," Elise joked.

Luke laughed.

"Hey, I heard that," Nate said, his mouth full of chips.

"I'm just kidding," she said loud enough for Nate to hear.

"You'd better be. I like you, FB. Don't make me change my mind."

"Is he going to call me that forever?" Elise asked with a sigh.

Luke winced. "Probably, but let's hope not. He didn't tell you what it stood for, did he?"

"Oh, he did."

Luke sent a death glare at Nate. "I told you not to call her that."

"What?" Nate looked confused before he must have remembered. "Ohh. Yeah, well, it's like a badge of honor. How could I not?"

Luke didn't say anything to Nate, but he did apologize to Elise.

She laughed. "It's fine. It's kind of funny if you think about it."

"If you say so."

"Well, I'd better go. Thanks again for coming today."

"No problem."

"By the way, I'm going to be thinking of you and Nate tonight when I'm alone in my room."

"Huh?"

Her voice dropped, becoming seductive. "Yeah, the whole giving-you-an-orgasm thing. I'll be thinking of that when I'm in bed tonight."

Luke was both horrified and turned on at the same time. "You're going to think about me and Nate? As in, us doing it?"

Nate's head whipped around at Luke's words. His eyes were round, and he paused mid chew. He leaned closer to the phone.

"Oh, yeah, baby. You wouldn't believe the number of male-on-male romance novels women read. It's fucking hot."

Luke swallowed. "Really?"

"Really. Now, I just have to decide who I'm going to picture blowing whom." She moaned ever-so lightly. "Since you know how much I love your cock, I think it's going to be Nate giving you head."

Luke was at a loss for words, and Nate seemed to be speechless as well.

Her voice returned to normal. "Oh, crap, I've gotta go. Make sure and invite me over if you two do end up having sex. Or at least take pictures. Have fun tonight. Bye."

And she was gone.

Nate sat up. "Holy shit, man. You'd better fucking marry that girl because, if you don't, I will."

CHAPTER TWENTY-TWO

Elise's alarm went off on her phone, and she threw back the covers. She practically jumped out of bed with excitement, despite the fact that she'd gone to bed late and only gotten five hours of sleep. Today was moving day, and nothing was going to ruin her enthusiasm.

She had closed on her new house yesterday, but because it had been Friday and everyone had to work, she had waited to move until today. She'd planned to hire movers, but when she'd told Rachel and Luke that, they had both been adamant about helping her move. So far, they had recruited Sean, Heidi, Tera, and Nate. Also, her sister and brother-in-law were going to come and help, too, and give their daughter a little time to spend with Grandma and Grandpa.

The day before, Elise's dad had insisted on helping her take over a few things that the two of them could manage. So, she was glad that her dad would be babysitting today and wouldn't be able to do any heavy lifting. She had appreciated his help the day before though. He'd gone with her to pick up the U-Haul, and he'd helped her take all her kitchen stuff over to her house and put most of it away. After that, she'd gone grocery shopping and stocked her fridge, freezer, and pantry, so she would be prepared to feed all of her helpers.

Knowing that today would be filled with sweat and grime, Elise threw on an old tee and shorts, put her hair in a ponytail, and didn't even bother with makeup. She went downstairs to find something to eat before everyone arrived. She wanted to be ready to go. She loved her mom and dad, but it was time to move out.

Elise had just poured her milk into her cereal when the front door opened, and Kristen, James, and Jennifer walked in.

"Aunt Elise!" Jennifer said, running over to her.

Elise leaned over and gave Jennifer a big hug. "How's my favorite niece?"

Jennifer pulled away and cocked her head. "I'm your only niece, Aunt Elise."

"Well, I'm pretty sure you'd still be my favorite if I had more."

Jennifer grinned. "You're right. I would be."

Elise laughed. "My, aren't you the modest one?"

"Where are Mom and Dad?" Kristen asked.

Elise picked up her cereal bowl and sat at the counter. "I think they're still in their room."

"We're right here," her mom said, coming down the stairs, tying the belt around her robe.

Her father followed, finger-combing his hair.

"Grandma! Grandpa!" Jennifer exclaimed.

Elise's mother held out her arms. "Hi, sweetie. How are you?"

"Good, except Mom and Dad made me get up early to come here."

Elise swallowed her bite of food. "That's my fault, Jen. I'm the one who made your mom and dad come here so early."

"We're more than happy to help. Aren't we, James?"

"Yeah," James said, but he didn't sound like he meant it.

James was standing as far away from Kristen as he could while still being able to say he was in the same room. It looked like things weren't any better between the two of them.

Poor Kristen.

"When is everyone else getting here?" her mom asked.

Elise glanced at the microwave. "About twenty minutes."

"Oh my. I'd better get in the shower. I can't let your friends see me like this."

"Mom, they won't mind," Elise said.

Her mom clucked her tongue. "Well, I mind." She turned around and started back up the stairs. "I'll be back as soon as possible. Come on, Ward."

"Suzanne, I look fine."

"Come on, Ward," her mom said again.

"Fine," her dad said, marching after his wife.

"Jennifer, why don't you get something to eat? I'm sure Aunt Elise bought some good cereal while she's been staying with Grandma and Grandpa," Kristen told her daughter.

It was true. Elise bought way better-tasting cereal than what her parents usually had stocked in the house.

Jennifer skipped over to the cupboard and started rummaging through it. "Lucky Charms. Score." She went to the next cupboard and pulled out a bowl and a spoon from the drawer.

"Jennifer, please find something else to eat," James said. "Kristen, I thought we talked about Jennifer's sugar intake."

"Dad," Jennifer whined.

"One day isn't going to hurt her, James. It's kind of a special day."

James threw up his hands. "I don't know why I even bother." He spun around and headed for the front door.

"James," Kristen called after him, her face red.

Elise tried not to look at her sister with pity in her eyes because that was not what she would want if their positions were reversed. "What's wrong with him?"

Kristen shook her head and lowered it, obviously upset. "Nothing. Everything." She looked up at her daughter, who seemed to be busy pouring her cereal. "It's complicated." She sighed. "I'm going to go talk to him."

After Kristen left the room, Jennifer hopped up onto the stool next to Elise.

"How's summer treating ya, kid?" Elise asked.

Jennifer took a huge bite of cereal. "Good," she replied, not bothering to swallow her food first.

"Don't let Grandma catch you talking with your mouth full," Elise joked.

"Mom and Dad are going to get divorced," Jennifer said, surprising Elise.

"What? Where did you hear that?"

"From my friend Becky. She said her parents were

sleeping in different bedrooms and fighting all the time before they got divorced."

"Your mom and dad don't sleep in the same room?"

Jennifer shook her head. "They never have. So, I don't think that counts."

What? How could Elise not have known this?

"But they have been fighting an awful lot. And Mom stays at Aunt Ashley's house a lot. And, when Mom's home, Dad goes over to Uncle Adam's house. They're hardly together anymore."

Adam was James's best friend. Elise had had no idea it was so bad that they weren't even staying the night in the same house with each other.

"How do you feel about that, kiddo?" Elise asked.

Jennifer stopped eating and appeared to be thinking about it. "I don't know. I think I'm supposed to be sad, but Mom and Dad don't love each other anyway. Not like Grandma and Grandpa do." She shrugged. "I don't think I would care if they got divorced."

Elise was baffled. Where was all this coming from, and how did a six-year-old get this insightful? And was Jennifer even right about Kristen and James? Had they really never loved each other? Elise didn't understand because, in high school, they had been inseparable. Back then, they had been each other's best friends.

The front door opened, and the two of them came back in. Kristen looked stressed, and James was frowning. They definitely weren't the same people they had been back in high school.

Jennifer picked up on their tension and shifted in her

seat. Elise ran her hand over Jennifer's hair and gave her a one-armed hug.

"You can always come and stay with me if it gets to be too much at home, okay?" she whispered in her niece's ear.

Jennifer looked up at her and grinned, Lucky Charms marshmallows stuck in her teeth. "Thanks, Aunt Elise."

Elise kissed Jennifer's forehead. She loved the kid.

Elise was just trying to figure out what to say to her sister and brother-in-law to break the silence when there was a knock at the front door.

Kristen went to open it, and Luke, Rachel, Sean, and Nate spilled into the house.

"Hi, Kristen," Rachel said, giving her a hug. "Do you remember my fiancé, Sean?"

Kristen nodded her head and held out her hand. "Hello, Sean."

Sean shook it. "Hello."

"This is my husband, James," Kristen said.

James stepped closer, offering his hand as well.

For the first time that morning, James smiled.

"These two are Luke and Nate," Sean told Kristen and James.

They shook their hands as well, and when James got to Luke and Nate, he seemed to blush slightly. It was the oddest thing. She didn't think James knew Luke or Nate.

Nate broke away first and came toward Elise. "Hey, FB, you ready to move today?"

When he reached her, she grabbed his T-shirt in her fist.

Nate just grinned as she lowered her voice and said,

"You'd better not call me that again. One, my sweet niece is behind me."

Nate's eyes flickered to Jennifer and back to Elise.

"Two, nobody knows about Luke and me, and we're going to keep it that way. Okay?"

Nate mockingly saluted her, still smiling. "Yes, ma'am."

She let him go.

"You're kind of kinky, you know that?" he said to Elise. He looked around her at Jennifer. "Is your aunt always this feisty?" Nate asked, grabbing an apple from the bowl on the middle of the counter without even asking.

Jennifer giggled. "Yes."

Elise's mouth dropped open. "Jennifer."

Nate rubbed the apple on his shirt. "That's what I thought." He took a big bite. "No worries, FB. I'll just call you Wildcat instead."

"Don't you dare."

"Don't you dare what?" Rachel asked, stepping into the kitchen with everyone behind her.

"Do you want to tell her, or should I?" Nate asked.

He isn't really going to say anything, is he? Elise's eyes flew to Luke, who looked as confused as she felt.

"Hall, you—" Luke started.

Nate cut him off, "Oh, you know, Jennifer over here asked me to be her boyfriend, and Elise's all like"—his voice rose an octave—"'Don't you dare.'" His voice dropped back to normal. "But Elise doesn't understand true love, does she, Jennifer?"

Jennifer was cracking up so hard, she could barely sit up straight. "You're funny," she told Nate.

"Funny, my a—butt," Elise said. "Jennifer, this is my friend Luke, and this is Luke's friend Nate. If you're smart, you'll stay away from both of them and any guys like them." Elise got up from the counter and carried her bowl to the sink.

"Hey," Luke and Nate said at the same time.

"She's right, Jennifer," Rachel said. Then, changing the subject, she asked, "Where should we start?"

"All my big stuff is downstairs. I was thinking we should do that first before we start with all the boxes, don't you think? I'm going to finish cleaning up breakfast, and then I'll meet you down there."

"Sounds good to me," Rachel said. "Let's go, guys."

"Come on, Jennifer. You can help us with the light stuff," James said.

Elise turned back to the sink and cereal boxes on the counter. She heard everyone trudging out of the kitchen and down to the basement.

Strong arms slipped around her waist and pulled her back against a hard male body.

"Mmm," Elise said, closing her eyes, as she melted into Luke. She put an arm up and back to curl around his neck.

"I hate having to stay away from you," Luke whispered in her ear.

"Me, too."

"What did Hall really say to you?"

Elise smiled. "I told him not to call me that ridiculous nickname, so he said he was going to call me Wildcat instead, and I told him, 'Don't you dare.'"

Luke nipped at her ear. "Well, if the name fits..." He turned her head and kissed her.

Elise was just getting into it, wanting to get Luke naked, forgetting all about her parents being upstairs and her friends being downstairs, when she heard a giggle. Elise pulled far enough away from Luke to see her niece sitting at the counter still, hand over her mouth, trying not to laugh.

"Jennifer, I thought you went downstairs," Elise said.

Her niece shook her head, as if Elise had asked a question. Then, she tilted her head. "Is Aunt Elise your girlfriend?" she asked Luke.

Luke let Elise go and walked over to Jennifer. He leaned down, putting his forearms on the countertop so that he could get closer. "Can you keep a secret?"

Jennifer's eyes rounded, and she nodded enthusiastically, excited to be included in a private adult conversation.

"Yeah, your aunt Elise is my girlfriend. But nobody knows, okay? So, don't tell." Luke held up his finger to his lips.

Jennifer pretended to zip up her mouth, lock it, and throw away the key.

"That's my girl." Luke stood up tall. "I'd better go help them before they wonder what happened to me," he told Elise. He winked at her and went to join the others.

"Your boyfriend's cute," Jennifer said, turning back to her breakfast.

At her niece's words, Elise realized she'd been standing there, staring at the doorway where Luke had disappeared. The two of them had never discussed boyfriend-girlfriend status before.

"Yeah, he is," she said, her mind still swirling on the little bomb Luke had just dropped.

"Is that why you're smiling, Aunt Elise?"

Elise looked at Jennifer. "Yes, kiddo. That, and so much more."

CHAPTER TWENTY-THREE

E lise shut the dishwasher and was headed for the basement when the doorbell rang.

Jennifer jumped off her stool. "I'll get it."

"It's for me," Elise said.

But her niece ran for the front door anyway.

Elise came up behind Jennifer right as she opened the door to Heidi.

"Hi."

"Hey, girl."

"Thanks for coming."

"No problem."

"Wait for me," Tera said, running up the walkway. "Sorry I'm late," she said when she reached them.

"You're fine. Everyone else got here about ten minutes ago. They just went downstairs a few minutes ago." Elise waved them toward her. "Come in, come in."

Jennifer shut the door behind her friends.

"Who's this?" Heidi asked with a smile.

"My niece, Jennifer."

Jennifer moved closer to Elise and leaned back against her.

Elise put her hands on her niece's shoulders. "Jen, these are my friends Heidi and Tera."

Jennifer waved. "Hi."

"Hi, Jennifer," Heidi and Tera both said with a smile.

"My aunt Elise has a secret boyfriend. His name is L—"

Elise slapped a hand over Jennifer's mouth and chuckled uncomfortably. "Kids," she said as a lame explanation.

"A secret boyfriend, eh?" Tera said, her eyes big and questioning.

"Ooh," Heidi said, "do tell."

Elise shook her head. *Think, think,* she commanded her brain. "Jennifer, can you go in the other room and finish your cereal?"

"But I'm done."

"Then, go and put your bowl in the dishwasher."

"I never get to hear the good stuff." She kicked the floor and then went and did as Elise had asked her.

That's because you can't keep the good stuff a secret, kid.

She'd lasted all of two minutes before telling the first person she saw.

"So?" Tera asked, practically bouncing up and down.

"Yeah, don't keep us waiting," Heidi added.

She felt bad for bursting her friends' bubbles, but it had to be done.

Elise lowered her voice. "Look, my sister and brother-in-law are going through a rough time. Jennifer thinks they're going to get divorced. She saw me talking to Nate and then to

Luke, and I think she got the wrong idea about one of them. I think she is looking for a healthy relationship to attach herself to right now."

Tera and Heidi both went from excited to frowning.

"That's so sad," Heidi said.

"Poor thing," Tera said.

"I know. It's so sad for everyone all around. I think my sister is really trying, but I don't know if my brother-in-law is anymore." Elise brought her voice up to a normal level. "Anyway, why don't you go downstairs? Thanks again for helping today."

"You're totally welcome," Heidi said.

"I am more than happy to help. But you have to tell me who this Nate guy is," Tera said.

Elise laughed. "He's Luke's friend."

"Ooh, is he hot like Luke?" Tera asked.

"Yes." *And No.* "He's gorgeous." *But not as gorgeous as Luke.* "The problem is, he knows it." *Although Luke does, too.* "I think they might be two peas in a pod." She headed for the stairs, waving her friends to follow. "Come on, you can come meet him."

Several hours later, the group had moved in most of Elise's furniture, and they had put a big dent in the pile of boxes. They'd actually had to leave some at her parents' and go back to fill the U-Haul again.

When she'd moved out of her house in Denver, she remembered how much she'd gotten sick of packing the boxes by room and labeling them. Now, she was grateful because no one had to ask what went where.

Rachel, Tera, Heidi, and Kristen were upstairs, working on the bedrooms and the bathrooms, while the guys brought in more boxes. She was very lucky to have friends and family who weren't just willing to move her furniture and boxes, but who were also willing to help her unpack.

Elise let them do their thing while she concentrated on bringing in other stuff from the truck. She trusted her friends to do a good job, and she didn't want to sound like a dictator, directing them to do this and that and to put things here and there. She could always move things around later.

Currently, the guys were working on her bedframe, headboard, footboard, mattress, and box spring. She even heard them arguing about tools. Sean had run home and grabbed his toolbox, so they could put her bed back together. She'd kind of forgotten about that stuff. Her guy friends in Denver had helped her move out and never even mentioned tools. Sometimes, she was such a girl.

The next thing in the U-Haul was a big garbage sack full of her dirty clothes that she'd been putting off washing until she got to her new house. She lugged it inside and down to the laundry room in the lower level. She'd decided a week ago that it would be easier to move dirty clothes than clean ones.

The only downfall of her new home was that her washer and dryer were in the basement, fairly secluded and away from everything else. While she'd love a main-floor laundry room or even an upstairs one, it wasn't a deal-breaker, and it was something she could easily live with. Plus, the upstairs bathroom had a laundry chute, which made getting clothes downstairs a whole lot easier.

After dropping off the soiled laundry, Elise went back upstairs to the main floor. She walked into the empty kitchen from the basement. Then, she headed back for the front door to go outside and grab something else from the moving truck when she ran into Luke. He and the other guys had taken their shirts off a long time ago. One of the bad things about moving in Minnesota in July was the humidity.

But he looked delicious.

Inspiration struck.

"Hey, Lise, we just—" Luke started.

Elise interrupted him by slipping her fingers into the waistband of his shorts. "I need you to come downstairs to look at my dryer," she told him with a sly smile as she walked backward, pulling him along.

"Okay. How can I help?" he said, giving her his cocky smirk.

They were at the door of the downstairs now, but just in case someone could hear them, she said, "I'm worried my dryer vent is clogged with lint. I don't think it's working." She looked up into his eyes. "I think you need to stick something in there and clean it out."

Luke opened the door and pushed her through. "Well, we'd better go take care of that then."

"Last one to the bottom has to make the other come first," Elise said as she took off down the stairs.

Luke quickly shut the door behind them and rushed after her.

They reached the laundry room, and one of them—Elise wasn't even sure which one—swung the door closed. They came together, kissing and touching. It was lips, tongues, fingers, and arms everywhere. They couldn't keep their hands off each other.

Luke walked them back toward the dryer, and when they reached it, he turned her around and pushed her forward. He reached over her and turned the dryer on. "We'd better just see if this works first, shouldn't we?" His voice was all business, but the next thing he did was yank her shorts and underwear down.

Elise squeaked at the cool basement air hitting her butt cheeks, but she quickly forgot it as Luke slipped two fingers inside her. "Oh, shit," she moaned.

"Already wet for me," he said as he removed his fingers. "God, I love your pussy," were the next words he spoke right as he pushed himself inside her.

They'd stopped using condoms the night her father went to the hospital, and she loved that they could have sex anytime, anywhere without worrying about protection.

Elise leaned forward and stuck out her ass to get Luke inside her as deeply as possible. He grabbed on to her hips and began pumping into her, full force.

Luke could be a sweet and gentle lover at times, and he often had her take control. But she loved it when he took what he wanted from her. When he fucked her hard, fast, and dirty.

Whenever he did this, it wouldn't take her long to come. Sometimes, that could be a bad thing because she wanted to extend their lovemaking. But, occasionally, like now, when they had a household full of people upstairs, it was amazing that Luke knew exactly what she needed.

Just to help her along and give that extra push, he glided his fingers between her legs and rubbed her clit one, two, three times before he pinched it between his finger and thumb.

Elise went off like a rocket, clutching on to the dryer for dear life, afraid her legs might give out underneath her. Apparently, she was rather vocal because Luke covered her mouth with his hand. She smelled her essence on his fingers, and it only kept her orgasm going, knowing he'd been touching her secret place mere moments ago.

Two thrusts later, and Luke was right behind her. His hand dropped from her mouth and slid around her waist. He held her close to him, biting down on her shoulder to keep himself quiet, as he poured himself inside her.

After several minutes later, when they both caught their breaths, Elise told him, "I think the dryer works."

Luke buried his nose in her neck and laughed.

CHAPTER TWENTY-FOUR

Luke pulled out of Elise's heat and turned her around to face him. He loved her spontaneity and her sense of adventure. But she deserved more than some quick fuck against the dryer in her laundry room. Not that she seemed to mind, going by how hard she'd come.

He picked her up, sat her butt on the dryer, and took her lips. He kissed down one side of her face and then her neck. She clutched the back of his head, pulling him closer. He opened his mouth over her pulse, feeling it throb against his tongue, and sucked.

Elise moaned, and that was all it took to make him hard again. Her shorts and underwear were still down around her calves, so he slipped one leg out, pulled her to the edge of the appliance, and entered her.

She drew back from him and opened her eyes. They were wide with surprise. "Again? Already? Now?"

"Again." *Now. Forever. Always.*

She affected him more than any other woman had in the past.

He withdrew and pushed back home. She was wet from him coming in her earlier, but she was tight from her climax, and even though they'd just done it, she felt incredible.

"How do you always feel so good?" he asked her.

Her head was thrown back, but she lifted it enough to look at him. "Me? How do *you* always feel so good?"

He chuckled and leaned her back over his arm. "I guess we'll have to agree to disagree," he said as he pushed her shirt and sports bra up.

He sucked her nipple in his mouth as he thrust, and she began softly chanting his name.

He was pretty sure that Elise didn't realize that she said his name over and over again when they had sex and that she usually got louder, the closer she was to coming. He loved it because then he had no doubt that she knew who was inside her.

Their relationship might have started out as fuck buddies, but it was more than that now. They'd moved from one-night stand to friends with benefits to sleeping exclusively with each other, and today, when he'd told her niece that Elise was his girlfriend, he'd meant it.

He might not have brought his feelings to Elise's attention in the correct way, but he was scared of things getting serious. Not because he was afraid of commitment, but because he was terrified she was. He was also worried about messing up the rhythm they had going. As if making the relationship serious would make it too serious, and she would think they couldn't have fun anymore, like they were now.

He had probed her more about the orgasm thing and about guys not being able to get her there. She'd been open about discussing it, but he wasn't sure if she realized that the guys she had gotten serious with weren't great in bed and that her non-serious relationships, encounters, whatever you wanted to call them, were the ones where she'd managed to climax. Considering how responsive Elise was in his arms, he had a feeling that he knew what category she'd put him in.

So far, she hadn't asked him about the girlfriend thing that had come up with her niece. Granted, they hadn't been alone very much, but he was going to let her bring it up. He wasn't sure if she was ready to take their relationship further, and he was afraid that, if he pushed her, she'd push back—and not in a way he'd like. He wasn't willing to risk losing her.

Luke released her nipple and pushed her breasts into his chest, so he could look into her face. He grasped her hair and gave a slight tug. "Elise."

"Hmm?"

"Open your eyes."

Her green eyes flickered open, and she smiled at him.

"Attagirl. I want you to look at me while I fuck you."

"Oh, Luke," she moaned.

Her pussy squeezed tighter over him.

"Come on, Lise, come for me."

Unable to keep her eyes open any longer, they slammed shut as her back arched, and she came around him. He loved how tight she got as she convulsed when he was inside her.

Unable to hold his orgasm off any longer, he let go and released himself deep within her.

He rested his forehead against her chest. "Damn, woman, I don't think I can walk."

Elise chuckled. "You can't walk? I'm the one who's going to be limping out of here later. I don't think we've had sex twice in a row like that so soon."

He jerked his head up. "Did I hurt you?"

She cupped his cheek. "No, it's just that you're not small, and I can get a little sore sometimes."

"Please keep talking about how big my dick is."

She laughed, causing her to tighten around him.

He groaned.

"I don't think you have any trouble with your ego and penis."

He pulled out of her. "Oh, babe, it's a dick or a cock. Not a penis."

She leaned up onto her elbows. "But that's the actual word for it."

"I know. It makes me think of work."

"Ah," she said as she understood. "Okay then. Your cock is huge."

"Thank you," he said, grinning. He pointed to the floor. "Are these clothes all dirty?"

"Yes."

He tore open the garbage bag, grabbed the first thing his fingers touched, and gave it to her. "Sorry, I think I left you extra messy."

She grabbed the shorts and put them between her legs to clean herself up.

Luke grabbed something else out of the bag to clean his

own body up. Right as he was done, he threw the garment on the floor and heard his name.

"Shit," Luke said. "Someone's coming. Quick. Make yourself look busy."

Elise had just pulled up her shorts, and she went over to her pile of clothes and started sorting them while Luke opened the dryer to make it look like he had come down there to inspect it.

He waited for his name to be called again before he answered, pretending like he hadn't heard the previous shout, "In here."

Right before the door opened, Luke looked at Elise. "Your hair," he told her.

Elise reached up and realized half of her ponytail had fallen out. She pulled out the band holding her hair up and let the rest of the tresses fall down around her shoulders.

"Hey, what are you doing?" Sean asked.

"Elise saw that post on Facebook about making sure the dryer vent is cleared out, so your house doesn't catch on fire." Luke tried to put enough inflection in his tone to make it sound like he thought Elise might be overreacting a bit.

"Hey, it can really happen. I don't want my new house to burn down because my dryer is in the basement, and I'm upstairs."

Luke gave her a thumbs-up behind Sean's back. She was really selling it.

She, however, shot him a look that said, *I'm half-serious, and if my house burns down, I will cut you.*

Elise stood up. "Well, I got all the clothes sorted. You're sure everything's okay?" she asked Luke.

"Yep." Luke stood and wiped his hands on his shorts, as if he'd really gotten them dirty.

"Okay. See you guys upstairs then."

As soon as Elise was gone, Sean looked at Luke. "You're fucking her, aren't you?"

Luke was taken aback. "Holy shit, Sean."

Sean shook his head when Luke didn't deny it. "How long has this been going on?"

None of your goddamn business, Luke thought as he gritted his teeth. What happened between him and Elise was between them.

"How did you know?" he asked instead.

"Because it smells like a brothel in here."

Luke cursed. He hadn't thought about that before Sean walked in. The room didn't have a window or any sort of ventilation, so he really shouldn't have been surprised that Sean smelled sex.

"Look—" Luke started.

"If you hurt her, man, and Rachel finds out I knew..."

Luke was grateful that he didn't even have to ask his friend for his loyalty in keeping their secret. But, at the same time, where was Sean's faith?

Luke stalked toward his friend and poked him in the chest. "Fuck you."

"Fuck me?"

"Yes. Why does everyone assume I'm going to break her heart? You know, I have had a long-term relationship before. My last girlfriend and I dated for two years before she broke up with me. I am not the same guy I was in college."

"Damn," Sean said, taking a step back, "I had no idea."

"Of course not because no one bothers to ask me. They just see me and assume that I'm the same player that I always was, but I'm not. A term that you all gave me by the way, not something I have ever called myself. I never fed false promises to anyone. Back then or now. Either way, I'm not the same guy I was in college. I mean, I wasn't ready to marry my ex or anything, but I loved her. Or I thought I did. Now, things are so clear." Luke shook his head. "But that's not the point."

Sean looked ashamed. "I'm sorry, man. I really am."

Some of the anger left Luke upon seeing Sean looking so guilty. "It's okay. I mean, it's not, but I can forgive and forget." So, not all the anger had left.

"So, you have no plans on breaking Elise's heart?"

"Well, first, she'd have to give it to me, but the answer is no. I don't have any plans to go anywhere, okay?"

Sean nodded. "Okay."

"Sean?" Rachel called from the stairs.

"Yeah?"

They heard Rachel's footsteps descend until she came through the door. "Hey, what are you guys doing?"

"Nothing."

"Talking."

Rachel looked back and forth between them, clearly picking up their tension. She went over to Sean's side. "Is everything okay?"

"Yeah," Luke said. "I've gotta go...do something," he finished lamely.

He left the laundry room and took the stairs two at a time. Elise was in the kitchen, pulling stuff out of the pantry. She'd put her hair back up in a ponytail, looking like she hadn't been doing the nasty with him less than a half hour ago.

For some reason, that really added to his disappointment and irritation.

She took one look at his face and asked, "What's wrong?"

"Nothing."

He didn't want to tell her about his conversation with Sean, only to have her worry about Sean saying something to Rachel, but maybe she'd already guessed, given his mood.

He couldn't help feeling a little resentful, preparing himself for her asking if Sean could keep a secret. Like that was the important thing here.

She stepped closer and touched his arm. She surprised him when she said, "I hope everything's okay. I'm here if you want to talk."

Her offer calmed Luke. He liked knowing she cared. He pulled her close and kissed her temple. "Thanks, babe. Maybe later. We still have stuff to bring in. Then, you and I have a lot more rooms to christen." He smiled at her. It wasn't his usual full smile, but he was trying to be his normal self.

Elise laughed, knowing he was trying. "Okay, but we might have to do the christening thing in steps. My house isn't small."

If it meant he got to see her over the next few days, that would totally work for him. "Deal."

CHAPTER TWENTY-FIVE

Elise went to her fridge to grab beers for everyone. They'd finally gotten all the boxes moved into the house, and they could relax. She carried the bottles into the family room where the guys were hooking up her TV, so they could watch Netflix. Thankfully, one of the things she had done the day before was get her internet set up.

Elise handed a beer to Rachel, who was lying on the floor, and one to Heidi, who was sitting next to her, leaning back against the couch. Tera and Kristen were sprawled out on each end of the sofa, and Elise gave them their drinks as well. James had left about half an hour earlier, saying he had other things to do, but Elise was pretty sure he just didn't want to be around her sister longer.

Elise set Luke's, Sean's, and Nate's bottles on the coffee table and plopped down in the recliner.

She studied Luke for a moment. He seemed to be in a better mood now than he had been after they had sex. She didn't know what, but something must have happened with Sean in the basement because Luke had not been in a good mood when he came upstairs. She suspected Sean knew about the two of them because he had looked skeptical when he walked into the laundry room. But, when she'd asked Luke what was wrong, he'd said nothing. She had seen he wasn't ready to talk about it, and she had decided to give him his space.

"Sorry, I don't have any other alcohol," Elise told the group. "I can run to the store and get something else if someone wants it. I was just so excited to be able to have beer in my fridge that I forgot about buying anything else."

Nate, not caring there was little room in between Tera and Kristen, picked up a beer and planted his butt right in the middle of the two before throwing his feet up onto the coffee table. "Why couldn't you have beer before?"

"Her parents are a little religious. They don't drink," Rachel explained.

Kristen snorted. "A little? More like ultra."

Elise grimaced. "I wouldn't say ultra. They are quite religious. Their church doesn't believe in drinking, but I have met people with stricter religions. I worked with someone in Denver who didn't own a television because their church frowned upon it."

Kristen's eyes got big. "I guess it could be worse. But Mom and Dad are pretty bad, especially Mom. Quite frankly, I'm surprised we were ever born, Elise. Mom acts like sex is evil, so the fact that she ever let Dad in her pants is a mystery."

"Is it really okay if we go visit?" Elise asked when she rejoined the rest of the group. "And should we shower and change first since we were working all day?"

Rachel waved off her concern. "Nope. I told Shelly we were coming, and she can take us as we are."

Luke stood from near Elise's entertainment center. "Just in time, too, seeing as how we finally got the TV set up."

Luke smiled as Elise fawned over Virginia Rose.

"She is so precious." Elise ran her hand over the baby's head as Rachel held her. "And look at all this red hair."

"I told you I couldn't wait to see their little ginger baby," Rachel said. "And look at those blue eyes. I know they'll probably change, but they're so beautiful."

Shelly and Joe laughed.

"I knew we'd have a redhead, obviously," Shelly said, "but I had no idea she'd be born with so much hair. I figured she'd be bald until she was two. And we thought the same thing about her eyes. I'm secretly hoping they stay that way."

Elise held out her arms. "Can I hold her now?"

Rachel pouted. "Okay, fine," she relented as she handed the baby over.

"Hi, sweet pea," Elise said. "I haven't held a baby in a long time." She looked up at Shelly. "You know, anytime you need a babysitter..."

Shelly smiled. "Good to know."

"Me, too, of course," Rachel said.

Elise bumped her hip into Rachel's. "We can do it together."

"Yay! We'd have so much fun."

"What about you guys?" Joe asked. "Are you going to offer to babysit, too?"

Luke and Sean looked at each other.

"Uh..." Sean said while Luke didn't say anything.

"I'm kidding," Joe said.

"Whew, because I have no idea what to do with a baby."

"Well, you'd better learn soon." Rachel kissed the top of Virginia's head.

When she looked up, everyone was staring at her.

Elise spoke first, "Rachel, are you trying to tell us that you're—"

"What?" Rachel looked confused at first until realization dawned. "No. I'm just saying that, as soon as the ring is on my finger, bye-bye goes the birth control."

Luke and Joe laughed at Sean's deer-in-the-headlights expression.

"You might as well start preparing yourself now, man," Joe advised him.

"It'll be entertaining for sure to see Sean with a baby," Luke said.

"Me? What about you?"

"I can handle a baby just fine," Luke bragged.

He didn't have any nieces or nephews yet, despite having three siblings, one of whom was older. But he'd grown up with a lot of cousins, and he'd had to do plenty of babysitting of them and his younger siblings.

Everyone looked at Luke like they didn't believe him,

which kind of chapped his ass. First, Sean had thought he was going to use Elise, and now, everyone thought he was a baby hater. Today was not Luke's day.

At that moment, Virginia started to fuss, and Elise's attempts to calm her weren't working. "Is she hungry?"

"I don't think so," Shelly said. "She just finished nursing right before you guys got here. She's been doing this on and off, and we can't seem to calm her down." Shelly sat up better on her bed and winced. "I can take her."

Luke stepped closer to Elise. "Give her to me."

Elise doubtfully looked at him. Luke tried not to let her uncertainty bother him, but it still rubbed him the wrong way.

He made a come-here motion. "Let me hold her."

Elise looked to Shelly, who nodded, and then Elise gave him the baby.

Instead of cradling the baby in the crook of his arm, he placed the baby on his chest. Luke was wearing a V-neck T-shirt, and he pulled it down, so little Virginia's head was on his skin. He turned away from everyone and began shushing her over and over as he bounced lightly on his feet. After several seconds, she settled down, closed her eyes, and went to sleep.

When Luke turned around, everyone was staring at him again.

"What?" he asked.

"You're, like, a baby whisperer," Joe said. "I'm calling you first to babysit."

"Screw that. I'm calling you in the middle of the night," Shelly added.

Luke smiled. "It's not that hard to do. I put her on my chest, so she can hear my heart beating, and I moved my shirt down, so she can have skin-to-skin contact. And then either rock her or bounce her as you make a *shh* noise."

"Nope," Joe said. "You're still a baby whisperer."

Luke laughed softly so as not to wake Virginia as he continued to bounce her in his arms. He kissed her downy head before looking up at Elise, and when he did, he couldn't quite read the expression on her face, but she looked like she was in awe.

CHAPTER TWENTY-SIX

Elise ran her hand down Luke's bare back and nude butt as she lay on her side, facing him, until she reached the sheet just under his ass and then went back up again. He was lying naked on her bed, facedown, with the leg opposite hers bent and one of her pillows covering the top of his head. She wasn't sure if he was falling asleep or just resting, and she didn't care either way as long as she could keep touching him.

He was so beautiful to look at. His back was muscular and tan, as was his butt. He had a slight farmer's tan where his shirtsleeves hit his arms and even where his shorts hit his waist, but it wasn't significant because he was already dark. She wondered if he had any idea how gorgeous he was.

Oh, he knew he was good-looking, but she didn't think he understood that he was perfection. She wanted to take a picture and put it on display at an art museum so that everyone would be graced with his beauty. Yet, at the same time, she wanted to take a picture and hide it away, so she didn't have to share it with anyone else.

Elise braced herself on one elbow and continued to skim her fingers over his back and buttocks, enjoying the feel of him. "Hey, Luke?"

"Yeah?" he said, his head still under the pillow. He was facing away from her, but his mouth was free, so she could make out what he'd said.

"You were great today."

"What part?"

"All of it. Being patient with my niece, helping me move all my crap, the laundry room, and the way you calmed Shelly and Joe's baby."

He didn't say anything at first, but she could see the corner of his mouth tip up.

She leaned over and kissed the middle of his back. "You're amazing. I hope you know that. I don't know what happened between you and Sean, but I know you were bothered by it."

Luke moved the pillow to under his head and rolled over, bringing the sheet up enough to cover his groin. He grabbed her hand that she'd been using to touch him and linked their fingers together while putting his free arm behind his head to prop himself up more.

"Sean knows about us."

Elise let herself fall back down on the bed. "Yeah, I figured."

"Are you upset?"

She looked into his face, and he seemed genuinely worried.

"No," she told him. "It was bound to come out sometime."

Her words seem to calm him.

"I don't think he's going to tell Rachel. That will still have to come from you."

"Darn it. Here I thought, I was getting out of doing it. But, at the same time, my phone hasn't been ringing off the hook, so I'm not surprised." Elise turned toward him. "I know Sean finding out isn't what upset you."

He gave her a half-smile. "You're right."

"Want to tell me what happened?"

Luke sighed with frustration and ran his hand over his face as he gazed at the ceiling. "Sean thinks I'm going to break your heart."

"What?"

"Yeah. I was insulted that he would think so little of me. I got upset and yelled at him because everyone thinks that I'm some womanizer who only cares about himself." He turned his head toward her. "For the record, I have no intentions of hurting you."

"I know," she whispered.

And she did know that. She one hundred percent knew that Luke wouldn't hurt her. On purpose. It was the accidental heartbreaks that people needed to be wary of.

"What did he say then?"

Luke grunted and returned to staring up. "I didn't give him a chance to talk. I yelled at him about the fact that I dated someone for two years, but nobody knew because everyone just assumes I'm an asshole."

"No one thinks you're an asshole," she told him. "And I'm sorry."

"For what?"

"For being one of those people who thought that you were a player. When I heard you were coming to dinner back in June, I immediately thought of how you were in college, despite several years having passed."

He picked up their twined hands and kissed the back of hers. "Thank you."

It was Elise's turn to sigh, but hers was due to anxiety. She'd wanted to ask Luke about Ava ever since Nate brought her up, but she didn't know how. She hadn't wanted to seem pushy or clingy. And, now that Luke had opened the door, Elise saw her chance and took it even if she wasn't sure that she'd like the outcome.

"This two-year relationship...was that Ava?"

Luke's head swung toward her. "How did you hear that name?"

"Nate."

"That fucker."

Elise laughed but was bothered at the same time. Did Luke not want Elise to know about his ex? "If you don't want to talk about her, I understand."

"No, she's not a secret or anything. It's just that, that guy has a way of always sticking his nose in other people's business."

"Oh," Elise said, mostly because she didn't know how else to respond.

"I met Ava about five years ago. Her father is a surgeon at the hospital. He introduced us while I was still in my residency, and I thought things were great between us. Then, she started dropping little hints about how much money her dad made and how he could get me into the surgical program. I told her that I was sticking with emergency medicine. I didn't choose it because I wasn't good enough to be a surgeon or something else. It's what I wanted to do ever since I was ten years old and broke my leg. She didn't get it though. Eventually, she broke up with me. Last I heard, she got herself that surgeon husband, and they live in some mansion."

"Oh, Luke." She squeezed their fingers.

To be made to feel like you weren't good enough by someone you cared about was a horrible feeling. Especially when you were more than good enough.

Poor Luke.

He shrugged. "I'm glad I got out while I could. If I had done what she wanted, I could only imagine what would have been next. I have a feeling that nothing would have ever been good enough for her.

"And I wasn't raised that way. My parents taught me to be happy and appreciative. Ava was always looking for something better. At first, I thought she was driven, but now, I see that she was constantly unsatisfied. I actually feel bad for the poor shmuck who married her because I doubt he makes her happy either."

They lay in silence for a few minutes.

Then, Elise asked the second question she'd been wondering about since she heard Ava's name, "Did you love her?"

He shrugged again. "I thought I did. Of course, now that I've been out of the relationship for two years, I see things in a new light. And you know what they say about hindsight. Plus, I'm really starting to see things differently."

"How so?"

Luke extracted his fingers from hers and rolled on top of her. "How about we don't talk about her anymore?"

Elise had about fifty more questions, but she could see that Luke was done, and she didn't blame him. She didn't want to talk about her exes either. At least, not for very long and not with the guy she was currently, literally, in bed with.

She reached up and ran her fingers through his hair. "What do you want to do instead?"

Luke smiled at her. "Well, we have several rooms left to christen."

Elise laughed. "Maybe we can hold off on that. I'm a little"—she looked down—"sore."

They'd had sex twice in her basement and then twice after they got home from the hospital. And, considering that Luke wasn't a small guy, she was feeling it down below.

Luke grimaced. "Sorry, baby."

She put a finger to his lips. "No apologies."

She didn't want him to feel guilty. She'd been a full and willing participant. He didn't need to apologize.

"We're not really going to have sex in every room in my house though, are we?"

Luke smiled. "The hell we aren't. I have some pretty creative ideas for your closets and pantry."

"Oh, really? Do tell."

"No way. You're just going to have to wait to find out."

"Well, if it involves you, then the wait will be worth it."

"Damn, woman, you always know the right thing to say." He leaned down and kissed her, slowly and gently.

She opened her mouth, and he slipped his tongue inside. She loved the taste of Luke. She wrapped her arms around him and pulled him closer. She continued to kiss him as she spread her legs, so Luke could settle between them. His cock hit her right on her clit, and she rubbed against him.

Luke groaned and moved to roll away from her, but she held him tight.

"Don't go."

"Lise, I have only so much control."

Elise didn't answer. She just kissed him again. She arched, and the head of his penis slipped inside her.

Luke broke their kiss and put his forehead against hers. "Elise."

"Luke."

"Are you trying to kill me? I'm going to die from the worst case of blue balls."

"We can't have that now, can we?" She tilted her pelvis, taking him more inside her.

"Jesus Christ. You are trying to kill me."

Elise laughed and coyly bit her lip.

"Baby, I love playing with you, but I really have to move to the other side of the bed now."

"But I don't want you to go," she said seriously.

"You said you're sore. I don't want to hurt you."

It was true. She was tender and swollen, but she still wanted him again. "Just go slow, okay?"

"Are you sure? Because, if you're not, you need to tell me now."

She touched his face, stroking his cheek. "I'm sure."

That was all it took for Luke to push the rest of the way inside her. She bit her lip again because there was a quick bite of pain, but it passed right away.

"You okay?"

She nodded. "Yes."

Luke kissed her again and softly moved, testing how much she could take. He tenderly shifted inside her, not thrusting, only moving their bodies enough to create a slight friction. He kissed her on her mouth, her neck, and her breasts, all while he rocked into her over and over again. He was sweet and gentle, and Elise was surprised but not really when Luke brought her to orgasm this way, too.

When they were done and Luke had come deep inside her, he gradually pulled out. There was a small tug, as if her body didn't want to let go of his. As he gathered her up in his arms, she completely understood. She didn't want to let go of him either.

And Elise knew it was time to tell Rachel about her relationship with Luke. She would take her friend out for lunch and tell her everything.

That was the idea anyway. Unfortunately, life sometimes had other plans.

CHAPTER TWENTY-SEVEN

A couple of days later, Luke stepped into the break room at work to grab a quick snack. So far, the morning had been pretty slow, which only made the day drag on. As much as he hated when there was an overflow of patients, he thrived on the adrenaline. That was why he loved being an emergency room doctor. Maybe, someday, he'd get into private practice, but that wouldn't happen for a long time.

Since Luke had a few minutes to kill, he pulled out his phone to see if he'd missed anything important.

What the hell?

There were seven missed calls from Elise within the last twenty-five minutes. Since there were several other people in the break room, Luke went to find a place where he could talk to her in private.

Finding an empty ER room, Luke dialed Elise.

"Lu-Lu-ke?"

Damn. She was crying.

His heart went into his throat. "Elise, what's wrong?"

"My-my dad. Can you come here?"

Luke closed his eyes. *Crap.* He had almost six hours of his shift left. "Lise—"

"*Please.* I need you. My dad is really si-sick. I don't know what to do."

Shit.

If her dad was really sick, then he should be brought to the hospital.

"Can you bring him here?"

"No. He's—" She didn't finish because she started crying harder.

Fuck.

He couldn't stay here when something was obviously wrong. With her father's history, he was at risk for so many serious conditions.

"Baby, listen, I'll be there as soon as I can, okay? Are you at your parents' house?"

"No-no, mine."

What was her father doing at her house? Had he gone over there because he didn't feel good? Or had something happened while he was there?

Elise would never forgive herself if she thought she was to blame.

"I'll be there in fifteen minutes."

"Th-thank you."

Luke hit End on his phone and went to talk to his coworkers. He needed to let them know that he had to leave for personal reasons. Now, he was thankful the morning had been slow. Hopefully, it would remain that way until someone came in to cover for him.

Luke didn't even change his clothes before leaving and heading for Elise's. If he had a patient to look after, he might as well keep his scrubs on.

Climbing into his SUV and taking off, Luke tried to keep all negative thoughts out of his mind and concentrate on his soon-to-be patient, but he couldn't deny that he was feeling uncertain. He understood that Elise trusted his skills as an MD, which he really did appreciate, especially after dating Ava. But would she have called him to come if he wasn't a doctor?

He knew that wasn't the important thing. Her father's health was, but he just couldn't ignore the doubt that lingered in the back of his mind.

Damn, am I turning into a woman? He might have to check his pants later to see if his dick was still in there.

Luke got to Elise's house in record time, hitting all green lights on the way. At least, now, he was in full professional mode, forgetting all about his qualms.

He knocked on Elise's door, wanting to be quiet at first in case her father was sleeping, but when she didn't answer, he rang the doorbell. When she still didn't come to let him in, he tried the knob to find it unlocked.

"Elise?"

No answer.

He walked through the whole main level, softly calling her name. Still nothing. He went upstairs and saw her bedroom door was slightly ajar, and he had a moment of hesitation about what he would find in there. He would hate to walk in and see something that Elise couldn't come back from, like her father dying.

He pushed the door open. Elise was lying on her side, facing away from him. He quietly approached the bed. She was sleeping. But, even in slumber, she looked tense. She had dark circles under her eyes and was frowning. It wasn't a peaceful nap.

He sat on the edge of the bed and shook her shoulder. "Elise?"

She slowly opened her eyes, blinking a few times from the bright sunlight streaming through her window. When she saw his face, the relief that fell over hers was so obvious that he couldn't help but feel humbled.

He rubbed a hand over her hair. "Hey."

Her lower lip quivered.

"Where's your dad, honey?"

She flew upright, threw herself into his arms, and started bawling.

Realizing he wasn't going to solve the mystery of her missing father with her so emotional, he pulled her onto his lap and held her close. He rubbed her back and tried to offer comforting words.

After most of her crying was finished, she pulled away and wiped the tears from her eyes. Luke snatched a tissue from her nightstand, so she could blow her nose.

She was sniffling some, but she was able to speak at least. "He's at Mayo."

Understanding struck Luke, as he realized that Elise hadn't called him to check on her dad. She had called him because she wanted him. Just *him*. Not the doctor.

He wanted to kiss her, but now wasn't the time.

"What's wrong?" he asked instead.

"My dad's really sick. He just had a small cough, and then he started to feel worse last night. He refused to go to the hospital because he had a doctor's appointment today, saying it could wait. My mom was barely able to wake him up this morning. He basically went from the bed to the car. But, instead of taking him to the local ER, she drove *two hours* away and had my dad sit in the waiting room for another half an hour. Thank God his oncologist took one look at him and had him admitted. But I can't help but be angry with my mother for being so negligent with him. If only I hadn't moved out..."

Luke met her eyes. "Hey. You are not blaming yourself."

"But—"

"No. This is not your fault." He raised his brow. "Okay?"

"Okay."

"I'm serious, Elise."

He wanted to tell her that it wasn't really her mother's fault either. Most people who weren't in the medical field didn't have the education to recognize certain things. He was sure Elise's mom was beating herself up pretty badly all on her own. But he wasn't going to say that to Elise. She was worried, and from having a mother and two sisters, he knew she just needed someone to listen to her.

"I tried to go and see him," Elise told Luke, putting her head down. "But, every time I tried to drive there, I would start crying and couldn't see anything. I didn't want my mother to have to visit someone else in the hospital."

Poor Elise.

She was feeling responsible for moving out and not being there last night, and now, she felt guilty for not going to the hospital.

"Do you want me to drive you?"

Her head whipped up. "You'd do that?"

"Course. Just let me change real quick."

She brushed her lips across his. "Thank you."

He kissed her back and moved her from his lap to the bed. "I'll be ready in five minutes."

She nodded, and he went to fetch his clothes from his vehicle.

Four and a half minutes later, they were pulling out of her driveway.

The drive to Rochester was about two hours, which seemed like a long way to go when there were numerous hospitals in the Minneapolis-St. Paul area. But, considering that people came from all over the country and sometimes all over the world to visit the Mayo Clinic, two hours was nothing.

"Why don't you try to nap some more?"

"Okay," she agreed as she put her seat back.

He turned up the stereo in his SUV, hoping the music would help lull her to sleep, but she continued to fidget every few minutes.

Keeping his eyes on the road, he took her hand and pulled her toward him. She didn't protest or question his motives. She laid her head down in his lap and adjusted her seat belt to make herself more comfortable. She still didn't fall asleep right away, but she did eventually let slumber take her.

When they only had about a half hour left of the drive,

Luke's stomach rumbled. He remembered that he'd never eaten anything on his morning break, so he hadn't eaten anything since about five a.m. It was close enough to lunchtime that he decided to stop and get food.

He searched for the closest drive-through, so they wouldn't have to waste time in getting to Elise's dad. He ordered food for both of them because, surprisingly, Elise didn't wake up the whole time he picked up their food. The guy at the drive-through window smirked when he saw Elise's head in his lap, but Luke ignored him. *Teenagers.*

When they were only ten minutes away—thank you, GPS—Luke woke Elise.

"Hey. Elise. It's time to wake up."

She stirred, and he put his hand on her hair.

"Be careful. Don't hit the steering wheel, babe."

Elise slowly sat up, still groggy. The circles under her eyes had lessened but were still there.

He reached into the fast-food bag and pulled out the cheeseburger he'd gotten her. "Here. I didn't know exactly what to get you."

She pushed his hand away. "I'm not hungry."

"Lise, you need to eat. When was the last time you ate?"

She scowled but snatched the burger from his hand. "Fine." She unwrapped it and took a big bite. She looked pained, but she chewed it up and swallowed. "Are you happy now?"

"No, but I'm better," he told her. "I don't want to worry about you getting sick, too."

He saw some of the anger leave her body as she took another bite—this time, with no coaxing.

He stared straight ahead at the road and told her, "Thank you."

"Humph. You're a meanie, Dr. L."

Luke chuckled. "As long as you're healthy and happy, you can call me whatever you want."

Elise didn't reply, but she took his hand and laced their fingers together while she managed to eat her entire sandwich.

CHAPTER TWENTY-EIGHT

Elise tightly grasped Luke's hand as they rode the elevator up to her father's room. She was so afraid of what she would find when she got up there. She knew her dad was alive, but beyond that, she had no idea what his condition was.

She gazed at Luke and squeezed his hand. He looked down at her and gave her a reassuring smile. She was so grateful that he was with her.

When she'd called him this morning, she hadn't even thought about it. She'd just known that she needed Luke, so she'd dialed his number.

Now that she'd gotten some rest, she remembered that he'd had to work today, so that meant he'd left to come and take care of her. She felt guilty but not guilty enough to wish she hadn't called him because he was the one who she wanted there with her.

He had taken such good care of her so far, and if it hadn't been for him, she didn't know if she would have found her dad. Despite being called the Mayo Clinic, it was anything but. It had two hospital campus locations and various buildings with numerous clinics in those buildings. Basically, if you didn't know where you were going, you were screwed.

She let go of Luke's hand and linked her arm through his as she rested her head against his shoulder. She hoped he knew how much she appreciated him, but she would have to make sure and tell him later.

When the elevator stopped, she kissed his shoulder before the doors opened for them to step out. Luke twined their fingers together again, and they followed the signs to the correct room.

When they got there, Elise saw her mom sitting next to her father's bed, staring off into space. There was a curtain pulled around the bed, so all Elise could see was her mother. The door was partially open, and Elise didn't even bother knocking before she pushed it open and entered the room.

"Elise," her mother said, rising to her feet when she saw her daughter.

Her mom held out her arms. While Elise was still angry with her mother, she didn't really blame her for her father's condition, and she willingly went into her arms.

"*Hello*, Luke," her mother said as she squeezed Elise to her.

Elise had to fight to hold back the tears. She didn't want to cry again. At least, not right now. Right now, she just wanted to talk to the doctor and find out what was wrong with her dad.

"Hello, Mrs. Phillips."

Her mom released Elise. "Please, call me Suzanne." She

took Luke's hand. "I'm so glad you could bring Elise here to visit."

Elise stepped around her mom and Luke and got a good look at her father for the first time. She gasped when she saw him. "Oh, Daddy," she whispered.

Her father had several IVs, a nasal cannula, a pulse ox, heart monitor, and several other things hooked up to him.

Elise collapsed in the chair next to him on the opposite side of the bed as her mother.

Her mom took her own seat, and Luke came to stand behind Elise. He put his hand on her shoulder, and she welcomed his strength at a time like this.

"Where's Kristen?" Luke asked.

Elise's hand flew to her mouth. "Oh my God. I didn't even call her." The only person she'd called was Luke. One more thing for her to feel guilty about. "We could have ridden together. I'm a horrible sister."

Luke squeezed her shoulder as her mom said, "Don't worry. I called her. She was at work but left. She's on her way."

A rush of relief washed over her. "Thank God."

The nurse came in to check on her father several times but wouldn't tell them much, saying that the doctor would be along any minute now.

Two hundred forty-three minutes later, the doctor walked in.

Any minute now, my ass.

The only good thing about the delay was that it had given her sister time to arrive. She was alone, and Elise didn't bother asking why her brother-in-law hadn't come.

"I'm Dr. Olson," an older gentleman with gray hair said after he walked into the hospital room, commanding attention.

He looked like he'd been doing this a long time. His eyes were all business. Dr. Olson wasn't mean, but he wasn't kind either. It was apparent to Elise that her father was just another part of Dr. Olson's job, not someone's family member.

"I'm the hospitalist on today. Mr. Phillips has sepsis, which is an infection in his blood."

"But he just had a cold," Elise's mom protested.

"That's how it started, but, Mrs. Phillips, your husband is on chemo. The chemo doesn't just kill the cancer; it also kills good things in the body. Because of this, your husband's immune system is very weak, and he was unable to fight off his cold like he normally would. Didn't your husband's oncologist inform you to seek medical attention at even the slightest thing?"

Her mom closed her eyes in regret. "Yes. But my husband was just in the hospital for a blood clot, and I didn't want to pressure him to come to the hospital again. He hates hospitals. And, since he had his appointment today, I figured it would be okay to wait." Her mother looked down at her hands as she wrung them. "Clearly, I was mistaken."

"Yes, well, next time, take him to the hospital right away."

What an asshole. Would it kill this doctor to reassure her mother just a little that it wasn't her fault?

Luke must have read her expression because he put his hands on her shoulders and lightly massaged her neck until she calmed.

"Mr. Phillips's condition has reached the point where he is neutropenic. This means, his white blood count—the cells that fight off infection—are very low. The next twenty-four hours are the most critical for him."

Elise's vision blurred as new tears formed in her eyes, and she heard her sister sniffle next to her while her mother used a tissue to blot her face.

And, with that, the doctor was gone. No parting words, no wishes for the best, nothing.

Elise turned around to Luke. "Please don't ever be an insensitive butthole like that."

"Elise, language!"

Oh, Mom, even when Dad is on his deathbed, you're all about propriety.

It was a good thing she hadn't really said what she thought about Dr. Olson.

"I agree," Kristen said. "Where's his compassion?"

"It's not an excuse," Luke said, "but some people have been doing this a long time, and they forget why they started in the first place."

"That's sad," Elise said.

"It is," Luke said. "I will do my best to never end up like that."

Hours later, the sun had fallen, and there was no change in Elise's dad. Her mom, Kristen, and she hadn't moved, except to use the restroom. If it hadn't been for Luke, none of them would have eaten anything. He'd gone out and gotten dinner for the three of them without anyone asking him to.

"You three should go home," Elise's mother told them.

"No way," Kristen said.

"Honey, you heard the nurse the last time she was in here. There won't be any change tonight, and you sitting here won't make your father better. He would want you rested."

"What about you, Mom?" Elise asked.

"I got a hotel room here earlier. I was lucky there was a cancelation for a single; otherwise, I would let you stay with me. Well, you girls, anyway. Sorry, Luke, but I couldn't have you staying with us."

Luke looked like he was trying not to laugh. "I understand."

Elise was about to offer to sleep in the car, but she'd ridden with Luke. And, while her sister had driven separately, it wasn't fair to ask her sister to stay overnight in her car. She probably wanted to get home to Jennifer.

Her mother sealed the deal when she said, "Elise, can you bring me some stuff tomorrow? I can give you a list."

"Of course, Mom."

The drive home was uneventful, and even though Elise's mind was going over and over her father's condition, she fell asleep. She vaguely felt Luke lift her out of his SUV and carry her into the house.

The next thing she remembered was waking up and seeing her alarm clock read 1:38 a.m. She was wearing a T-shirt and her underwear. She didn't remember Luke changing her.

She wondered when he'd left and why he hadn't said good-bye. Even if he'd wanted to let her sleep, it would have been nice.

She rolled onto her back and was surprised to look over into Luke's sleeping face. He hadn't left after all. She shouldn't be feeling any happiness with her father in the hospital, but she couldn't help but feel joy upon seeing Luke in bed beside her.

He must have sensed that she was awake because he opened one eye. "Are you okay?"

"Yes," she said. And she meant it. She brushed her hand down his chest. "I'm sorry I woke you."

He pulled her close and kissed the top of her head. "No worries."

She snuggled into him, and they both fell back to sleep.

CHAPTER TWENTY-NINE

L uke woke to the sound of his alarm going off early in the morning. He snatched his phone off the nightstand and hit Dismiss before it could wake Elise. It was set for working the day shift, and he'd forgotten to turn it off before he went to bed last night. He had already taken care of his shift today, so he didn't have to worry about going into work. But, now, he was awake and wouldn't be able to go back to sleep.

Luke was lying on his side with Elise curled up behind him, her arm slung over his waist. Her fingers were clutching his boxers, as if she were worried he would leave. He carefully extracted her hand and rolled her onto her back, so he could slide out of bed. He grabbed his phone and then slipped on his jeans, not bothering to button them, as he left the room and closed the door behind him.

He went downstairs and started the coffee. Elise had been in her new home for only a few days, but she'd taken the week off from work to unpack, and she had made good progress. Although now she would be using her time off to visit her sick father. Maybe Elise could drive to Rochester today by herself, and Luke could help out by doing some more unpacking for her.

Luke rummaged around for something to eat for breakfast. This was only the second time that he'd stayed at Elise's house. He'd spent the night the day she moved in, but since he'd had to work early on Monday and Tuesday, he'd stayed home.

It was kind of crazy to think that Elise and he hadn't actually spent that many nights together. With her living at her parents', she would come to his house but always went home to sleep, except for their first night together and when her dad had been in the hospital the first time. Elise having her own place was going to make it a lot easier for them to be together.

Luke found bacon and eggs, but it was still too early to make them. He wanted Elise to sleep longer because she needed the rest. But, since he was still hungry, he selected a banana, picked up his coffee, and headed for the family room to turn on the morning news.

He didn't make it far before there was a pounding at the front door. Who in the hell would be making so much noise at six fifteen in the morning? Luke rushed to the door, setting his cup on the counter on the way, before whoever was out there woke up Elise.

He took a quick peek out the window in the front door before opening it. It was Rachel, and she looked upset.

Luke swung the door open. "Is everything okay?"

Rachel scanned Luke from head to toe, probably taking in his messy hair, his bare chest, his unbuttoned jeans, and his bare feet. There was no denying that Luke had slept there, so he didn't even try to hide it. He was going to own that shit. He did, however, button up his pants.

"No," Rachel said, pushing Luke out of the way and barging into the house. "I don't even know where to start," she practically yelled.

Luke held out his hand and pushed it down. "Shh, Elise is still sleeping." He walked past her and motioned for her to go with him. "Come on, I'll pour you some coffee. I'm guessing you have some questions."

Rachel followed, stomping behind him. "You're damn right I do."

"How do you take your coffee?" Luke asked before taking the last bite of his banana and tossing the peel in the garbage.

"Black is fine."

Luke poured Rachel a cup while she took a seat at the kitchen table. He set it in front of her and then sat across from her.

"What can I do for you?" he asked.

"First, how is Elise's dad?"

"Critical. Hopefully, things are better this morning, but we haven't heard anything since we left the hospital last night." Luke leaned back in his chair. "Didn't Elise tell you?"

Rachel scowled. "No. She didn't tell me anything. The only reason I know anything is because Sean told me, and Sean knew because you'd canceled your plans last night and told him."

Whoops.

Luke wasn't sure if he had messed up or not. He'd texted

Sean to cancel, and he had just assumed Elise had told her best friend about her father right away. And, since Sean knew about Elise and Luke, he hadn't bothered to keep anything private. And he really couldn't imagine Elise wanting to keep Rachel in the dark about her dad, which meant that Elise had probably forgotten to call her, like she'd forgotten to call her sister.

The realization that Elise had called him and only him made him want to smile, but he wouldn't dare in front of Rachel right now.

Not only had Elise called him when she was in distress, but she also hadn't asked him to do one doctor thing at the hospital yesterday. When her father's doctor had left and she'd called him a butthole, Luke had briefly wondered if she'd ask him to go talk to him, doctor to doctor. But she hadn't even hinted that it was what she wanted from him. He'd wanted to kiss her right in front of her mother.

Focusing back on the current conversation, Luke told Rachel, "I'm sorry she didn't tell you. She was very upset. She even forgot to call Kristen."

"I tried calling and texting her several times."

"She turned her phone on Do Not Disturb when we left the hospital, so only her mom's and sister's phone calls would come through."

Rachel crossed her arms. "Yet, somehow, you knew, and you were there."

"Yeah, about that. That is something you and Elise need to talk about. I'm not going to get in the middle of it," Luke said as he lifted his cup to take a sip of coffee.

"You mean, the fact that you're fucking one of my closest

friends like she's one of your whores?" Her voice dripped with hostility.

Luke slammed his cup on the table and pointed a finger at Rachel. "Don't you dare talk about Elise like that."

Rachel blanched at his words, dropping her arms. Her face showed surprise and then softened. "You're right. That was completely uncalled for. I shouldn't have suggested that..." She waved her hand for Luke to fill in the blank in his head.

Except Luke wasn't going to let her off that easily. "That she's a whore. No, you shouldn't have."

Rachel grimaced. "I'm sorry."

As she should be.

"Look, I just don't want her to get hurt."

This time, Luke crossed his arms.

"Sean told me that this isn't some fling to you, but I wouldn't be a good friend if I didn't look out for her."

"Why does everyone think I'm such a bad guy?"

Rachel sighed. "It's not that we think you're a bad guy. We're just thinking of your history." She held her arms off, as if to ward off his protests. "I know college was a long time ago, but it's what most of us know."

"Well, how about this? Did it ever occur to anyone that I didn't get serious in college because the girls didn't want to, not because I didn't want to?"

Rachel looked at him like he'd grown another head.

"Yeah, I'm not saying I wanted to date every chick I slept with, but most girls just saw me as some conquest. Some big hockey player to add to their roster. It wasn't even just the puck bunnies. There were a few girls in there who were more on the serious side and didn't follow hockey. But they pretty much laughed in my face when I brought up seeing them again. Apparently, I was only good enough for a roll in the hay."

Luke hadn't even told Elise this. Let's face it; it was downright embarrassing to only be wanted for your dick.

"I...I had no idea."

"Well, now, you do. I really have no intentions of hurting Elise. If anything, I'm the one who could end up being the injured party."

"Why do you say that?"

"You're going to think I'm crazy, but has Elise ever talked about other guys she's slept with?"

"You mean, how all her boyfriends are duds in bed?"

Luke didn't know why he was surprised that Rachel knew this, but he was.

He cleared his throat. "That, and the only guys she was able to...achieve a climax with were not boyfriend material, according to Elise."

"Yeah, I've noticed that, too."

"Well, I don't mean to toot my own horn, but let's just say that Elise is satisfied in that area with me. Very satisfied. So, I can't help but wonder how long I'm going to last. What I don't understand is why."

"I think it has something to do with her parents and how she was raised. She seems so different from them, but it seems like there must be some weird things ingrained in her that she doesn't even know about."

"I noticed." Luke stood, took his coffee cup to the sink, and rinsed it out.

Rachel didn't say anything more as Luke put his cup in the dishwasher, and she got up to use the bathroom. He grabbed the bacon and eggs out of the fridge when he heard soft footsteps coming from the front of the house and then up behind him. A pair of feminine arms slipped around his waist.

"Are you going to cook me breakfast?" Elise asked.

Luke turned around and pulled her close. "That was the idea."

Elise stood on her tiptoes and kissed him. "You're so sweet."

"Did you find out anything about your dad?"

"No, I'm going to call my mom in a minute. I just wanted to say good morning to you."

Luke rubbed her back. "So, does this mean that you haven't checked your phone at all?"

"No...why?"

"Because Rachel's here."

"Uh-oh."

"Uh-oh is right," Rachel said, appearing from around the corner.

CHAPTER THIRTY

E lise hit End on her phone from her spot in the recliner and looked up at Luke and Rachel, who sat on opposite ends of the couch.

"How's your dad?" Luke asked. He was close enough to reach for her hand and give it a reassuring squeeze.

"Better, but he's not out of the woods. I'm going to go see him again today. And I need to stop by my parents' house before I go, so I can get my mom a change of clothes and some other stuff." Elise looked at Rachel. "But I suppose we should talk first."

"That would be nice," Rachel said.

"I'll just go upstairs and shower while you two talk." Luke stood and kissed Elise on the forehead.

"Thanks," Elise told him.

After Luke left the room, Rachel said, "He even keeps clothes here?"

"No, he keeps extra clothes with him all the time because of work."

"Oh," Rachel said. "But he's your boyfriend?"

Elise had never said it out loud, but that was exactly how she thought of Luke. "Yes."

Rachel looked crushed.

Elise's shoulders sunk under the weight of guilt. "Rachel, I'm—"

"Why didn't you tell me?" Rachel asked, her voice small and laced with pain.

Elise got up and moved to the sofa to sit, facing her friend. "Oh, Rachel, I'm so sorry. When it started out, I didn't want you to be mad at me for sleeping with Luke after you warned me not to. Then, it seemed like the longer I waited, the worse it would be to tell you. And Luke and I were having fun, keeping it private. It was our own little secret. Did you really have no clue?"

"I don't know. I thought something might be going on but nothing definitive. I thought you might be seeing someone because you were busy a lot of nights, but that could also be explained by living with your parents."

"And I was busy with them a lot," Elise reassured her. "You know I didn't go on our girls' weekend trip because of my dad, not because I was hanging out with Luke."

"I know. I wasn't even sure if there was some guy. And I did notice that you and Luke seemed to be becoming better and better friends. You played pool with him that first night, you hung out with him quite a bit at our Fourth of July party, and then Luke had asked Nate to help you move before Sean even brought it up. So, while I wasn't thinking you might be seeing someone, I thought you might be developing a crush on Luke. But, when you told me you'd never sleep with him, I thought you meant it."

Elise blushed. "Well, I did at the time. I really wasn't planning on sleeping with the guy."

"So, when did it happen, and how did you guys get from there to here?"

Elise laughed uncomfortably. "Well..."

Rachel cocked her head to the side. "You didn't."

Elise winced. "I did. But, in my defense, it was mostly the alcohol talking. I still don't remember half of that night."

Rachel raised her brow.

"I know, I know. Alcohol is not an excuse. But it is," she whined.

Rachel laughed, so that was good. "So then, what happened?"

"He texted me the following Monday. I thought he'd just done it to sleep with me again, but you could say that's when our friendship really started. You know, I even hung out at his house without having any physical contact."

"Really?"

"Really."

"Then, Luke kissed me in your garage at your party, which kind of made me realize that I wanted to sleep with him again. You remember when I spilled my drink on him?"

Rachel nodded. "Oh, yes. How could I forget? That was funny."

"Well, I hadn't realized Luke was a doctor and that he was in doctor mode when he was looking at Tera's leg. I'm ashamed to admit, I got a teensy bit jealous, and I might have purposely let my cup tip over until the contents landed on Luke."

Rachel threw her head back and laughed. "Oh my God, that is hilarious. I thought it was an accident."

"Well, I wasn't going to admit that it wasn't."

"Is that why you went to his house to apologize?"

"Yes."

"I always wondered why you couldn't have just waited until he came back to the party."

"I felt really bad and immature about the whole thing. I couldn't have it eating away at me."

Rachel nodded. "I get it. But it sure took you a long time." A look crossed her face. "You two got it on at my party, too."

Elise held up a finger. "It really wasn't at your party, just during. You were the one who got it on *at* your party. With guests waiting no less."

"Guilty." This time, Rachel blushed. "So, how did you end up with Luke being the one to take you to see your dad?"

Elise shrugged because she didn't know what to say really. "I don't know. When I found out he was in the hospital, I just knew I needed Luke. I'm sorry I didn't call you."

"It's okay. I guess."

"Are you really mad at me?"

"Not *really* mad."

Elise stuck out her lip. "So, just mad then."

Rachel sighed. "No. I want to be, but I'm not."

"I really am sorry for everything."

"I know, and I forgive you. Except you know that I am on summer vacation, so I wouldn't have to take time off work to go with you to see your dad."

"Oh, great. Make me feel worse, why don't you?"

Rachel shrugged, her expression saying, *Sorry, not sorry.*

"So, you told me everything about now, but did anything ever happen back in college that you didn't tell me about?"

"No, absolutely not. I wanted nothing to do with him."

"So, why now?"

"Well, if I'm honest with myself, I was attracted to him back then, but I think I knew I couldn't handle anything with Luke."

"But you had one-night stands in college."

"I know, and call it intuition or something, but I guess I knew it would end up being more than that with him. I guess I thought I could handle a strictly sexual relationship now because I'm older, maturer, and more in touch with myself and what I want. Because, even though I blame a lot of it on alcohol, I'm the one who drank with him and let myself drink too much. I suppose a part of me thought sex could happen, and if I had really been afraid of sleeping with him, I wouldn't have gotten drunk."

"But you're glad everything happened the way it did?"

Elise leaned against the back of the couch. "I am."

Rachel smiled and leaned back, too, putting her head on Elise's shoulder. "Does he make you happy?"

Elise smiled. "Yeah, he does."

"Who'da thunk? You and Luke dating and him making you happy."

"Right?"

Rachel lifted her head. "I just have one more question."

"Shoot."

"How big is it?"

"*Rachel*," Elise scolded while trying not to laugh.

"I'm sorry. But, no, really, how big is it?"

Elise smirked at her friend and held up her two hands a distance apart to show her.

"Damn, no wonder he makes you happy."

Elise laughed and wiggled her eyebrows. "That, and he knows how to use it."

"Ha. I knew it. Like a rock star, right?"

Elise pushed her shoulder into Rachel's. "Not that you have anything to complain about. Little Ms. My Man Is Short But Not *Short*."

"What are you ladies talking about?"

They both shrieked and jumped in their seats. They hadn't heard Luke sneak up behind them.

He looked adorable with his dark hair wet and his brown eyes twinkling, but Elise tried to look mad that he had scared them when she really wanted to kiss him.

Before either of them had to come up with some lame topic to disguise their real conversation, Elise's front door burst open, and Sean came rushing in. He was wearing a suit, minus his jacket, with his tie askew, and he had sweat spots on his armpits. He stopped when he saw the three of them, and then he bent over at the waist to catch his breath.

"You okay, man?" Luke asked.

Sean stood, breathing hard. "No. *Someone* told me she was going to wait to confront Elise but then snuck off when I was in the shower and busy getting dressed. Then, when I realized she was gone, I found out my keys and my spare were missing, too."

"Holy shit, did you run all the way here?" Luke asked.

"No, I had to ride my bike," he said accusingly at his fiancée.

Elise stifled a laugh.

"Be right back," Luke said.

"Rach, did you really leave and take Sean's keys?" Elise asked.

Rachel stuck her chin up. "Yes, I did. I didn't want him to stop me from coming over here."

Sean shook his head. "You're going to get it later."

"Ooh," Elise said to her friend. "You're in trouble."

Luke returned with a bottle of water for Sean.

Sean drank half of it in one gulp and then wiped his mouth with the back of his hand. "So, what did I miss? You all looked pretty serious when I walked in." He lifted the bottle to take another drink.

"Oh, I just caught the *ladies*—and I use that term loosely —talking about our dicks."

Sean started coughing on his water, practically spitting it across the room. "Holy shit."

"*Luke*," Elise said.

But he continued on, "Yeah, what you saw was guilt on their faces because I'd busted them."

"That's not true," Rachel lied.

"You don't know what you're talking about," Elise protested.

Sean shook his head in mock disappointment. "You two are dirty, dirty girls."

"Yeah, you're a bunch of perverts," Luke said, grinning.

Elise and Rachel turned back around, facing away from the guys, and smiled at each other.

"Then, I guess you're never going to find out whose is bigger," Elise said.

"That's easy," Luke started.

"Mine is," both guys said at the same time.

Rachel rolled her eyes, and Elise laughed.

CHAPTER THIRTY-ONE

O ver the next couple of days, Luke and Rachel took turns in going to the Mayo Clinic with Elise. She had a great friend and boyfriend. Now that everyone knew about her and Luke, she had no problems saying boyfriend, and what was even better was that Luke had no problems calling her his girlfriend. If someone had told Elise when she moved back to Minnesota that she'd be dating Luke Long, she would have laughed in their face, but here she was.

Elise's dad was making a slow recovery, but he finally got well enough to go home, and so far, he was doing pretty well. Thankfully, Elise had already taken time off work to move, and she had explained about her father before she'd taken the job, so they understood that she might need time off at the last minute. She could never thank her former boss enough for the recommendation.

Today, Elise was meeting her sister for lunch, per Kristen's request to talk. They were going to have dinner tonight with their parents and Kristen's husband, and Elise had a feeling that something important was going to happen.

While waiting for Kristen and an available table, Elise stood in the entryway of their favorite restaurant when her phone began belting out "Kung Fu Fighting." Everyone turned their heads to look at her, and she laughed nervously while she cursed Luke out. He'd changed her ringtone for him, which had made her laugh. But he was forever turning her volume up to the max because he'd found the loudest recording, so when she was out in public, everyone would hear her phone and look at her.

Elise got the hostess's attention and pointed to the front door, so she would know that Elise hadn't left.

After she stepped outside, she answered her phone and greeted Luke with an, "I'm going to beat you."

Luke laughed in her ear, and she tried to not smile at the musical sound.

"What's wrong, Lise?"

"I told you I was going out to lunch with my sister, and I know you turned my ringer up and waited to call me when you knew I'd be at the restaurant. Sometimes, Lucas, I question your real age."

"Babe, if you haven't realized that there is a ten-year-old little boy in every man, lying dormant until the time is right, then you're in for a big disappointment."

Elise sighed. "Yeah, I know." At least, that had been her experience with men. "What did you need?"

"Nothing."

Nothing? "Then, why did you call?"

"I thought we just went over this."

Elise rolled her eyes. "I really am going to beat you."

"Sounds kinky."

Elise smiled. "What am I going to do with you, Luke?"

"So, you're not going to beat me? Damn."

"You know I'm not going to hurt you, no matter how mad you make me."

"You could tie me up and ride my cock until you came."

Elise's vagina clenched deep inside at the thought, and she struggled to keep her voice straight. "That doesn't sound like much of a punishment."

He lowered his voice. "It is if you don't let me come, and you get yourself off over and over again." He groaned in her ear. "Trust me, watching you use my cock as your own personal sex toy would be the ultimate punishment."

Elise stepped farther way from the entrance even though she was the only one outside. "Stop talking like that. I'm getting turned on."

"Then, you'd better get your ass over here later."

Elise saw her sister walking toward the building. "Deal. I'll try to come after dinner tonight. Gotta go though. Kristen's here."

"Okay. Later, babe."

Elise hung up the phone and waved at her sister. She could see lines of stress around Kristen's eyes.

Elise hugged Kristen, hoping she would realize that she could trust her sister with whatever was bothering her. They entered the restaurant, and thankfully, they only had to wait a couple of minutes for a table.

After they were seated and the server brought their drinks and taken their orders, Elise was over the small talk.

The longer Kristen waited to say something, the more worried Elise became. While she figured this had to do with her sister's marriage, Elise couldn't help but think of other bad things. The worst possible scenario would be that Kristen or Jennifer was sick, and if that were the case, Elise didn't know what she'd do.

Right before Elise was ready to tell her sister to spit it out, Kristen said, "I asked you to lunch because I really need your support tonight at dinner."

Elise didn't know what for, but she didn't have to. "You have it. One hundred percent."

"You don't even know what I'm going to say yet."

"I don't have to. You're my sister. I love you. I'm here for you."

"Still."

"I can guess. Things aren't working out with James."

She nodded. "He filed for divorce."

Elise leaned forward and took her sister's hand. "I am so sorry."

"Me, too."

"Why did you think I wouldn't support you? We'd already talked about this a while ago, so it's not like you're taking me by surprise. And I know Mom and Dad will be disappointed, but they will get over it. Eventually."

Kristen withdrew her hand from Elise's. "There's more."

More? How could there be more? "Are you pregnant? Because having a baby out of wedlock might give Mom a heart attack. But just a mild one. She'd recover."

Kristen chuckled at Elise's joke but only for a few seconds. "No, James says he doesn't want to live a lie

anymore. And, if I don't tell Mom and Dad the truth, then he will. To be honest, I don't want to lie anymore either."

Elise ruminated on the words. "I'm sorry. I don't know what you're talking about." Elise thought about it some more.

"He doesn't want to live a lie."

"Wait, does this mean that..." Elise sat back in her seat. "Does this mean, James is gay?"

Kristen swallowed. "Yes."

"That makes so much sense."

"What?"

"You know, I have never seen James check out a woman. And he was blushing around Luke and Nate when you guys helped me move. I'm not that surprised really."

"Huh?"

"I'm so sorry, Kristen. It must be awful to be married to someone you love who doesn't love you the same way."

Kristen just stared at Elise.

"What's wrong? Why are you staring at me?" *Do I have something on my face?*

"You don't think James is a bad person?"

Elise tilted her head to the side. "In what way? The fact that he's gay? No, not at all. The fact that he married a woman when he's into dudes? Then, yes, he should have never led you on."

Kristen looked down at her hands and muttered, "He never led me on."

"What?"

Her sister looked up at her. "I said, he never led me on."

Elise was confused. "I don't understand. Then, why did

you get involved with him? Why would you put yourself through that?"

"One, he was my best friend. Nobody got me like he did. We were each other's cover," her sister said.

And the light bulb went off in Elise's head. Suddenly, all these little details began to fill her mind. James was the only guy she'd dated, her super-close relationship with Ashley, and why she didn't look at guys, like James didn't look at girls.

"Oh, Kristen, you're gay, too."

Kristen nodded as tears began to roll down her face. Elise grabbed her sister's hands this time.

"You've been living with this inside you all this time? You must have felt so alone. Sweetie, I am so sorry."

Elise could not even imagine what it was like for her sister to live with hiding a big piece of who she was like that. Especially with their parents and their old-fashioned ways.

"So, this is why you want my support?"

Kristen looked so sad. "Yes."

"You still have it. I would never leave you to face Mom and Dad alone in this. That's what big sisters do. They protect their little sisters."

Kristen let go of Elise's hands and wiped her tears. "Thank you."

"Of course. But can I ask you something?"

"Sure."

"How do I have a niece?"

Kristen laughed through her tears. "James was my best friend. We both knew what the other one felt like because we were the only homosexual kids at church, and we thought, if

we tried to have straight sex, maybe we would like it, and all our problems would be solved."

"Oh, Kristen."

"Yeah, needless to say, our little experiment failed miserably. We both hated it, and we couldn't look each other in the eye for, like, a week. When I missed my period, it was the icing on the cake. Honestly, back then, I was kind of relieved. I knew our parents and James's parents would force us to get married. And, since I'd be married to my best friend, I figured everything would be great. I knew his secret, and he knew mine. And we got a beautiful daughter out of it. But the older Jennifer gets, the harder it is to hide stuff from her. She knows we don't have a normal marriage."

"Uh, yeah, I think she said something about how you've never shared a bedroom and how, lately, you've been going to Aunt Ashley's and James has been going to Uncle Adam's quite a bit."

"See! We're horrible parents."

"No, Kristen, you are not horrible parents. Yes, lying is wrong, but if you both come out now, you will show Jennifer that it's okay to be who she is. That everyone is different, and people love who they love."

"Man, you're insightful."

"Eh, maybe I should have been a psychologist," Elise joked.

The server brought their food, and they thanked him, letting their conversation pause momentarily.

After they dug into their food, Elise asked, "So, Ashley?"

Kristen blushed. "She's my girlfriend." She raised her

eyebrows. "Wow, I never thought I'd be able to say that to you."

"Doesn't it feel good to tell me?"

"Yes."

"And Adam is James's boyfriend?"

"Yes."

"So, why does James want a divorce now?"

"Adam wants to get married, and he's tired of waiting. I honestly don't blame him."

"Why now? Same-sex marriage has been legal in Minnesota for almost four years."

Kristen shrugged. "I think because it's legal in the whole US now. Plus, I think Adam is sick of being the other woman, so to speak."

Elise could understand that. It would be tough to not be able to be with the person you loved because they were stuck in a farce of a marriage.

"Kristen?"

"Yeah?" she said around a bite of food.

"Why didn't you ever tell me all this before? Did you think I would judge you?"

Elise's feelings were hurt because her sister hadn't trusted her. The irony was not lost on her that she and Rachel had had almost the same conversation, and now, Elise was on the opposite side. But Elise had kept her secret for about two months. Kristen had kept her secret for *years*.

"I can't really explain what it's like to be me and grow up in our church and with Mom and Dad. And society isn't as great as some people think it is. There is still a lot of judgment and prejudice. It's scary to tell people. Plus, I didn't

want you to have to keep it from Mom and Dad. I didn't want to put you in that position because I know how that feels."

"You know I'm not a saint. There are plenty of things I do that Mom and Dad would definitely not approve of."

"But are you a lesbian who got pregnant out of wedlock by a gay guy?"

Kristen had a point.

"Touché. You got me there. But I still wouldn't have judged you, and I would have kept your secret."

"I know." Kristen smiled at her. "I appreciate it." She sighed. "Now, I just have to get through telling Mom and Dad."

"I'll be right there with you."

"I'm glad because I'm scared shitless."

CHAPTER THIRTY-TWO

At dinner that night, Elise arrived at the restaurant after her parents. Kristen and James had chosen a restaurant where they would have some seclusion, but it was still a public place, so hopefully, it would keep the conversation civilized. James's parents were watching Jennifer for the night, so she wouldn't have to be involved.

Elise sat at the end of the table and noted her father looked well for having been on his deathbed recently, but he still didn't look completely like his old self. Elise feared he never would, and she worried what the stress of tonight's news would do to her father.

Her dad wasn't quite as conservative as her mother because, while her mother had grown up in the church, her father had married into it. Her mother hadn't grown up with a television in her home, and Elise probably wouldn't have had one either if it weren't for her father. But he wasn't exactly liberal. He had married her mother and converted to her religion after all.

Kristen and James walked into the restaurant a few minutes later, holding hands. Now that Elise's eyes were open, she could see that they were best friends supporting each other and not lovers, like everyone assumed just because they were a man and a woman. Elise had been as guilty as everyone else, and she was ashamed for not knowing her sister better.

It appeared, now that Kristen and James weren't fighting about getting divorced and had come to an agreement, their relationship was on the mend.

When the two of them arrived at the table, they sat across from her parents.

After their orders were put in, Elise could see how nervous Kristen was, so Elise grabbed her hand under the table and gave it a supportive squeeze.

Elise had reassured her sister prior to dinner that, no matter what the outcome, there were worse things in the world. Mom and Dad would recover from this. They loved their daughter, and they had gotten over Kristen getting pregnant before she was married. They would get over this, too.

At least, Elise hoped they would.

She knew her parents were conservative and close-minded, but they weren't mean. She couldn't see them disowning their own daughter or anything.

So far, her parents were making casual conversation while Kristen looked at James and then Elise. Elise nodded.

It was like a Band-Aid; Kristen just needed to rip it off.

"Mom, Dad?" Elise said.

Her parents stopped talking about whatever they'd been discussing and looked at her.

"Yes?" her mom said.

"Kristen needs to tell you guys something, and she really needs you to listen, okay?"

Their mom looked at Kristen. "Is everyone okay? No one else is sick, are they? Is Jennifer okay?"

"Mom, everyone is fine, health-wise."

Their father looked relieved.

Their mother put her hand on her chest. "Thank the Lord."

Elise mentally winced. Why did her mom have to bring up God right now?

When Kristen didn't continue, their mom asked, "What is it, dear?"

Kristen looked at James again and then back at her parents. "James and I are getting divorced."

Their parents looked more worried than mad. Okay, this was a good sign. Maybe they would take the rest of Kristen's news better than Kristen had originally feared.

"Well," their mother said, "we can fix this. We'll help you go through counseling. We'll have you talk to our pastor. This will all be fine."

"Yes," their father said. "We can also sign you up for one of the church's couples retreats. Your mother and I have done those before. They are very enlightening."

Elise's spine slumped in defeat for her sister already. Their parents weren't listening to Kristen. She'd said divorced, not that their marriage was in trouble.

"Mom, Dad, you don't understand. We don't want to be married to each other anymore."

Her mother shook her head. "No, no, no. This can't be

happening. You can't get"—her mother looked around and lowered her voice—"divorced."

"Mom, it's not a dirty word," Elise said. "Plenty of people get divorced nowadays."

"And that's what's wrong with this world, Elise," her father said. "People don't take marriage seriously or understand that God disapproves of divorce."

"I agree," Elise said, "to an extent. But what if the husband is abusive or if someone cheats on the other person? Are you just supposed to stay married if your husband is beating you?"

"I don't have the answers for that," her father said.

"It's not for us to decide," her mother said.

Elise was flabbergasted. Her parents hadn't said yes, but they hadn't said no either. That they actually considered it acceptable for someone to stay with an abusive spouse was more than Elise could comprehend, and it left her speechless.

James steered the conversation back to where they'd left off. "Ward, Suzanne, Kristen and I love each other very much. But we're not in love with each other, and we never have been."

"But there is still time," her mom said. "You could fall in love with each other."

Unbelievable.

They'd been married for seven years. Even if they weren't gay, they weren't going to fall in love with each other now if they hadn't in the last seven years.

"No," James said, "you don't understand. It's not going to happen."

"Then, explain it to us," Ward said.

Kristen and James exchanged looks.

"There is someone else, isn't there?" Ward said. He pointed his finger at James. "If you cheated on my daughter..."

Elise didn't even know how they were supposed to respond to that. Technically, yes, they'd both cheated on each other. But was it really cheating when Kristen and James weren't truly married—at least, in their hearts—to each other? And cheating meant secrecy and deception. Kristen and James knew about Ashley and Adam. Kristen had told Elise that she and James were best friends, and they didn't keep any secrets from each other. In fact, they confided in each other and looked to one another for guidance.

"Dad," Kristen spoke up before James had to say anything, "James didn't cheat on me. At least, not in the way you think. And, whatever James has done, I have done the same."

Their father began to stand before his wife grabbed his hand.

"Sit down, Ward. We're not making a scene."

Their father reluctantly took his seat.

"Mom, Dad, James and I can't stay married to each other because we're each in love with someone else."

Their mother closed her eyes and clapped her hands together.

Elise thought she might be praying, but then she said, "Please don't say it, Kristen. I'm begging you."

Elise looked at her mom again. Did she know?

"I'm sorry, Mom. I can't. James and I are tired of lying. I like girls, Mom and Dad, and James likes guys. We can't stay together because we're gay. We will always love each other, just not in the way you want."

Neither of their parents responded. Their mother started praying out loud, and their father sat in silence, looking at anything and anyone but Kristen and James.

After several minutes of no response, Elise couldn't take it anymore. "Are you going to say anything? Your daughter just poured her heart out to you—something that was very, very hard for her to do—and you're just going to ignore her?"

Her parents were being completely unreasonable.

Her mother looked at Elise with so much rage that she sat further back in her seat. "You knew about this?"

It was on the tip of her tongue to say that she'd found out just today to defend herself from her mother's wrath, but she didn't think that would be fair to her sister, so she settled for a simple, "Yes."

"How can you condone this sort of thing? The Bible says it's wrong."

Elise fought the impulse to roll her eyes. "Mother, the Bible was written thousands of years ago by men."

"It's the word of God."

"No, it's how each individual person *interpreted* the word of God."

"It's not an excuse to...to...choose to be..." her father started.

"To be gay?" Elise said. "News flash—nobody chooses to be gay; they just are." She turned to her sister and clutched her hand. "It's how Kristen was born, and I wouldn't change a thing about her."

"Thank you," Kristen whispered.

"I'm sorry," her mother said, "but we just can't accept this."

"Except you're not sorry. Not really. Because, if you were, you would accept Kristen the way she was."

"Elise," Kristen interrupted, "you might as well save your breath. They won't understand."

Elise was too angry to stop. "No, they don't *want* to understand." She turned back to her parents. "You know, nobody is perfect."

"Kristen got pregnant out of wedlock, is getting divorced, and is now gay. We raised you girls better than that," their mother said.

Her parents were clueless.

"First, Kristen has always been a lesbian, and she got pregnant because she didn't want to disappoint you, so she had sex with a man. And she might not have gotten pregnant if you had discussed birth control with us."

Her mother stuck her nose in the air. "I don't regret how we raised you girls. Sex before marriage is wrong. And, obviously, one of you listened to me."

Elise laughed loudly, causing her mother to jump. "You honestly think I would sit here and not defend Kristen and James? That I took everything you'd told us growing up and lived by it? You're more delusional than I thought." Elise shook her head. "Mom, I am not a virgin, and I haven't been for a long time. Actually, I've had more sexual partners than Kristen."

"Elise," Kristen said, grabbing Elise's arm, "please stop. You don't have to take yourself down with us."

Elise shook her sister off. She was on a roll and too livid to stop. "Did you know, Mom...Dad, that I like sex? So much that I've had one-night stands and fuck buddies?" She purposely used the F-word to shock her parents. "And guess what? I'm still the same person I always was. There is nothing wrong with me." She held out her hand to her sister and her soon-to-be ex-brother-in-law. "And there's nothing wrong with Kristen or James."

Her mother slowly stood and set her napkin on the table. "Ward, I think it's time we go."

Her father rose from the table as well.

The two of them turned to go, but then Elise's mother turned around and said, "I don't know why either of you thought I'd be okay with finding out that my daughters were going to hell." Her mother wasn't saying that to be mean; she truly believed it.

"Kristen, the Bible says that homosexuality is a sin, and your father and I will never condone it."

Her mom looked at Elise. "And, Elise, why you think any man would ever value you as a wife and mother after you have had numerous sexual partners is beyond me. The Bible says you are supposed to save yourself for the sanctity of marriage for a reason. No man will ever be able to take you seriously or see you as anything other than someone who gave her body away freely. How is your husband supposed to see you as special when you have lain with other men? I can only hope that you find someone who looks past your errors and takes pity on you."

With those parting words, her mother spun around and left.

Their father didn't say anything. He just followed his

wife out the door, as if Elise and Kristen didn't exist.

CHAPTER THIRTY-THREE

Elise was avoiding Luke. The last time he had spoken to her was right before she had lunch with her sister several days ago. She had planned to come to his house after she had dinner with her family that night, but she had sent him a text saying that she was going to hang out with her sister for the rest of the night because Kristen was upset.

He understood that her sister needed her. Elise had told Luke about her sister's impending divorce and how they would be dropping the news to her religious parents. Luke could only assume that the whole situation hadn't ended well.

What he couldn't understand was what had happened to have Elise blow him off. She hadn't been answering his phone calls, and she'd barely returned his texts. He'd kept thinking over the last few days, trying to figure out what had gone wrong, and he could not understand what had happened between the two of them. All he knew was that he couldn't go on like this.

Luke had messaged Elise earlier and asked if she wanted to get dinner and hang out tonight. She had responded with, *Some other time. Some other time* was not a positive response, especially from the girl you were supposed to be dating.

He had tried to get together and talk to her several times, and today was the last straw. He wasn't going to wait around for her to come to him. There were two people in this relationship, and he didn't like being kept in the dark. He deserved...something. To not be ignored at the very least.

Since Luke's shift ended before Elise was done with work, he went home and showered. Then, he made his way to her house about the time she usually got home. He'd thought about warning her that he was coming, but he didn't want her to flee or tell him not to come.

Luke arrived at Elise's just in time to see her pulling into her driveway. Luke exited his SUV and approached the end of her driveway just as she got out of her own vehicle. He yelled her name, but she didn't turn around. She reached inside her car and grabbed her purse and another bag as he called her name again. She either hadn't heard him or was ignoring him, so he pressed on. He reached her just as she touched her door handle to go into her house.

"We need to talk."

Elise jumped and spun around. "Holy crap, Luke, you scared me."

"Sorry. I called your name twice."

"I didn't hear you."

Luke looked her over. Her blonde hair was pulled back in

a ponytail, and her green eyes looked flat. He wanted to pull her into his arms, but he sensed that it would not go over well.

"Can we go inside and talk?" he asked.

She tried to look cheery, but he saw right through it.

"Now's not a good time. Can I call you later?"

"No. Lately, everything has been *later* or *some other time*. You can't avoid me forever."

Elise's smile faded. "Luke—"

"Now, Elise. And, if you want to do it right here, in your garage, fine. But I'm not leaving until we talk."

Her shoulders sank, and he knew he'd convinced her.

She turned back to her door and opened it. "Come on in," she said.

Luke stepped in behind Elise and closed the door behind him.

"Just give me a minute to go change, okay?"

He met her eyes. "Five minutes. Then, I'm coming after you."

Elise changed out of her work clothes and tried really hard not to cry. When she had realized that Luke had come up behind her in her garage, she'd wanted to throw herself into his arms. He looked so good and smelled amazing. Like Luke and soap. But his eyes. His beautiful brown eyes had been hard, and he had never looked at her that way before.

She knew it was her own fault. He was right. She had been avoiding him. She hadn't meant to, but she hadn't been able to get what her mother had said out of her head.

"No man will ever be able to take you seriously or see you as anything other than someone who gave her body away freely. How is your husband supposed to see you as special when you have lain with other men?"

She knew her mother had been upset and had had a lot of things thrown at her at once, but there was a part of Elise that wondered if her mother was right. As much as she tried to tell herself that her mother didn't know what she was talking about, she couldn't get rid of the huge cloud of doubt that now hung over her.

She kept thinking, *Luke will never love you because you don't deserve it.*

Then, she'd tell herself to shut up, but the thought lingered. And it was still there.

It didn't help that she'd done the stupidest thing possible and Googled relationships and a male perspective, focusing on one-night stands and how she and Luke had started. The most damning article she'd found was full of so many things that she didn't even know where to start.

Supposedly, men had one-night stands because they liked sex—*duh*—but they also did it for bragging rights or because they were still hung up on an ex. Luke wasn't a bragger, but Elise just couldn't stop thinking about Ava.

Then, there were things like guys wanted girls who they could bring home to meet the family, and being on a list of girls they'd screwed wouldn't lead to that. Elise couldn't help but notice that she had yet to meet Luke's parents. And, considering how hot the sex was with Luke, he probably wasn't in any rush to bring home a slutty lover to introduce to his mom.

Also, in these articles, men didn't sleep around to find the women of their dreams; they often slept around because they had commitment issues. And women shouldn't get their hopes up because men could have trouble taking their casual partners seriously.

The big one was that men wanted to work to get a girl to prove she was worth him and his time, and a girl giving in too easily told them she was only in it for a good time. And they definitely didn't take girls who liked sex a lot and obviously slept around sincerely.

By sleeping with Luke right away, she had told him that she wasn't worth it and that all she wanted was a good time. Yes, all she'd wanted was a good time in the beginning. Now, she wanted more, but it was too late. Now, she wasn't worth it, and he wouldn't take her seriously. He probably didn't realize it, as it was subconscious, but it was bound to come up, and the longer she was with him, the harder it would be for her.

Her mother was right. Her horrible, backward, old-fashioned mother was right. It pissed Elise off and made her utterly depressed.

It was the twenty-first century, but apparently, some things were never going to change. This was why Elise usually kept her naughty side locked away from her boyfriends. So what if sex with them had all been boring? At least they had introduced her to their parents.

Elise looked at the clock and realized that she was almost out of time. She absolutely *could not* let Luke come into her bedroom. He already thought she was easy and just another girl he slept with. She couldn't prove that was true once again.

Elise practically dragged her feet as she went back downstairs. She walked into her kitchen to find Luke waiting for her. Once again, there was a burning in the back of her eyes. She could not let Luke see her cry.

"What's going on, Elise?"

Just like Luke to not beat around the bush.

She supposed she owed it to him to do the same, so instead of pretending like she didn't know what he was talking about, she answered his question, "I think we need to take some time apart."

"Excuse me?"

"I said, I think we need to take some time apart."

"Oh, I heard you. I just don't understand why you think that."

She looked down at her hands. "I need some time to think."

She looked up to see Luke's mouth set in a firm line.

"You need time to think?"

"Yes. This all started so fast. It was never supposed to go past one night. That one night wasn't even supposed to happen." That was when she hadn't known she could feel this way about him.

"I see," he said.

But she didn't think he did.

"So, you regret what happened between us?"

How was she supposed to answer that? She cherished all the time she'd spent with Luke, but if she hadn't gotten involved with him, then she wouldn't be standing there with her heart breaking.

Luke put up a hand. "You know what? Don't answer that. Your lack of a response says it all."

"No." She couldn't let him think she regretted their relationship. "You don't understand."

He put his hands on his hips. "Explain it to me then."

Elise searched his face. The sweet Luke she knew was gone. All that was left was this angry man. Not that she could blame him. But it was better this way. It was better for it to end now—before Elise got in deeper and then realized she wouldn't be good enough for Luke to be with long-term. She wouldn't be good enough to meet his family, be his wife, or be the mother of his children.

If only she'd made him wait...

If only she'd gotten to know him first...

If only she hadn't shown him how dirty she was...

"It's my fault. I was the one who slept with you that first night. I never thought we'd get this far, but it's too late. I had no idea it would mean..." She just couldn't say she wasn't good enough in front of Luke. She couldn't admit she was unworthy of him, not to his face. It was too humiliating. "I had no idea it would mean our relationship wasn't good enough to last. That having a lot of partners and one-night stands would doom a relationship."

A look crossed over Luke's face. He finally understood where she was coming from.

"It's better to end this now rather than later, don't you think?" she whispered, her voice wobbly and her tears threatening to spill.

"I guess so. It sounds like there is no changing your mind."

Elise looked him in the eye because she might be unworthy of a serious relationship, but she was still human. "No, there isn't."

Luke gave her a single nod, and then he left. The door shut quietly behind him, and a few seconds later, she heard the sound of his SUV starting. As the sound of the engine faded, Elise slipped down against the cupboards onto the floor where she buried her face in her hands and let the tears finally flow.

Luke slammed his fist against the steering wheel and cursed his fate.

After Ava, he'd thought he would never get involved with another girl like that again, yet here he was. All the things Elise had said about their relationship were really about him. She knew he'd slept around in college, but now, apparently, it changed things.

He didn't know what had made her change her mind, but at this point, it didn't really matter. He shouldn't want to be with someone who thought that way about him.

Luke picked up his phone and dialed Nate.

"Yo?"

"You up for drinking tonight?"

"Sure. Any special reason?"

"Nope," he lied.

"Text me the deets, and I'll meet up with you."

"Good." Luke hung up his phone and threw it on the passenger seat.

Luke was going to get rip-roaring drunk tonight. Then, maybe he'd forget that, once again, he wasn't good enough for the girl he loved.

CHAPTER THIRTY-FOUR

Elise stared at her television, not really paying attention to what was playing. She was tired, but she knew she wouldn't sleep. She had been like this for the last week. Since Luke had walked out of her house. Despite going to work every day and then coming home and working on her new house until she was exhausted, sleep had been eluding her.

Every time she lay down, she would go over and over her last conversation with Luke. And then she would question whether or not she'd done the right thing. But, whenever she thought about picking up the phone to call him, she would hear her mother's voice in her head. Over and over again. It was a vicious cycle, and she was seriously considering a lobotomy.

Elise heard her front door open and close, and even though she knew it had been locked, she couldn't muster up any fear that someone was breaking in.

Bring it on. She was ready for a fight.

Rachel came around the corner and stopped when she saw Elise. Her expression turned to pity, and for the first time, Elise wanted to punch her friend. Pity was the worst.

"Remind me to take your key away," Elise said.

Ignoring Elise's bad mood, Rachel came further into the room and sat next to Elise. "What the hell is going on?"

Elise looked around the room and back at Rachel. "Uh, nothing. Just watching some TV."

Rachel raised her eyebrows. "Don't be a wiseass. You know what I mean. What's going on with you and Luke?"

Elise sank down into the couch. "Nothing. I don't want to talk about it."

"Too bad. When I come in here on a Friday night to see you staring off into space with your sweats on, your hair looking like you didn't brush it all day, and tearstains on your cheeks, I'm going to talk to you. All you're missing is a bucket of ice cream and a roll of cookie dough. So, what gives, Elise?"

She absolutely *did not* want to talk about this. Besides Kristen and James, no one knew what her mother had said to her at the restaurant. It was humiliating, and Elise was too ashamed to tell her friend.

"Nothing."

"What if I told you I already know? Some of it anyway."

No way. "How?"

"I called your sister."

Elise groaned. "Why?"

"Because you won't talk to me. You don't want to hang out. You just sit at home every night."

"I do not. I've been busy unpacking and putting all my crap away."

"That's just an excuse not to deal with anything."

"Whatever."

"Do you want to talk about what your mother said to you?"

Fuck no. "Fuck no."

"Tough."

Elise realized Rachel wasn't going to leave until she talked to her. "Fine. My mother said some mean things to me, yes. She really hurt my feelings, and what's worse is that she is right."

"What did she say to you, Elise?"

"I thought you already knew."

"I want to hear you say it."

Elise sighed. "She basically called me a slut and said no man would ever take me seriously or see me as a wife and mother. That she hoped that someone would take pity on me and marry me someday. I just couldn't let things get any further with Luke, knowing it would eventually end anyway."

Rachel grimaced. "Oh, man, Elise, that is harsh."

Elise shrugged. "It's true."

"Wait a second. If that's true for you, then it must be true for me, too."

Elise vehemently shook her head. "No. You and Sean dated for, like, a month before you slept with him. You made Sean wait. You made him work for it. You showed him that you were worth it in the end. I think you even met his family before you slept together."

Rachel put her fingers to her temples. "I am a little confused. I need to process this for a second." After about a minute, Rachel said, "Okay, so you think, because you and Luke had a one-night stand, he will only ever see you as someone like that and will never see you as someone good enough to bring home to his mom and dad."

"Yeah. You get it. It's not that confusing."

"That's bullshit. You know your parents are archaic in their thinking."

"I thought so, too, so I decided to look up articles on the internet. Instead of reassuring me, they basically confirmed what my mother had said."

"Don't you think that should be for Luke to decide instead of you just assuming he felt that way?"

Elise wanted to cry again. If she looked at Rachel, she would, so she focused on the TV instead. "But what if it's all subconscious? What if he doesn't even realize he feels that way? Not until years later when he meets some nice virginal librarian who makes him wait a year before having sex with him, and when she does, it's strictly missionary and for procreation only. And he realizes that he doesn't want to be with some dirty slut who put out the first night."

"Holy shit. Your parents screwed you up more than I thought. And I swear to God, Elise, if you call yourself a slut one more time, I'm going to slap you."

Elise shrank back, a little afraid of her friend. Elise had several inches and several pounds on Rachel, but she had a feeling her friend would win if they actually got in a fight.

"Do you really think women who sleep around are sluts?"

Elise sighed. "No. Of course not. Women should be able to be with who they want, when they want."

"Good. Now, did you know that, when Sean and I started

dating, he was the one who made me wait? I was ready to sleep with him on the first date."

"No. I had no idea."

"That's because I was a little embarrassed that he'd turned me down, and I didn't want anyone to know."

"Wow."

"Yeah. So, do you think I'm a slut?"

"*Of course not.*"

"Now, we're getting somewhere."

"What do you mean?"

"So, if I'm not a slut and women who sleep around aren't sluts, why are you?"

Elise knew Rachel had a point, but she didn't have an answer. "I don't know."

"Going all the way back to college, did you ever notice that the guys you liked having sex with were never really serious relationships? And that you only seriously dated guys who were boring in bed?"

"Yeah, I kind of realized that this summer, but so what?"

"Luke is the first guy you've enjoyed sex with, the first guy you've been yourself with, and the first you've dared to call your boyfriend. And I think it scares the shit out of you. I think your parents have gotten so far in your head that you don't even realize that you have some weird thing where you think you can't be yourself in the bedroom and be worthy of dating. You want to be this twenty-first century feminist woman who does what she wants, but deep down, you think that a wife and mother has to be sweet and demure in the bedroom."

Elise put her head back against the couch and thought

about what her friend had said. Had she really thought that? It would explain her sexual and dating history.

"Elise?"

She lifted her head and looked at Rachel.

"It's really okay to like sex. And I bet that is one of the things Luke likes about you. He likes you because you like sex, not in spite of you liking sex. Elise, so what if you're dirty in bed? Just because you're dirty, it doesn't mean you're *dirty*. No matter what your mother would like for you to believe."

Elise didn't reply because her mind was spinning. She never really realized how much her upbringing had affected her. She'd thought that she had thrown that all aside, but it clearly still influenced the way she thought about herself.

"Look, hon, I just want you to think about what I said, okay?"

"I will."

Rachel looked at her with speculation.

"I promise. You really have given me a lot to think about."

Rachel sighed with relief. "Good, because I hate to see you and Luke miserable."

"Luke's miserable?"

Rachel nodded sadly. "Sean can't get much out of him, but apparently, you and Luke have a lot in common because Luke has been working doubles at the hospital. Sean thinks he's been using work to try to forget about you. What did you say to him?"

"Something along the lines of how we shouldn't have jumped into bed and that I didn't realize it would mean our relationship wasn't good enough. And that having multiple partners was bad for our relationship."

"Did you say *you* having multiple partners or Luke having multiple partners?"

"Neither. I was a little general on the whole subject because I was too embarrassed to come out and say that my sexual history was the reason our relationship was doomed." Elise thought about it. "My mom and dad really did kind of mess with my head, huh?"

Rachel snorted. "Ya think? But back to you and Luke. Do you think he might have thought you meant *him* and *his* sexual history?"

"What?" Elise was shaken. "No. Why would he think that? Guys sleep around all the time. It's women who have the stigma attached to them."

"Well, hon, you didn't get involved with Luke in the past because he was a player. Maybe he thinks that it made you change your mind about him. Did you ever think that maybe Luke thinks he's not the one who is good enough to marry? That maybe, because of his past, he thinks that you think he's not worthy of being a husband and father?"

Elise shook her head. "No, he can't." She did not want to think of Luke feeling the horrible pain she had this past week.

"He can, Elise, and there's a big chance he does."

Elise just couldn't wrap her mind around it. Everyone loved Luke. How could he ever think badly of himself?

Rachel patted Elise's knee. "I see I've given you even more to think about. I'm going to go for now."

Elise looked at her friend from where she'd been staring off into space.

"Call me next time you feel this way. I won't judge you,

sweetie. That's why we're friends. You don't judge me, and I don't judge you. Okay?"

Elise nodded once. "Okay."

Rachel hugged her. "I love you."

"I love you, too. Thank you."

Rachel leaned away. "You're welcome."

Rachel left, and Elise shut off her television and walked slowly up to her bedroom. She had a lot of information to process, and she knew she needed to talk to Luke. No matter what, she needed to make sure he understood where she'd been coming from.

For the first time all week, Elise actually slept.

CHAPTER THIRTY-FIVE

The next evening, Elise got home from visiting Kristen and threw her purse on her kitchen counter. It had been a good visit. Kristen was doing well. Her sister and James's news to his parents hadn't gone very well either, but it had ended better than their conversation with Elise's parents.

Kristen and James had sat Jennifer down and told her they were getting divorced, and she had taken the news amazingly well. Then again, Elise hadn't expected much less from her awesome niece.

Kristen had asked Elise how she was doing, and she had ended up pouring her heart out to her sister. They'd cried together, and Kristen had agreed with Rachel one hundred and ten percent. Kristen hadn't realized how much Elise had been affected by their parents, too. The two sisters had really bonded over everything they'd been through lately, and Elise had never felt closer to her sister. It was the one good thing to come out of it all.

Elise's phone chimed with her text message notification, and she hoped that it was Luke. She'd been trying to contact him all day, but she hadn't heard anything back. She pulled her phone out of her purse and saw that it was Nate. When she hadn't been able to get ahold of Luke, she'd resorted to using his friend.

Nate: Hey, I found Luke.

Elise: You did? Why won't he answer me?

Nate: I honestly don't know if he's looked at his phone much. He might be avoiding it.

Crap.

That wasn't a good sign. He had to have either called Nate or answered Nate's phone call. He had to have seen that Elise had texted and called him. She suspected Nate was trying to be diplomatic.

Nate: But, listen, I need you to get dressed and come downtown to the nightclub Pulse.

Elise: Why?

Was Luke even with Nate?

Nate: I don't have time to explain, but if you care about Luke at all, you will come down here right now.

Oh no. What was going on with Luke? Was he okay? Had something happened to him?

> Elise: You have to give me something. I can't walk in blind.

Elise waited, but Nate didn't reply right away. When he did, it only worried her more.

> Nate: Promise you'll come, no matter what.

Wild dogs couldn't stop her.

> Elise: I promise.

> Nate: Ava's here, and she's trying to get Luke to leave with her. She's using Luke to cheat on her husband. If this happens, Luke will never forgive himself. I need you to get your ass down here. Now.

> Elise: I'm on my way.

Elise walked into Pulse, ready to take on the world. She'd put on her makeup, giving herself a sexy nighttime look. She'd found her slinkiest dress and her favorite heels. But, before that, she'd dressed herself in her favorite bra and underwear.

A few days after Luke had come to her house, she'd received a package in the mail with the underwear she'd lost at Luke's all those weeks ago. He had sent a simple note with them.

Cleaning lady found these. Thought I'd better return them to you.

—Luke

Tonight, she'd put them on with the intention of giving them back to him.

Nate met her at the door, kissing her cheek. "Damn, girl, you look good. Luke is going to come just from seeing you." Nate had to talk loud to be heard over the music.

Elise laughed and couldn't deny that the compliment lifted her spirits. "Thanks, Nate. You know just what to say to a lady."

"Yeah, well, I told Luke, if he didn't marry you, I would."

Elise swallowed and forced a casual laugh. She knew Nate and Luke had been joking around, but she still anticipated Luke's response. "What did he say?"

"He told me that, if I touched you, he'd break both my arms."

Elise couldn't help it. She grinned.

"Come on," Nate said. "Let's go find Luke. Just giving you a warning. I might need to talk to him first."

She nodded. That didn't sound promising.

Nate put his arm around her. It was more friendly than sexual. It was easier to stay together with the crowd of people there tonight, and it seemed like Nate was offering Elise his support.

As they moved to the other side of the room, she saw Luke before he saw her. He was sitting in a booth, and there was a beautiful woman with long dark hair next to him. She was one of those lucky people who could have black hair and pale skin and make it look good. Elise had dyed her hair dark once, and she'd looked like a vampire. This woman also managed to pull off a deep red lipstick and made it look classy. And her breasts, which had to be fake, were on display in a fashionable way. She was way prettier than Elise, and she knew this was Ava.

Elise hated her on sight.

Part of it was jealousy, and part of it was because Ava had made Luke feel less than when he was way better than her.

Luke gently eased the other woman away, as if he was trying to be polite yet, at the same time, letting her know that he didn't want her touching him.

Elise snickered to herself. Luke didn't want Ava, even with Elise out of the picture.

The closer they got to the booths, the softer the music got, so it was a little easier to hear conversations over on this side of the room.

"Luke, my date is here," Nate said with a joking voice as they approached.

Luke looked up from his phone.

So much for him not seeing my messages.

His look went from anticipation to what Elise could only describe as no emotion. His eyes were so cold that it made her want to get on her knees and beg for the old Luke to come back.

Elise quickly shook her head to let Luke know she wasn't Nate's date, but he stared right through her, and she began to doubt that it had been a good idea for her to come here. She didn't know if Luke would hear her out.

Ava looked Elise up and down and then smiled, but it was filled with judgment, obviously finding Elise lacking.

Bitch.

"Ava," Nate said, "I have to talk to Luke alone."

"Nah, I think everyone's said everything they wanted to," Luke said, finally meeting Elise's eyes.

Nate ignored Luke. "Ava, go."

Ava huffed, but she got up. She looked at Elise. "We might as well get a drink."

Elise looked to the guys.

Nate waved Elise off. "Give us five minutes."

"Sure," Elise said to Ava.

They walked away, and Ava introduced herself. She obviously had no idea who Elise was.

"I'm El—"

Some drunk guy crashed into Elise, almost knocking her over.

Ava gave the man a bitchy look, but he was too intoxicated to care. "Come on, Elle, let's go."

It was on the tip of Elise's tongue to correct Ava, but she decided against it in case Luke had told Ava about her. Ava might be more open this way, and Elise wanted to thank the person who'd run into her.

They reached the bar and ordered their drinks.

"So, you're dating Nate?" Ava asked.

"Oh no, we're just friends."

"That's too bad. He's a stud in bed."

Elise almost swallowed her tongue. "You've slept with him?"

Ava smirked. "Yeah, after Luke and I dated."

What a bitch.

Sleeping with Luke's best friend was low. And Elise lost a little respect for Nate as well.

"Luke and you dated?"

"Yeah, for two years. Fucking best sex of my life. Too bad he wasn't great outside the bedroom."

Elise wanted to claw this chick's eyes out. Luke was more than great outside of the bedroom.

Instead, Elise managed to say, "That is too bad."

"Nah. I'm married now." She wiggled her left ring finger, showing off her ginormous rock.

"So, what are you doing here—" Elise put her hand up. "Never mind. None of my business." Except for the fact that Luke was hers, and he was her business.

"I found out my husband has a little side piece, and I'm all about getting even. I saw Luke here tonight and figured, if I'm going to cheat on my husband, I should do it with someone who knows what he's doing. My husband has nothing on Luke when it comes to fucking, so his little mistress can have him as long as the checks keep coming." Ava laughed.

Elise pretended to laugh, but it was really, really hard. How Luke could have ever dated this woman was beyond Elise.

"And, if Luke isn't game, I figure Nate is a very close second. You don't mind, do you? You did say you're just friends."

"No, I don't mind." Elise hoped Nate minded and turned Ava down. But there was no way Luke was sleeping with this chick.

The bartender brought their drinks, and they headed back to Luke and Nate's table.

When they reached the guys, Luke stood up and grabbed Elise's hand as she set her drink down. "Come on, Elise."

"*Elise?*" Ava said as Luke dragged her away.

So, Ava had heard of her.

Elise smiled, shrugged, and gave Luke's ex a little wave as he dragged her away. It was petty, but she couldn't help herself.

Ava started after them, but Nate grabbed her arm. Elise focused her attention on Luke, wondering where he was taking her. He was still upset, the anger practically radiating off of him, but she couldn't ignore how much she loved just being able to hold his hand again.

She hoped he would listen to what she had to say and forgive her because she missed him something awful.

CHAPTER THIRTY-SIX

Luke pulled Elise out the back door of the nightclub and into the alleyway. He pushed her against the wall. He let go of her hand and crossed his arms.

"Nate said you wanted to talk."

"I do," Elise said.

"So, talk," he said rather rudely.

And he instantly winced with guilt. Then, he was mad at himself for feeling bad. This girl had stomped all over his heart.

"I came to tell you, I'm sorry."

Luke winced. *Ouch.* So, now, she pitied him. *Could this day get any worse?* First, his old ex, and now, his new ex.

When Luke had seen who Nate's *date* was, his first thought was that he'd been so glad to see Elise. His second thought was to wonder how Nate could do that to him. When Nate had asked him why he'd given up on Elise so easily, he'd told Nate that life was too short to spend it with people who didn't appreciate him and thought of him as unworthy. And, if you had to change someone's mind about that, then it wasn't really worth changing their mind in the first place. Ava had taught him that. Luke knew Elise wasn't really Nate's date, but Luke was smart enough to know that Nate had set him up since Luke had been avoiding Elise's calls and messages.

When Luke didn't say anything, Elise said, "I've done some thinking the last two days, and I've talked to Rachel and Kristen."

As far as apologies went, Elise's was horrible. Now, her friend and sister pitied him, too.

"I should have let you make your own decisions instead of telling you how you should feel," Elise continued. "My mom said some pretty horrible things to me and made me doubt myself and our relationship. The worst thing is that, for a while there, I thought she was right."

Luke dropped his arms. He knew something must have happened at her family dinner, but she had refused to tell him what had happened.

Luke wanted to stay mad at Elise, but he was dying to hear more. "Go on."

Elise's demeanor changed, and she suddenly seemed nervous. "This is really hard for me to say, and I know you're upset with me, but please don't think badly of me."

He wanted to refuse, but he still cared about her, so he nodded. "Okay."

Elise looked down at her hands, over his shoulder, at his shirt —basically anywhere but his eyes. "She said that no guy would ever seriously want me or ever see me beyond being someone they just had sex with. That no one would think of me as marriage and mother material. And that she hoped, one day, some guy would take pity on me and marry me, despite my slutty ways."

Luke was furious. "What the actual fuck, Elise? Your mom really said that shit to you?"

Elise grimaced. "Yes. It sounds much worse out loud. And, to make matters worse, my father just stood there and said nothing."

Luke took a deep breath. "I'm going to kill them."

Elise finally met his eyes. "Please don't. I don't want to visit you in prison," she joked. "They're really not worth it."

"They hurt you, Elise. Nobody hurts you and gets away with it." Luke was too irate to realize he'd just given his feelings away until Elise smiled.

"So, you don't agree with them?"

"Fuck no." What kind of guy did she think he was? "I thought you knew me better than that?"

Elise threw herself in his arms. "I do. I was just so confused. I mean, it was my mom. I can't just ignore what my mom said. But I should have trusted myself to trust you more."

Luke hesitantly hugged her back. "I'm glad you got it all figured out." Luke let go and set her away from him. "But this doesn't solve the reason you broke up with me."

Elise wrinkled her nose. "Yes, it does."

So, it was obvious that one of them was clueless.

"Elise, you broke up with me because of my past and because I slept around too much. That hasn't changed."

Elise added eye-squinting to her nose-wrinkling, looking even more confused. "No, I didn't."

Luke laughed, but it was without any humor. "Elise, I was there. I remember what you said."

"I was there, too. And, apparently, I wasn't very clear in my explanation. I broke up with you because *I've* had too many sexual partners, not because *you've* had too many. I broke up with you because we'd started as a one-night stand and because you know how much I like sex, and good girls don't like sex. At least, that's what my mother had me believing. I know—"

Luke cut her off, "Wait, wait, wait. I don't get it."

"My mom scared me off. I thought you would never really want to be with me because you would always, deep down, see me as some girl you screwed, and you wouldn't respect me. I didn't think *I* was good enough for *you*. Not that you weren't good enough for me." Elise put her head in her hands and moaned. She looked up at Luke. "I'm a horrible person. Luke, I *never, ever* meant to make you feel bad about yourself. You are the best person I know."

Luke stood there, stunned.

Elise took a step back. "Why are you grinning like that? It's kind of scaring me."

Luke hadn't realized he had been smiling like a fool. He started to laugh. It was a real laugh, too, not something he had to force for the people around him.

He pulled Elise into his arms and kissed her.

Without any hesitation, Elise kissed him back. She ran her hands up and down him—his arms, his chest, his back, everywhere—as if she was checking to make sure he was real. Luke backed her up against the wall. He rubbed his realness between her legs. She wrapped her legs around him and ground her crotch against his.

Luke pushed her skirt up until he skimmed the seam of her underwear, and she moaned. Her panties were already soaked, and he wanted to pull her underwear off and push inside her. It had been too long since they were together.

Instead, Luke set her down and took a step back to create some distance between the two of them. Both of them were breathing hard, and he hated that they were outside, in the back of a nightclub. No one else was back there, but that didn't mean someone couldn't come along, just like the two of them had.

"Elise, I have never thought less of you because we had a one-night stand. I love how free you are"—he pulled her close —"and I love how much you love sex. I love how dirty you are. I love you. Your mother doesn't know what the fuck she's talking about."

Elise looked like she was going to cry. "Did you just tell me you love me? Or was that *love* like you love Die Hard movies?"

Luke laughed. "That was an I-love-you I love you. I am completely and utterly in love with you, Elise."

She pulled his head down and soul-kissed him. When she was finished, she said, "I love you, too. I'm sorry I listened to my crazy mother and broke up with you."

"I'm sorry you listened to your mother, too. But mostly because she made you feel bad about yourself. You are one of the best people *I* know. And you are going to make a great wife and mother someday."

She smiled. "I know. It took me a little while, but I know that now. But thank you for saying it."

"Let's go back inside and find Nate."

Luke took Elise's hand once again, but instead of dragging her behind him, they walked inside next to each other.

When they reached the restrooms, Elise stopped. "I'm going to go in here for a minute. I'll meet you back at the table."

Luke kissed her. "Don't be long."

She smiled. "I won't."

Luke found his and Nate's table, and it was blessedly empty. He didn't want to deal with Ava, but he couldn't leave without talking to Nate.

Elise slid in next to Luke a minute later and picked up the drink she'd set there earlier. She was about to take a drink, and then she set it down. "I probably shouldn't drink that, huh? Ava probably spiked it with something."

Luke laughed and pulled her into his arms. He kissed her again. Elise slipped something into his hand and shifted her hips so that she straddled him. This area of the club was dark, and the booths were only lit with small LED lights that looked like candles. It gave plenty of couples the opportunity to make out in the dim lighting, and they were far from the only ones.

Elise kissed him as she spread the bottom of her dress around them like a mini blanket. Then, she reached underneath and went for his fly. Before he could question her, she had his cock in her hand and started stroking him.

"Holy shit, babe." He was all for an apologetic hand job

in public. He'd rather have sex, but he could wait. But he should have known that Elise didn't want to wait either.

"Are you ready for more?" she asked in between kisses.

"Yes. No. Yes. I'm afraid this might kill me. I don't know if I can handle anything more."

Elise laughed as she shifted her weight and sat down right on his dick. Her laugh turned into a moan as she took him to the hilt.

"Holy fuck, Elise," he panted. "I can't believe I almost forgot how incredible you feel."

She chuckled. "Maybe it's just one of those heart-grows-fonder sort of things."

"I don't think so."

She kissed him again. "Then, I'd better make sure you never forget."

She rocked her hips over his to create just enough resistance for it to feel good. To everyone else around them, it probably looked like they were just having a hot make-out session.

"I want to flip you over and pound inside you. I want to put myself so deep inside you that I never really leave," he told her.

She moaned softly and clenched her pussy around him. She smiled. "Later," she said breathlessly. "I'm going to hold you to it."

Elise continued to kiss him and milk him with her inner muscles. There wasn't a lot of friction because they were trying to be discreet, but it wasn't long before a tingling in his nuts signaled the beginning of an orgasm.

"Baby," he said as he clutched her hips in his hands hard enough to leave marks, "I can't hold off much longer."

"Tell me you love me again."

Luke smiled and put his mouth to her ear. "I love you. Always and forever."

And Elise came. She pushed her face into his neck and tried to make it look like she was relaxing there, but her body shook with her orgasm. Thankfully, Luke seemed to be the only one paying attention. Not that he would really know because he was busy emptying his balls inside her.

After several minutes passed, Elise got up further on her knees so that he slipped out of her. He was immediately disappointed. He missed her pussy already. She didn't move, so he was still covered, but he didn't know how he was going to clean himself up from their lovemaking.

Luke looked at the table for napkins.

"Check your hand."

He'd forgotten she'd put something in his palm before she got on his lap, and he was surprised to find it was still there. He looked at it more closely and laughed.

It was her underwear. The ones she'd worn to his house the first night.

Man, he loved his dirty, dirty woman.

He used them to clean himself up and then slipped them in his pocket. He buttoned up, and Elise slid off his lap to sit beside him, resting her head on his shoulder.

"What about you?" he asked, knowing he'd left quite a mess inside her.

She shifted, so she could look into his eyes. "I'm fine. I

like walking around, knowing there is a part of you inside me."

And Luke was already getting hard again. *Damn.* How could she ever think he didn't love this side of her?

Just then, Nate returned to the table with Ava behind him. She scowled when she saw Elise and Luke sitting so close together. What he had ever seen in his ex, he would never truly understand.

Luke nudged Elise to get out of the booth, so he could follow. "We're going to take off," he told Nate.

Nate grinned. "I was hoping you'd say that. Everything better now?"

"Yes. Are you going to be okay with that one?" Luke asked, referring to Ava.

Nate nodded, his ice-blue eyes shining. "Don't worry; I know how to get rid of her. You get out of here."

"You don't have to tell me twice." Luke grabbed Elise's hand. "Come on, Lise."

Elise let him direct her toward the front door, but she paused to say something in Ava's ear. When Elise was finished, she smiled knowingly, and Ava looked pissed.

Once they were outside, Elise asked, "Did you know that she slept with Nate? After you were together?"

"Yes."

She looked surprised. "You did?"

"Yes, Nate doesn't hide anything from me. After we broke up, he asked me if it was okay, and I gave him the go-ahead. I think I knew it would make it easier for me to cut ties with her. And I think that's why Nate did it, too. He never really liked her in the first place."

"Okay. As long as you know and you're okay with it, then I'm okay with it. How guys can sleep with someone they don't like makes no sense to me."

"We're a different breed, baby."

"You know you can do much better than her, right?"

"I know. I'm with you after all."

She smiled. "Good answer."

"What did you say to her anyway?" Luke asked.

Elise grinned. "I told her that my birthday was this week, and all I wanted was you. And then I told her my wish already came true."

Luke put his arm around her and pulled her close. "God, I love you."

She grabbed on to the hand around her neck and linked their fingers, looking up at him. "I love you, too."

CHAPTER THIRTY-SEVEN

"**N**o peeking."

"Please?" asked Elise.

Luke had picked up Elise to take her to get her birthday present. He'd explained that he couldn't bring it to her, that he had to take her to the present. And the blasted man was making her wear a blindfold.

Her thirtieth birthday had technically been a couple of days ago, but Luke had worked evenings all week, so that was why he had waited until Saturday. She'd tried to tell him that she'd already gotten her present last weekend when they got back together, but he'd insisted.

"Can you give me any hints?"

Luke had told her to dress casual, and that was the only information she'd gotten when he picked her up.

Luke took her hand in his. "Nope. Then, it wouldn't be a surprise."

"You're no fun," she said, sulking.

She tried to cross her arms, but he refused to let go of her hand.

"That's not what you said last night."

The night before, Luke had come over after work. Elise had already been sleeping, and Luke had snuck into bed and woken her with some phenomenal lovemaking.

"I blame lack of sleep and a post-orgasmic haze. Today, I'm in complete control of my faculties."

"You're cute when you're pouting."

She stuck her tongue out at him. She didn't even know if he could see, but he laughed, so he must have been looking at her.

After what seemed like an hour of anticipation, they were finally there.

"I got the name of this place from someone, so I'm trusting them to do good work."

Good work? Elise rolled the words around in her head. She'd assumed that they were going to a restaurant. But then wouldn't he have said something about good food instead of good work?

"Can I see now?"

"Nope."

The excitement was too much. "I'll give you a hummer if you let me look."

Luke laughed, and she let the rich sound roll over her. She couldn't believe she'd almost let this wonderful man get away.

He kissed her, a quick peck on the lips. "You're probably going to do that sooner or later anyway."

"Dang it."

He was right.

"Just sit tight. I'll come around and get you out."

She heard his door open and close. Then, her door opened, and the warm August heat hit her as Luke helped her out. He took her arm as he guided her to a sidewalk that she had to step up onto and then a little farther to a door that dinged when it was opened.

There were voices all around, and Elise heard what sounded like buzzing.

Luke led her to a counter and rested their hands on it. "Hi, yes, I have an appointment."

"Name?"

"Luke. For Elise."

"Ah, yes."

Elise could hear the smile in the woman's voice.

"I'm Trinity. Why don't you come back here? We'll let her decide what she wants."

Now, the suspense was killing her.

"Come on, baby."

They walked a little ways and stopped.

"Are you ready?" Luke asked her.

"Does a bear shit in the woods?"

Trinity laughed next to Elise.

Luke removed her blindfold, and that was when Elise saw they were in a tattoo shop.

Elise looked at Luke.

"We're getting your nose pierced."

"*What?*" Elise was excited and nervous instantly.

"I knew you would never come here on your own, so here we are. It's the perfect birthday present."

"What about my parents?"

Luke lifted an eyebrow.

"You're right. It can't get any worse."

Elise and Kristen still hadn't talked to their parents. Both of them were willing, but they'd decided they weren't going to be the first to initiate anything. Their parents would have to reach out to them.

"Let's do it."

Luke clapped his hands. "Yes."

Trinity pointed to a display case. "We have a lot of selections for you. Just pick what you want, and I'll start setting up while you fill out the paperwork."

There were so many choices, but Elise settled on a tiny lavender opal stud to go in her right nostril.

"Do you like it?" she asked Luke. "Do you think it'll look good on me?"

He pulled her to him. "I think you'll look sexy. And I love that you'll be wearing something I gave you, even when you're naked."

A throat cleared behind them, and Elise's face heated.

"Did you decide on one?"

Elise pointed to her pick. "This one."

"All right, let's do this," Trinity said.

A half an hour later, Elise and Luke walked out with Elise's new addition. She couldn't believe she'd actually gone through with it, and she had Luke to thank.

"Does it hurt?"

"Just a little. Not as much as it did right away."

They reached Luke's SUV, and Elise instantly pulled

down the sun visor, so she could examine her nose. It was so cute, and she loved her piercing.

Luke smiled at her. "You like it?"

"I love it." She leaned over and kissed him. "Almost as much as I love you."

Luke grinned. "I'm glad. Part of me thought you'd hate the idea."

"Never. Even if I hadn't done it, I would never hate the idea."

"Good."

"Thank you by the way."

"You're welcome, Lise. I just want you to have everything you want."

"Have I already told you, I love you?"

"Yes, but you can always say it again."

Elise smiled. "I love you."

Luke kissed her again.

"So, where are we going now?"

"We're going to eat."

"Where?"

Luke shook his head.

"Another surprise?"

"Yep."

"Ah, poop."

Luke laughed, but at least he didn't make her put the blindfold back on. Not that it mattered because Elise was too busy admiring her nose ring. He took a picture and sent it to Rachel and Kristen. Both gave her positive reviews and asked to hear the details later.

Before she knew it, they were pulling up to a two-story

home in a middle-class neighborhood.

"Where are we?"

"Just follow me," was Luke's only answer.

They exited Luke's SUV as another car pulled up, and a younger version of Luke got out.

"Hey, Luke," he called out as he ran up to them.

When he got closer, Elise could see that his hair and eyes were lighter than Luke's, but there was no denying that they were related.

"Hey, Cade. This is Elise. Elise, this is my little brother, Cade."

"Little, my ass." Cade flexed his impressive biceps.

Elise held out her hand for Cade to shake. "Nice to meet you."

"Same here. Come on. Mom's making bacon-wrapped chicken tonight. Yum." Cade took off into the house.

Elise stopped Luke. "We're having dinner with your family?" she asked, starting to panic.

Luke shrugged. "Yes. It's about time you met them, don't you think?"

He started to walk, but she stopped him.

"But I just got my nose pierced."

"Babe, my parents don't care about that. Wait until you meet Sydney."

Elise remembered Luke's phone call with his sister back in LA. "She's home?"

"Yep. That's why it's the perfect time. You can meet all of them at once."

"Oh, great," she said sarcastically.

Luke had three siblings—two younger, Cade and Sydney,

and one older sister, Alyssa. So, with his parents, that was five people. That was a lot of people to impress.

Luke laughed. "It'll be fine. You've already met my brother, and he was totally cool with you."

He had a point.

"Okay, let's do this."

They headed for the house.

"How old is Cade?"

"Sydney is twenty, Cade is twenty-four, I'm thirty-two, and Alyssa is thirty-three."

"That's an odd spread."

"Yeah, I was an *oops*. They wanted to wait longer to have their second baby, but I guess I was impatient. That's why they waited eight years to have their third. And then Sydney was an *oops*, too, I think, but Mom won't admit it."

Luke led Elise into the house and introduced her to his parents. His mom had dark blonde hair and blue-eyes, girl-next-door pretty, and his father was the most muscular Asian man Elise had ever seen. He was very handsome and still looked good for his age. And, while Luke's dad, Jin, was the tallest in the family, he was an inch or two shorter than his wife, Beth.

When she'd asked him once how he was so tall, Luke had said that he figured he'd gotten it from his mom's side.

Elise met Luke's sisters last. They were completely different from each other.

Luke told Elise that Alyssa was a researcher and had a double PhD in microbiology and pharmacology. She had shoulder-length hair that she kept pulled back in a look that spoke of convenience, not style. Luke explained that his sister lived and breathed work.

Sydney, on the other hand, was a free spirit who would rather enjoy life than work. Her hair was dyed platinum blonde with pink, purple, and blue streaks in it. She had her septum and lip pierced. Elise now understood why Luke said no one would care about her new piercing.

Cade worked with computers. He did IT work for a bank.

Even though Luke's siblings were all different from one another, they were all very nice to her. Luke's dad even gave Elise a beer as soon as she sat down, and his mom had made her a birthday cake. The whole family joked and had fun with each other over dinner, and the two of them didn't leave until after ten at night because they were having such a good time. The whole experience was very different from Elise's family, and she could see why Luke loved them all.

On the drive home, Luke asked, "So, what did you think?"

"They are all great. Was your dad born here?"

"Nope, he came to America when he was five. He can speak some Cantonese with my grandparents, but he has to insert English in there because he's not quite fluent."

"That would explain the phone conversation."

Luke laughed. "Yeah, my grandma is stubborn and hard of hearing, so sometimes, Dad has to yell at her."

Elise laughed. "I was a little surprised though."

Luke looked at her. "Oh? What about?"

"This is embarrassing, but I guess I always assumed your mom was Chinese, and your dad was white. You never said their names until I met them today, and I don't know why I thought that."

"That's because some white guys have a fetish with Asian females. Also, unfortunately, Asian men have a bad reputation as being skinny, nerdy, beta males. Ha. They never met my father."

"I'll say. All the men in your family are good-looking."

Luke glanced at her. "Don't get any ideas. I know some women like younger men."

"I like my men older."

Luke scowled.

"But only a little bit older, like say two-and-a-half years."

"Good," he said.

He was trying to be serious, but she saw a smile peeking through.

She put her arm through his and leaned against him. "You don't have to worry. I'm not going anywhere," she told Luke.

He kissed her head. "Me either, babe. Me either."

CHAPTER THIRTY-EIGHT

About two months later, Elise received a phone call. She was leaving work, so she didn't bother looking at the display before answering, too busy loading her stuff into her car, "Hello?"

"Elise, this is your father."

As if she didn't know her own dad's voice, no matter how long it had been since she talked to him.

"Dad?"

He cleared his throat. "I would like you to come to lunch this coming Sunday after church."

Elise didn't miss the fact that he had said, *I*, and not, *Your mother and I.*

"Sure, Dad. I'll be there. Is Kristen coming?"

"I don't know. I haven't called her yet."

Elise closed her eyes, so grateful that he wasn't going to ignore his other daughter. She opened her eyes and realized she was still standing outside her car with the door open.

"Is Mom okay with this?" she asked as she got behind the wheel.

"She will be."

Great.

"It doesn't matter. It's my house, and I'm inviting you."

For someone who lived by the Bible, her mom really did usually wear the pants in the relationship.

"Thanks, Dad. What time should I be there?"

"Noon, sharp."

"See you then." Elise ended the call and rang Luke right away.

Sunday rolled around, and Kristen picked up Elise before they drove off to their parents'. They'd decided it would be better for them to show up together, as a united front.

"What do you think's going to happen today?" Kristen said.

"I have no idea," Elise said.

The two of them had had variations of this same conversation many times this week.

"The anticipation is killing me. I could barely eat breakfast this morning," Elise said.

"Oh, I know. Me either. And I have a feeling we're not going to eat lunch either."

Elise snickered. "You're probably right. But maybe we'll feel better when it's all over. What's the worst that could happen? I'm sure we're already out of the will."

Kristen laughed. "Agreed. Let's go do our own thing if it ends badly."

"It's a deal."

"Did Dad even tell you happy birthday?"

"Nope."

"Ouch."

"Yeah."

Neither of her parents had made contact with her on her birthday. Elise was trying not to let it bother her, but it still hurt after two months.

When they got to their parents' house, their dad let them in. He looked good, and Elise was itching for some news on his cancer. She might be mad at her parents, but they were still her parents, and she loved them.

Their father led them into the living room where their mother was already waiting. She sat on the sofa, hands clasped, and was so tense that she looked like she might break if someone touched her.

"Sit, girls," their father said as he sat next to his wife.

Elise and Kristen each took an armchair across from them. They exchanged a look.

Elise said what both of them were thinking, "What's going on?"

Their mom started crying, and their father patted her arm.

"Girls, the cancer's spread."

Elise jumped to her feet. "What? But I thought they were getting it."

"Peanut, please sit."

Elise did somewhat reluctantly.

"We all thought I was doing well, but my latest scan showed the cancer has gotten worse."

Their mother pulled out a handkerchief and covered her face as she cried harder.

"Oh, Daddy," Kristen said.

"How-how much time do you have?" Elise asked.

"Six months to a year."

With that news, the three women in her father's life were crying in the living room.

Elise and Kristen rushed over and gave both their parents a hug. Elise saw her mom hesitate for just a moment before she hugged her tight.

When they had gotten the majority of their tears out, their father announced that it was time to eat.

"Dad, how do you expect us to eat at a time like this?" Elise asked.

"Because I'm a dying man, and it's what I want. Every Sunday from now on. And you can bring your Luke, and you can bring"—he fluttered his hand around as he looked at Kristen, as if trying to find the word—"your girlfriend."

"Actually, she's my fiancée," Kristen said.

Elise squealed. "Yay, I'm so excited for you," she said, giving her sister a hug. "Why didn't you tell me?"

Kristen laughed and hugged her back. "Thank you. It just happened last night. I wanted to tell you in person."

The two sisters pulled apart and looked at their parents.

Her father cleared his throat. "We're happy for you, too."

Kristen looked skeptical. "Why the change of heart?"

"Because I'm not going to live forever, and I don't want to miss out on anything by being a stubborn fool." He grabbed his wife's hand. "And I don't want your mother to be alone after I'm gone."

"Oh, Ward," she said.

"Mom won't be alone," Elise said. "We'll be here for her."

"That's right," Kristen said.

For the first time, their mom looked at them with a tentative smile.

Could their mom be ashamed of how she had treated them and that was why she hadn't looked at them until now? Because she thought her daughters were mad at her?

"I made your favorite, girls. Chicken and dumplings," their mom said.

"Oh my, that sounds delicious," Elise said.

"I can't wait to eat," added Kristen.

"Let's go to the kitchen then," their father said.

The four of them sat down at the table where Elise and Kristen had grown up and held hands to pray.

Elise spit out her toothpaste. "And then, Luke, my mother apologized. To both of us." She rinsed her toothbrush in the sink and put it in the toothbrush holder. "I apologized for some of the things I said, and then they told me they were sorry they missed my birthday. I think I'm still in shock," she finished as she walked out of the bathroom. "The best part was, I don't think they even noticed my nose."

Luke chuckled. "That's amazing, babe. I'm so happy for you guys. You both deserve it," he said from his spot on the bed. He was wearing boxers and a T-shirt and was reading a medical journal.

The first time she'd seen him doing that, she'd told him that he didn't have to impress her with his smarts anymore. He'd replied that he actually found them interesting.

She remembered back to the night she and Luke had first slept together and how she liked brains in a man. She still did. But a medical journal? *Bo-ring*.

Elise changed into her pajamas and lay down on her side of the bed. She and Luke had been together long enough now for her to have a side, which made her smile inside. She rolled onto her stomach as Luke set his reading material down.

"I'm sorry about your father though," Luke said as he slipped down on the bed beside her.

"Me, too. I'm sad about the things he's going to miss. My wedding day. He won't get to walk me down the aisle. He'll never get to meet my kids." She scrunched her pillow up under her head, so she'd have something else to do besides cry.

"Well, how about we take care of one of those things? And we can try really hard to start working on the second."

Elise laid her head back down. "What do you mean?"

"Let's get married. He can walk you down the aisle and be at your wedding. And then we can try for the baby-making. Unfortunately, I can't speed up that process."

Elise got up on her forearms. "Are you serious?" She held her breath as she waited for him to answer.

"Yeah, babe. Sorry, science has come a long way, but babies still take nine months. Ten, if you're counting weeks."

Elise pursed her lips and playfully pushed him. "You are such a tease."

Luke caught her arm and pulled her over him. "Yes, I'm serious. I was going to ask you anyway—although a little more romantically—but I think we should do it."

Elise kissed Luke, and they rolled around on the bed as the kiss turned hot.

Just when she was about to take off their clothes, Luke drew away. "Does that mean yes?"

Oh, yeah. She'd forgotten to answer because she was so in love with this man that she'd skipped to the celebrating.

"That's a hell yes."

Luke laughed. "Good. Now, I have something for you."

There was no way he'd bought a ring yet. He'd had no idea her father had gotten sicker.

"Okay," she said.

"Prop the pillows up and lie back."

Elise did as he'd asked while Luke grabbed the TV and DVD remotes. She had no idea what he was up to.

"You didn't tape us having sex, and now, you're showing me the video, did you?"

Luke cough-laughed. "No, but now, you've given me an idea."

"I don't know if I'd like watching myself, but I would definitely love watching you."

Luke just looked at her with amazement.

"What?"

"How'd I get so lucky?"

"It's because you think like that. That's why we're blessed. Don't ever change."

"Yes, ma'am."

Luke settled back, and Elise curled up next to him.

"Are you ready, Lise?" He made it sound so serious.

Elise giggled. "Yep."

Luke hit play on the DVD remote, so the movie already started playing before he turned on the TV.

And the tears came back as Elise saw the opening credits of *Love Actually*. Luke really had been thinking about marriage before she told him about her father because he'd once told her that he'd only watch this movie with his future wife.

Elise sniffled.

Luke asked, "You okay, babe?"

She kissed his neck. "Yes. I just love you so much."

"I love you, too. Now, let's watch this movie, and as we go, you can explain to me why it's your favorite."

And they did.

The best part? Luke loved it, too.

EPILOGUE

SEVERAL YEARS LATER

L uke grabbed Ariel's two-and-a-half-year-old hand and helped her step through the sliding glass door and into the house.

"Daddy, why do we have to go inside?"

"Because it's almost bedtime."

"But I see the sun."

"It's still the same time, sweet pea. The days are getting longer now."

"No, Daddy."

"Yes, Ariel."

She let go of his hand and ran over to Elise. "Mama, Daddy says it's bedtime."

Elise looked up to the clock on the microwave from where she was helping their five-year-old daughter Lili do her reading homework. "Daddy's right, sweet pea. It's almost eight o'clock." She looked up at Luke. "Thank God because this kindergarten homework is brutal. Is it summer vacation yet?"

Luke chuckled. "Soon, but then we're going to have even more work, so you might want to hold off on that thought."

"True," she said with a sigh. She ran her hands down both girls' heads.

Both their daughters had ended up with blue eyes, thanks to both of the grandmothers' recessive genes, but Lili got his dark brown hair while Ariel's was a dark blonde.

"Will you read me a story, Mama?" Ariel.

Elise turned her attention to Ariel and rubbed their noses together. "Yes, sweet pea."

"Me, too, please," Lili said.

Elise did the same to their older daughter. "Of course, honey," she said.

But Luke could see the exhaustion weighing her down in her face.

"You know what, girls? Daddy's going to read you a story tonight, and we're going to let Mama rest," Luke announced.

"Because Mama is busy cookin' Baby Edward?"

"You're a dummy, Ariel. Mama's not cooking the baby. She's growing him in her belly."

Technically, neither of their daughters was right, but they had plenty of time for anatomy lessons later.

Ariel stuck her tongue out at her older sister. "That's what Grandma said."

Elise snickered. "Yeah, well, sweet pea, I wouldn't listen to everything Grandma tells you," Elise said as she stacked Lili's homework in a pile and put it in her backpack.

Ariel cocked her head to the side. "Because Grandma's a bitch?"

Startled, Elise dropped Lili's backpack. "Ariel Long, we do not use that word in this house."

At least, not as long as you were under the age of sixteen because his wife used it all the time.

"Where did you even hear that word?" Elise asked.

Case in point...

"From you, Mama," Ariel said, as if the answer was obvious.

Luke tried not to laugh at Elise's horrified expression.

Suzanne had come a long way in changing her ways and accepting Kristen's lifestyle, especially after Ward had passed away, but sometimes, she would resort to her old habits. Elise was known to use some colorful language to complain about her mom when it was just her and Luke, and Luke was grateful that his own mother was close with Elise.

"I don't think so," Elise disputed.

"Ariel is right, Mama. You told Daddy that Grandma was a bitch."

"Stop saying that word. You're not allowed to use it either." Elise looked up at Luke with help-me eyes. "They're five and two," she said through clenched teeth.

Luke clapped his hands together. "All right, young ladies, let's go get ready for bed. We can talk tomorrow about what kind of language we use in the house."

The girls willingly went with him, discussing what story they wanted him to read to them tonight.

After two rounds of toothbrushing, three glasses of water,

one bathroom break, two pairs of pajamas, and four bedtime stories, the girls were finally asleep.

Luke closed Lili's bedroom door and quietly stepped away, hoping to not wake either of them.

Luke walked the short distance to his and Elise's bedroom.

When she had called Luke all those years ago to come and look at this house, he'd never imagined that he'd live there one day.

He pushed open the door to find his seven-month-pregnant wife naked, wearing only the stud nose piercing he'd gotten her for her thirtieth birthday, and snoring. It was a cute female snore, but it was still snoring, and he was going to give her shit about it tomorrow.

They'd always slept naked until the girls were born. But, now that Elise was hot all the time with pregnancy, she'd gone back to sleeping nude almost every night—although she did try to cover up when the girls were around.

He loved that she didn't care if he saw her like this. He had friends whose wives who wouldn't let their husbands see them naked once they started showing, which Luke found ridiculous. His wife's body was amazing, and she was sexy, no matter how big she got with pregnancy.

Even though Luke had gone to med school and learned all about how babies were made, he still found it fascinating that Elise grew their children inside her. How anyone could not find the maternal form beautiful was beyond him. And the fact that she trusted him to see her like this made her all the more attractive to him.

Luke went into the master bathroom and got ready for

bed, being careful to stay as noiseless as possible in order to let Elise sleep. After he brushed his own teeth and stripped down to his boxers, he got into bed beside her, pulling the covers up and over them.

"Are the girls sleeping?"

"Yeah," he said, rolling over to put his arm around her. "Sorry I woke you. I tried to be quiet."

Elise slipped her hands into his underwear and wrapped her fingers around him. He immediately grew hard in her hand. Some things never changed.

"I tried to stay up for you, so I'm glad you woke me up. And speaking of waking up..." She squeezed his hard-on. "Why do you have your boxers on?"

"I thought you needed the rest."

She moved closer and said softly in his ear, "I need you to fuck me more."

Luke loved when his wife talked dirty. He absolutely loved it when she asked or told him to fuck her. It had taken her a while to realize that she could be dirty in bed and still be a good wife and mother. Once she had understood that, she didn't hold back.

"I want to taste you," she whispered before biting his earlobe.

Luke groaned at her words and kicked off his boxers. He slid his hand between her legs and pushed a finger inside her. She was already wet, and he loved how turned on she was.

"I want to taste you first."

Not waiting for her to respond, he threw back the covers and pulled his wife onto her back. He spread her legs wide as he stretched out on the bed, putting his mouth at her secret place. She tasted spicy and hot, and her musky scent surrounded him, making his dick impossibly harder.

She tasted different, and her scent changed when she was pregnant. She was always wetter, too. It fucking turned him on in a way he couldn't even explain. The fact that her body was altered because of him, because of something he had left inside her, was the ultimate marking of his territory. He just couldn't control the caveman satisfaction inside him when he thought about it.

He sucked on her clit, which was super sensitive when she was pregnant, and released it before she came. He sucked her pussy lips in his mouth and licked her from bottom to top. He fucked her with his mouth, letting her know much he loved going down on her, and after he'd tortured her enough, he let her come.

She cried out, "Luke, Luke, Luke."

He let her ride his mouth, encouraging her on, until she was finished.

She gently pushed his head away when she couldn't take any more pressure down below, and Luke sprawled next to her. He turned her on her side and pulled her leg up and over his, so he could bring her close. He waited for her to catch her breath before he entered her in a single thrust. He groaned at how tight she was, even after two kids. Not that he would have judged her if she wasn't, but he wasn't going to deny that it was one more thing to put in the Plus column of his amazing life.

Elise put her arms around his neck and let him fuck her while she arched her back and enjoyed the ride.

"You doing okay?" he asked.

She kissed him. "God, yes. You always know just what I need."

And didn't that make him feel like he was seven feet tall.

He kissed her again, and as he grew closer, he pushed her leg up higher, so he could get inside her even more deeply. Although he didn't think he could ever really be deep enough for his complete satisfaction. Sometimes, he wished he could live in her pussy.

"Harder, baby," Elise told him. "Please."

She didn't have to ask him twice.

Elise began to contract around him, and he knew she was close to another orgasm, so he kept thrusting inside her, just the way she liked. His climax could wait because, as much as he loved coming, he loved making his wife come even more.

When she did reach her peak, she came so hard that Luke had to slap a hand across her mouth, so she didn't wake the girls. Her pussy squeezed him so tight, she pushed him right out of her. He wanted to wait a few seconds before he slipped back inside her wet heat, but she pushed him onto his back and got on her knees.

She scooted down and took his cock in her mouth, not caring that she could taste herself all over him. Before Elise, Luke had only ever seen that in porn. Elise had admitted that she'd always wanted to do it, but she'd always been afraid of being judged. He'd asked her once if she really liked doing it or if she did it because it obviously rocked his world, but she'd confessed that she loved tasting the two of them together. He supposed it was her way of marking her territory. Because there was no doubt that he belonged to Elise.

She sucked him down as far as she could go, taking him to

the back of her throat, and he knew he wouldn't be able to hold out much longer, no matter how much he wanted to keep her phenomenal blow job going.

"Baby, I'm going to come."

Elise hummed around his dick in approval.

His cock throbbed as his impending orgasm came to a crescendo, and she must have sensed it, too, because she wrapped her lips around his head and let him come down her throat. When he was done, she licked everywhere, including the crease in his head to make sure she got all of him.

"God, I love you."

Elise stuck him back in her mouth and deep-throated him again.

"Holy shit, Lise."

She carefully released him, knowing how sensitive he was after coming, and plopped down beside him.

"You're just saying that because I give world-class head."

Saying what? Oh, yeah, that he loved her.

He yanked her close and kissed her nose. "You know that's not true."

Yes, he loved the blow jobs and the great sex, especially when other women wouldn't let their husbands touch them while they were pregnant. Elise let him touch, and she actually liked it. And she liked it dirty. But he also loved her because she was a wonderful person, a great mother, and the best partner Luke could have ever asked for.

Elise cuddled into him, her belly pressing against his side. "Yeah, I know," she said with a smile.

"I mean, if I was going to marry someone for their blow-job skills, I would have married—"

Elise whipped her head up and gave him a warning look. He still loved giving her shit after all these years.

"You, the first night we had sex." Luke feigned confusion. "What did you think I was going to say?"

Elise laid her head back down. "You're lucky I love you, Luke."

Luke kissed the top of his wife's head. "I know, baby."

He felt Elise smile against his chest.

Less than five minutes later, she was out.

Luke lay there, letting happiness wash over him. He had his wonderful wife sleeping in his arms, their beautiful daughters snuggled in their beds just down the hall, and his unborn son kicking him in the side through his mother's abdomen.

Luke couldn't have asked for anything more.

Want to know what happens between Elise & Luke that first night? You can download ***One-Night Stand*** and find out now!

MEANT TO BE SAMPLE
CHAPTER ONE

Piper closed the lid of her laptop and rubbed her temples. The pounding in her head matched the pounding of the hammer outside. She reached for the bottle of ibuprofen that had taken up permanent residence on her desk and shook out four tablets.

After Jordan's death, she had thrown herself into her work, but lately, it hadn't been bringing the same fulfillment. She still loved her job. She was a women's advocate at a women's and children's abuse shelter, and she would always find satisfaction in helping women or children get away from their abusive spouses or parents.

But she had slowly begun to realize that it couldn't be her only source of happiness like it had been for the last thirteen months. She'd been exploring jobs for one of her clients today, despite it being Saturday, and even though she enjoyed doing research, a headache hadn't taken too long to make its appearance.

Piper heard shouting coming from her backyard and pushed her feet into the carpet so that her desk chair rolled back and she could look out the back window. She couldn't make out the words, but it was obvious that Nate was arguing with Luke about something. He shook his bald head along with the hammer in his hand, as if trying to make a point, and Piper found herself smiling. The two of them were both alphas and often butted heads about what should and what should not be done.

She scanned the backyard. The veranda was coming along somewhat slowly but nicely, and it would be done before fall. She was excited to see the conclusion, but it also brought a deep longing to the surface.

Jordan should have been the one outside, working with Nate. It had been Jordan's idea in the first place. When they had purchased the house, everything had been perfect, except for the backyard. Jordan had promised her he was going to make it the best yard on the block for their future children, and all the neighborhood kids would want to come over to their house to play.

They'd moved into their home in January, and it had been too cold to start a big project. But, four months later, Jordan was dead, the supplies he had purchased to start on the project a reminder that he was gone.

They'd sat in the garage for almost a year when Piper decided they needed to go. When she'd asked Nate if he wanted any of it, he had proposed to finish what Jordan had barely started. She'd tried to tell him not to bother. After all, there wouldn't be any children to play back there now, but Nate had insisted.

She didn't know what had transpired between Nate and Jordan while they sat in the wrecked car, waiting for the first responders to show before Jordan passed, but she suspected that her late husband had made Nate promise to take care of her.

Nate was always available when she needed him. He'd fixed her broken sink and helped her winterize her car and other things like that. She honestly didn't know what she'd do without him. In a way, he'd become her new husband—if you could count someone who lived in a different house and slept with other women while you were abstinent your husband. So, he might not have become her replacement spouse, but he had definitely become her best friend.

He'd been there for her as no one else had when Jordan passed. Not just fixing stuff but letting her literally cry on his shoulder. She knew he was a womanizer and a commitment-phobe, but to her, he was simply Nate.

Piper continued to watch the two men outside as their argument heated up. One might be worried they would hurt each other, but even though they were trying to act tough, both of them were smiling. Nate swiped his shirt off over his head, and Luke did the same. They looked like they were getting ready to brawl.

Both men were tall and nicely built. Very nicely built. Luke Long was half-Asian and already had a tan that she wouldn't get if she sunbathed every day of summer. His dark hair was wet with sweat, and she could almost see laughter gleaming in his brown eyes. But that wasn't the only thing gleaming on him. The sun shone off the ring he wore on the third finger of his left hand, telling all single women that this man was taken.

And Nate...well, Nate was pure sex on a stick. She might have been married when she met him, but she hadn't been blind. Nate was a mix of African American, Mexican, and Caucasian. He wasn't extremely dark, but his beautiful, bronzed skin definitely showed his mixed heritage. And thanks to his recessive genes, he had the lightest crystal-blue eyes that stood out from his tan complexion. He was just over six feet, and on his left arm, he sported a collection of tattoos. He kept his head clean-shaven, yet his face wore a sexy layer of stubble.

As a woman, she'd never understand why a man would shave one part of his head but not the other. She wasn't complaining though. It looked good on the man. And, if her libido hadn't died along with Jordan, she'd probably be drooling.

Actually, no *probably*. She would have been. Piper had always loved sex, and if she were single, she'd be hitting on Nate daily. But she was a widow with a dead sex drive and now only appreciated attractive men from a more objective point of view.

There was a knock at her front door just as Nate crouched down, put his shoulder into Luke's abdomen, and lifted the other man off the ground.

"Hello? Piper?"

"Back here," she called out to Elise Long, Luke's wife. "Hurry. You have to come see this."

Piper's office was directly off the dining room, so she had a view straight through to the kitchen. She watched as Elise set down a couple of bags from the local fast food place and then scrambled in to join Piper at the window.

Elise's belly bumped against the window as she practically pressed her nose to the glass. "Oh my God, what are they doing?" she asked with a laugh.

Piper shrugged. "Fighting."

"Put me down, motherfucker," Luke shouted loud enough for the two women to hear.

"I swear, those two act like children when they're together," Elise said. "I think it's because they've known each other since they were kids. It's like part of them can't grow up."

Nate set Luke down. He wasn't rough, but he wasn't gentle either. He dropped Luke on his ass, but Luke must have been ready for Nate because, before Nate could straighten, Luke pulled him to the ground and put some sort of wrestling move on him.

Elise was still chuckling, but she sighed. "We'd better go out there."

"Were they like this when they fixed up your house?" Piper asked as the two of them went to the dining room and then out the sliding glass door.

She curled her lip. "Yes. I'm pretty sure it took months longer than it should have to finish. I'd complain, but they worked for free, and it's obvious they love fighting with each other. Who am I to deny them their fun?"

They stepped down from the deck.

When their feet hit the grass, Elise shouted out, "Food's here, boys."

Piper snickered at the other woman's use of the word *boys* when the two were obviously more than men.

Both guys froze at Elise's announcement and looked over at the women.

"Hi, honey." Luke grinned. He threw Nate's leg off of him and rolled up onto his knees. He was about to stand when Nate wrapped his arm around Luke's neck and pulled him back to the ground.

Elise made a sigh of annoyance, but she smiled. She approached the two men and raised her brow. "Nate?"

Nate looked up at Elise, smiling as he used his other hand to pull his arm around Luke tighter. "Hi, Elise. How can I help you?"

"Can you let go of my husband?"

"Yeah, asshole. Your dick is rubbing on my ass," Luke complained.

"No can do, sweetie," he said to Elise while he lifted his hips and brushed himself against Luke even more.

Piper put her hand over her mouth to stifle a laugh.

"Gross, dude," Luke shouted and tried to get away while simultaneously reaching back to punch his friend.

"That's what you get for calling me a pussy," Nate told Luke. He looked to Elise again. "I'll let him go when he learns his lesson."

Elise rolled her eyes. "Luke, will you please apologize to your friend before I give birth to our firstborn? I really don't want our child to grow up without a father."

Piper knew Elise was joking; the woman hadn't said anything that anybody else wouldn't say, and part of Piper did think it was funny. There was also a small portion of her, deep inside, that was stung by the words. Because, if she'd had a child, it would now be fatherless.

"Elise," Luke said, trying to pull Nate's arm off of him, "I can't let our child think I'm a total wuss."

Elise raised her brow again, this time without a smile, and she saw Luke's body relax as he stopped fighting.

"Fine," he muttered. "I'm sorry I called you a pussy..."

Nate immediately released Luke.

Luke jumped up and finished his sentence. "Loud enough for you to hear. Next time, I'll whisper it behind your back."

"Fucker," Nate said and made a swipe for Luke.

Luke took off and ran around to the front of the house, and Nate followed.

Elise turned and looked at Piper as she shrugged. "I give up. If they want cold food, that's their fault. Let's go eat."

Piper led the way back into her house and pulled the food out of the bags. She separated her order from the rest, and Elise did the same. The two pulled out the stools at the counter and sat.

"Would you be more comfortable at the table?" Piper asked her.

"Nah, I'm fine here," Elise said with a wave of her hand. "I have a while left before I'm really big." She tilted her head. "At least, I hope I do. I'm only twenty-two weeks."

Luke and Elise had been married for a few months, and Elise had told Piper that she was pregnant before they'd gotten married. Elise's father had cancer, and they had hoped to have at least one child before he passed away. Piper hadn't gone to their wedding because it was a small ceremony, and she hadn't known the couple that well yet.

Piper and Jordan had moved to the area in January the

previous year, and when they had first moved, it had been all about getting situated. Jordan had settled into his new job while Piper had to search for her own. Then, before she had known it, it had been May, and she was a widow.

After that had come his funeral and sorting out all the paperwork after someone passed, all while trying to deal with grief. For a while, the only people Piper had seen outside of work were her mom and Nate. She had just wanted to be left alone. Socializing took too much energy.

But she'd slowly started coming back to life a few months ago, and that was when Nate had really started bringing his friends around. She knew he'd been afraid that she'd be lonely with no family in the area. She felt like she was almost back to normal. Well, her *new* normal because she was never going to be the same person she had been before Jordan passed away.

And, now, she was grateful that Nate had introduced her to Elise. The two of them got along great, and while Nate was her best friend, sometimes, a lady just needed some girl time. They still didn't know each other that well, but Piper hoped that could change.

Nate and Luke burst through the front door, shirtless, sweaty, and laughing. They went straight to the food without a word to either of the women and dug in like they hadn't eaten for a week. Neither of them bothered to sit either; both stood on the other side of the counter.

"I apologize for my husband's table manners—or lack thereof," Elise said.

Luke looked up from stuffing his face. "*Wha—*" he said

around a mouthful of food, his brown eyes gleaming with humor.

"You're a pig," Elise said.

Nate nestled in the corner of the counter and laughed.

Luke swallowed and smiled. "But I'm your pig."

Elise shook her head and rolled her eyes, but Piper saw she was hiding a smile.

"Apologies, Piper," Luke said. "I'm hungry."

Elise turned to Piper. "Do you care if I get a glass of water?"

Piper jumped from the stool, feeling like a terrible hostess. "Oh my God, I'm sorry."

"No, you don't have to get up," Elise protested, also rising from her seat.

"Yes, I do. My mother would pass out from shame if I didn't take care of my company."

Elise sat back down and laughed. "I understand."

She looked around to the two guys. "Water okay with you guys, too?" she asked as she walked around to Nate and Luke's side.

"I can get my own, you know," Nate said.

It was true. He wasn't really a guest in her home anymore. He raided her fridge whenever he was hungry and helped himself to whatever he needed without asking anymore.

"That's okay," she said as she opened the cupboard and reached up for the glasses.

But Nate went for them at the same time she did. As he reached from behind her, she felt his naked chest against her back. A tingle went down her spine, straight to her belly, and she dropped her hands to the counter as she tried to fight a slight tremor.

Apparently, her libido hadn't died with Jordan. It had just gone dormant. And she didn't know what to do with it if it was coming back.

AUTHOR'S NOTE

Dear Readers,

Out of any other book, *Friends with Benefits* is probably the book I have put the most of my personal life in. When Lara and I got the idea for the story, we didn't know what the characters were going to look like yet. I don't know exactly how the idea of Luke's appearance came to me, except that I was driving to visit my husband at the Mayo Clinic where he had elbow surgery. I guess I was thinking about him and our kids, and I realized, in all my years of reading, I had *never* read a romance novel where the hero was Asian. I have read books with heroines who are Asian or half-Asian, but even those are few and far between.

Unfortunately, Asians, especially males, have a lot of stereotypes about them. There is a Tumblr blog, Writing With Color, that tells it best, but some of the stereotypes include that Asian men are submissive and asexual. Asian men are often the beta males to their non-Asian counterparts. They are frequently thought of as skinny nerds who excel at math. Not only is it racist, but it is also simply not true. My husband was a jock in high school, didn't get great grades, was kind of a player in his younger years, and even got in fights—something not to be proud of though. He works as a machinist—blue-collar work—and is definitely not skinny but muscular. Although I will admit that he is good at math.

So, as I was driving, I thought about making Luke Asian, but then I thought of my two sons, and ultimately, I decided to make Luke half-Caucasian and half-Chinese because that's what my own children are. And, thankfully, I have a wonderful cowriter who didn't object.

So, going back to what I said above, while Asian females seem to be found attractive by many men of all races— although they have their own stereotypes to battle—Asian males are often thought of as being nerds, unattractive, and not well-endowed. I look at my handsome sons, and I don't want people to automatically think those things about them. I figured Luke was the perfect candidate to show the world something different. He's sexy, fun, smart, loving, and well-endowed—just sayin'. Although I admit, as a mother, I don't really want my boys to grow up to be players.

Many of the things I used for Luke's family are from my and my husband's family. Not all of it, but a lot of it. In fact, Lara laughed when she read what I had written about Luke's family. So, if anyone feels like I was inaccurate, I did go by my own personal experiences of what it's like to be married to an Asian man and to have a whole family of Asian in-laws.

I hope you all enjoyed the book, and perhaps you will look at Asian men differently now. I know I do.

Until next time, happy reading!

Love,

Renae

R.L. Kenderson

P.S. Need a Luke visual? Google Hideo Muraoka, and sit back and drool. Or check out this article about him.

FRIENDS WITH BENEFITS PLAYLIST

1. Inside You – Hoobastank
2. #1 Crush – Garbage
3. Addicted – Saving Abel
4. Addicted – Simple Plan
5. Animal I Have Become – Three Days Grace
6. Animals – Maroon 5
7. Animals – Nickelback
8. Call Me When You're Sober – Evanescence
9. Casual Sex – My Darkest Days
10. Closing Time – Semisonic
11. Dirty Little Secret – All American Rejects
12. Faded – SoulDecision
13. Get Lucky – Halestorm
14. I Get off – Halestorm
15. I Miss You – Blink 182
16. I Miss You – Incubus
17. My Immortal – Evanescence

18. Porn Star Dancing – My Darkest Days
19. Spaceship – Puddle of Mudd
20. Thnks fr th Mmrs – Fall Out Boy

Click her to listen to the Friends with Benefits Playlist on YouTube!

ACKNOWLEDGMENTS

First, we'd like to thank our fans for sticking with us during our two-year hiatus and for taking a chance on our contemporary romance. We promise not to go missing like that again.

Then, of course, we have to thank each other because we couldn't do this the way we do if we didn't do it together. We motivate, console, and inspire each other during the whole process.

Thank you to our beta readers, old and new, for your input. You truly made our story better. We're lucky to have all of you and your help.

And thank you to our ARC readers and bloggers who helped spread the word. You guys are great, and we appreciate everything you do!

Thank you to our editor, Jovana Shirley, for putting in the hard work to make *Friends with Benefits* the final piece of work it is. We really couldn't have done it without you!

Lastly, thank you to all our family members who put up with us when we are hard at work. We are lucky to have such supportive families. We love you!

ABOUT THE AUTHOR

R.L. Kenderson is two best friends writing under one name.

Renae has always loved reading, and in third grade, she wrote her first poem where she learned she might have a knack for this writing thing. Lara remembers sneaking her grandmother's Harlequin novels when she was probably too young to be reading them, and since then, she knew she wanted to write her own.

When they met in college, they bonded over their love of reading and the TV show *Charmed*. What really spiced up their friendship was when Lara introduced Renae to romance novels. When they discovered their first vampire romance, they knew there would always be a special place in their hearts for paranormal romance. After being unable to find certain storylines and characteristics they wanted to read about in the hundreds of books they consumed, they decided to write their own.

One lives in the Minneapolis-St. Paul area and the other in the Kansas City area where they both work in the medical field during the day and a sexy author by night. They communicate through phone, email, and whole lot of messaging.

You can find them at http://www.rlkenderson.com, Facebook, Instagram, TikTok, and Goodreads. Join their reader group! Or you can email them at rlkenderson@rlkenderson.com, or sign up for their newsletter. They always love hearing from their readers.